A DANGEROUS LIFE

A DCI Jack Callum Mystery

LEN MAYNARD

First published as *Prime Evil* in 2016 by Joffe Books
First published as *A Dangerous Life* in 2019 by LMP

This edition published in 2020 by Sharpe Books.

DEDICATION

To the memory of Lonnie Donegan, Wally Whyton,
and Paul Lincoln aka Dr Death.
Pioneers to a man.

AUTHOR'S NOTE

Certain liberties have been taken with the geography of Hertfordshire for the benefit of the story. Hopefully the residents of that beautiful county, home for many years, will be forgiving.

CONTENTS

Chapters 1 – 33

1 - TUESDAY MARCH 17TH 1959

"…So it's important you remember these three simple rules. One, don't talk to strangers. Two, never go off with anyone you do not know personally, and three, remember that the police are your friends. We are here to listen and help you whenever we can." Jack Callum looked up from his notes on the dais at the rows of faces staring back at him with expressions of total apathy.

Cynthia Arnold, the school's headmistress, sprung to her feet and walked to the front of the stage.

"Very informative," she said. "I'm sure, School, that you would like to show your appreciation to Chief Inspector Callum for giving up his valuable time to speak to you today." She started a round of applause that rippled listlessly around the assembly hall and quickly died. "Now, if you could all make your way out, in an orderly fashion, to the playground, where…" She looked down at the piece of paper clutched in her hand. "Where Sergeant Grant and Constable Cooper will explain to you how you can stay safe on our roads."

There was a hubbub of grumbling voices and shuffling feet as the hall gradually emptied.

"Thank you for that, Mr. Callum," the headmistress said. "I'm sure your words found a receptive audience."

"Well, those that stayed awake for long enough might have learned something," Jack said as he folded his speech and tucked it into the pocket of his jacket. "And can I apologise again that Superintendent Lane couldn't be here today."

The headmistress clucked her tongue. "Never to worry," she said. "I'm sure it couldn't be helped. In any case, you proved to be a very successful last minute substitution. Full marks."

"You're very kind."

The truth was that Henry Lane had been trying to wheedle his way out of this speaking engagement for weeks. More comfortable swinging a golf club than standing in front of a microphone, a last minute attack of laryngitis meant that Jack had to take his place, much to his own chagrin. He enjoyed public speaking even less than Lane.

"Well, excuse me," the headmistress said. "I hear your men

have brought a police car along with them to help with their demonstration. I have to see. It's all rather exciting."

Jack watched her bustle, *excitedly*, out of the hall, and then made his way to the side of the stage and the short staircase to freedom.

He trotted down the stairs and pulled up short when a voice spoke from out of the shadows. "Did you mean it?"

Someone was standing a few feet away, hidden by a fold in the curtain.

"Did I mean what?" he said, and a teenage girl stepped out from behind the folded brocade and stood in front of him.

"That the police were our friends and that we should come and talk to you, and you will help?"

Jack smiled indulgently. "We'll always listen, and help if we can…sorry I didn't catch your name."

"Gerry…Geraldine Turner."

"Well, Geraldine, do you have a problem you wish to discuss?"

The girl looked tearful. She nodded, a lock of her curly blonde hair falling out from beneath her Alice band and dropping down over her face. "It's my brother," she said.

"Well, what is it you want to tell me about your brother?"

"He's dead," she said, biting at her lip pensively. "I killed him."

"I'm sorry that your time has been so cruelly wasted, Chief Inspector," the headmistress said. "But our Miss Turner is one of Hatfield County School's greatest fantasists."

"So she's done this kind of thing before?" Jack said quietly, glancing across at Geraldine who sat in the corner of the office, biting her lip pensively and staring down at her shoes, doing her best to avoid meeting his eyes.

"With almost monotonous regularity," the headmistress said tiredly.

Jack continued to stare at the girl. He couldn't shake the feeling that, by involving the headmistress, he had betrayed Geraldine's trust in the most profound way, but he'd had no choice. Being alone in the office with a thirteen-year-old girl would have been seen by most as dangerously inappropriate.

"Still, the school secretary has been in touch with her father and Mr. Turner is on his way in now to take her home. He shouldn't be long. They live in a lovely house called *Elsinore,* on the Broadway in Letchworth," the headmistress said with a smile, gazing wistfully over Jack's shoulder, through the window to the playground where his junior officers were putting the black Wolseley through its paces, demonstrating stopping times to an audience of bored schoolchildren.

Jack, keeping his voice low, said, "And as far as you're aware Geraldine doesn't have, or has never had, a brother?"

The headmistress shook her head. "In our records we have her down as an only child. I'm afraid, Mr. Callum, that teenage girls have a great capacity for making up stories."

"I have two teenage daughters myself," Jack said, finding the headmistress's condescending attitude towards her charges irritating.

"Then I don't need to tell you, do I?" she said. "You don't have to stay, you know. I'm sure I can deal with Mr. Turner when he gets here."

"I'll hang on. I'd like a few words with him. Besides, I have to wait for my men to finish the demonstration. Sergeant Grant is my lift back to the station."

"I see," the headmistress said and, dropping all pretence, stood up, walked to the window and stared out at the car as it performed an elaborate skid on the playground's tarmac surface. Jack would have to have a quiet word with Constable Cooper about his tendency to showboat.

"Ooh," she said. "It *really* is quite exciting."

Jack went across and sat down on a hard chair next to Geraldine. Apart from her initial pronouncement that she had killed her brother, the girl had said nothing more to him.

"Are you all right, Geraldine?"

"I told you, it's Gerry," the girl said without looking at him.

"Sorry, *Gerry*. Are you feeling okay now?"

Geraldine finally turned her head, a look of contempt in her eyes. "You're just like the rest of them," she said. "I trusted you."

Her words cut deep, increasing the feeling that he'd betrayed her.

Thirty minutes later the school secretary knocked on the door of the office.

"Mr. Turner's here, Headmistress."

"Well, don't keep him waiting, Sandra. Show him in."

Anthony Turner was a tall man in his mid-thirties with lush, wavy brown hair and matinee idol looks. He nodded a hello to Jack and the headmistress, and folded himself into the chair next to the girl, grasping her hand and holding onto it tightly. "Geraldine, do we have to go through all this again?"

"It's Gerry," the girl said and wrenched her hand away from him.

Jack watched the colour spread up from Turner's neck, turning his face an angry puce. The anger was reflected in his eyes and in the fingers of his free hand that were clenching and unclenching.

Jack cleared his throat. "Excuse me, Mr. Turner," he said. "Chief Inspector Callum, Welwyn and Hatfield CID."

Turner turned his ferocious glare on the hapless Cynthia Arnold. "You called the police? Even though I told you that I would be down here within the hour to sort this matter out?"

"I...I..." the headmistress spluttered.

"You mustn't blame Mrs Arnold, sir. I was here anyway, giving a talk to the school. Gerry approached me with her confession."

"And you haven't got enough common sense to realise when you're being led up the garden path?"

Jack refused to rise to the bait. He found Turner to be a conceited, arrogant bore, but he kept his feelings to himself. "I'm afraid we have to take all such confessions at face value," he said evenly. "We'd lose all public sympathy if we didn't."

Turner opened his mouth to speak again and then, after consideration, shut it and got to his feet. "Come on, Geraldine. I'm taking you home."

"Actually," Jack said to him, "I'd like a quick word with you, if you can spare the time. Mrs Arnold, could you take Gerry into the outer office and wait with her until we're finished?"

"Of course," the headmistress said. She came across and took the girl's hand. "Come along, dear. Let's give your father and the Chief Inspector some privacy." She led Geraldine out into the secretary's office and closed the door behind them.

Jack went around the desk and sat down in the headmistress's chair. "Take a seat, Mr. Turner. This won't take long."

Grumbling, Turner sat down on the hard chair opposite him and glared across the desk.

"A day off from work is it, sir? Only I was wondering why the school called you and not your wife to come down here?"

"Not that it's any of your business, Chief Inspector, but I've just come off a long and arduous run at the *Lyric* I'll be resting until my next film role starts rehearsing in a fortnight."

"Ah, you're an actor," Jack said.

Turner nodded curtly. "Furthermore, my wife is not a well woman. She can't leave the house."

"I'm sorry to hear that. Is she bedridden?"

"My wife suffers from a psychological condition. She's an agoraphobic."

"That must be very distressing for you. She can't leave the house at all?"

"Not without very severe panic attacks," Turner said.

"It must be very difficult, with you being away at work in the theatre all the time. How do you cope with Gerry's needs?"

"We have a woman who lives in during the week."

"And she makes sure Gerry gets to school?"

Turner nodded. "And does the shopping and any other errands that would necessitate my wife leaving the house." He glanced at his watch. "Are we going to be much longer?"

Jack leaned forwards, crossing his hands on the desk. "Do you have any idea why Gerry told me she had killed her brother?"

Turner sighed. "Geraldine in an only child, Mr. Callum. We were never blessed with another child. I can't honestly say where this latest fantasy has come from. Geraldine is, what is it they say, highly strung?"

"She seemed very… convincing."

Turner barked a laugh. "I'm afraid that's something she gets from me. I come from a family of actors. My mother used to be very highly regarded. It's in the genes, you might say."

"Yes," Jack said. "That must be it. In the genes."

"Are we finished here?"

"I think so. I won't detain you any longer. You can take your daughter home now."

Turner nodded sharply, stood up and walked to the door.

"Just one more thing," Jack said as Turner's fingers closed around the door handle.

Turner turned back to him. "Yes?"

"I take it your daughter has done this type of thing before."

"What are you implying?"

Jack smiled "It's just that when you arrived you said to her, 'Do we have to go through all this again?' Which suggests to me that what happened today wasn't an isolated occurrence."

"Please understand, Mr. Callum, that dealing with my wife's…condition, puts a huge strain on us as a family. Geraldine is going through a difficult time of life, puberty. That's really enough for her to be dealing with. It's hardly surprising that she seeks refuge in fantasies."

"Oh, I can understand the pressures teenage girls are under. I have two daughters myself, but it's a bit extreme isn't it? Confessing to the murder of a sibling she doesn't even have?"

"What can I say? Only that I bow to your greater experience in such matters. Good day." Turner turned on his heel and left the office.

Jack listened to them in the outer office as Turner gathered up Geraldine and left the school.

"What a charming man," the headmistress said as she bustled back into the office. "And *so* talented. I was lucky enough to catch his *Hamlet* at the *Old Vic* a few years ago. It was right up there with Gielgud and Olivier, in my opinion."

"Strange," Jack said. "I've never heard of him."

"Well, of course, he's not as widely known, or as highly praised for that matter, but he's just as talented. It was a real coup when we found Geraldine a place here, especially as we were so far outside her local catchment area, but Mr. Turner was insistent. He wanted only the best for his daughter."

"I'm sure he did." Jack smiled indulgently at the foolish woman. "I'm sure he did."

2 - TUESDAY

"So why would a thirteen-year-old girl confess to killing a non-existent brother?" Jack said to his wife, Annie, as they washed up the dinner things.

"Is she troubled in other ways?" Annie said.

"She might be. Her mum's an agoraphobic, It's an almost pathological fear of open spaces. That can't be easy to live with."

"It sounds like the daughter's seeking attention," Jack's eldest daughter, Joan, said. She was sitting at the kitchen table sewing. "Perhaps her mother's illness is overshadowing her. Does she get much attention from her father?"

"Probably not enough," Jack said. "I don't think he's there much. He's an actor."

"An actor?" said Annie. "Is he famous?"

"I wouldn't know," Jack said shaking his head. "I've certainly never heard of him. Joanie, do you still read those trashy gossip magazines? Does the name Anthony Turner mean anything to you?"

"Anthony Turner doesn't," she said. "But Tony Turner does."

"Really?"

"Yes. He was quite the rising star, once upon a time," Joan said. "He graduated from the Rank Charm School and for a little while magazines were full of him. They had him in the same mould as Dirk Bogarde, and predicted that he would go on to have similar success. They ran features about him. You know the kind of thing; *At Home With Tony Turner*, *Meet Tony Turner and his Beautiful Family*."

"Well, he needs to get his money back from Rank, because they certainly failed him in the *Charm* stakes," Jack said almost to himself. "You do read a load of tripe, Joanie. So, what happened to him? Why is his star no longer rising?"

"Why are you so interested in tripe?" his daughter said with a smile.

"Call it prurient curiosity."

8

"The best kind," Joan said. "His wife died a few years ago and he remarried. It caused a heck of a stink."

"I remember him now." Annie finished washing a plate and came back to the conversation. "Didn't he marry Lois Franklin, the *Cadence Girl*? She used to be in all the magazines persuading us to buy their beauty products."

"You're right, Mum, he did. A month after his first wife died. Rumours began flying around that they had been carrying on while his wife was fighting for her life with cancer. The scandal killed his film career stone dead."

"He's still acting," Jack said.

"Yes, he went back to the theatre. He still pops up here and there in the odd film, but mostly in character parts as the hero's best friend or the heroine's husband. Nothing to set the box office alight these days, but as far as I've read, the theatre is his main source of income these days, that and television commercials. He did one for cigarettes a couple of years back."

"Then I shouldn't think Gerry's home life is a barrel of laughs," Jack said. "Losing her real mother to cancer, her stepmother unable to leave the house for psychological reasons, and her father treading the boards night after night or away on location."

Annie's soapy fingers entwined with his. "Why are you so concerned? Surely it's a case for the school board or the family doctor. It's hardly a police matter."

"I feel that I let her down, Annie," Jack said. "She sought me out today after I told her and the entire school that the police were their friends and that if they had any problems they should come and speak with us, and the first one to do so I couldn't help. I just batted her back to the school to let them deal with it."

"You did the right thing," Annie said.

"Did I?"

"Of course you did."

"Did mum tell you? I've got a job," Joan said, changing the subject abruptly.

"I haven't had the chance," Annie said. "You tell him."

"Avril is taking me on as her apprentice."

"Avril the hairdresser? What do you know about hairdressing?" Jack said.

Joan looked affronted. "Hey, I can shampoo and set with the best of them. I used to do some of the customers at the pub for pin money. Avril said I can help her out on her rounds, and she'll teach me to cut and everything."

"That's good, isn't it, Jack?" Annie said.

"Yes, splendid," he said distractedly, his mind still on Tony Turner and his family. "Don't expect me to stop going to the barbers' though. Carlo's been cutting my hair since we first moved up here."

"Well, I suppose he'll get it right one day," Joan said.

Jack spun around and threw the tea towel at her.

Joan ducked. "Hey, only joking," she laughed. It lightened the mood in the kitchen. He didn't like to bring his work home with him but, for some reason, Gerry Turner had got under his skin today. He'd be thankful to get to work tomorrow and go back to chasing down and arresting some *real* criminals.

He sat in his favourite armchair listening to the *Archers* on the radio. "An everyday story of country folk", or so the BBC would have their listeners believe. He *had* believed it, and the soap opera had spurred his eventual move from the smoke and noise of Tottenham in North London to the greener, semi-rural setting of Hertfordshire. So far he hadn't been disappointed, but his date with the Archer clan in the idyllic village of Ambridge was still required listening whenever he could spare the time.

The doorbell rang and he swore softly under his breath while he waited for someone else in the house to answer it. When it became evident that everyone else was more concerned with their own pursuits and not at all interested in seeing who was at the door he said, "Bugger!" and pushed himself out of his armchair.

As he stepped out into the hallway the bell rang again. "Coming!" he called irritably. "Keep your hair on."

Detective Sergeant Eddie Fuller stood on the doorstep.

"Christ, Eddie, haven't you seen enough of me for one day?"

Jack said.

"Sorry to disturb, guv," Fuller said. "I was against it but Chief Superintendent Lane insisted I come and get you."

"Come in and tell me all about it," Jack said.

Fuller shook his head. "I'll bring you up to date while I drive."

"That urgent, eh?"

Fuller glanced at his watch and nodded.

"I'll get my coat," Jack said.

"Where are we headed?" Jack said as they pulled out onto the main road.

"Norton Common." Fuller's face was grim and he had offered no information since getting the car. "The team's already there."

His sergeant's reticence was beginning to annoy Jack. He'd found the talk he delivered to the school today to be quite draining, and that, combined with Geraldine Turner's spurious confession and the uneasy confrontation with her father, had left him feeling tense. He'd hoped to drain the stress from his system with a quiet evening at home with the *Archers* and perhaps some music later. He'd bought the new David Whitfield long player at the weekend and so far hadn't had a chance to play it. Instead he was being driven through the dull Hertfordshire night, on his way to Norton Common and its sixty acres of rolling greens, thick woodland. Home to muntjac deer, Letchworth's own black squirrel colony, and one of the most unlikely crime scenes he could imagine.

"So are you going to tell me what's waiting for us when we get to the Common? Or is this your idea of a mystery tour?"

Fuller glanced around at his boss. "Sorry, guv," he said. "My mind's on other things. I was meant to be taking Judy to the pictures tonight, but the Chief Super caught me just as I was heading home. I wouldn't mind but I've had to cancel our last three dates because of work and I don't think she'll put up with it for much longer."

"A messed up social life goes with the job, Eddie. You know that," Jack said, but he sympathised with his sergeant. The job had put a lot of strain on his relationship with Annie during the early years of their marriage. "Try to put your love life out of your mind and just tell me what the case is."

"A particularly nasty murder," he said.

"Anyone we know?"

Fuller shook his head. "No identification so far. A man, mid-forties, found by a dog walker just after six tonight."

"So what makes this murder so nasty?"

"At first the dog walker only saw him from a distance and thought it was just someone taking a leak against a tree, but he got closer to him and the man didn't move away. He couldn't. He'd been nailed there and his throat had been cut."

Suddenly the peaceful idyll of Ambridge seemed a million miles away. Jack blew through his teeth. "You'd better step on it, and use the bell."

Fuller pressed down on the accelerator, switched on the *Winkworth* bell and the Wolseley tore noisily along the main road to reach its grisly destination.

By the time they reached Norton Common the body had been taken down from the tree and was laid out on the grass with police doctor, Barry Fenwick, crouched over it conducting the preliminary examination. One of the team had driven his police car onto the common. Its engine was idling and its headlights turned night into day.

There were a handful of CID officers searching the scene by torchlight for clues, and another taking photographs, the blinding light from his flash bulbs adding occasional illumination to the gory scene.

Jack looked from the blood-spattered tree, to the sticky pool of red slowly sinking into the earth at its bole, to the body lying on the grass. "Any idea how long ago this happened, Barry?" Jack said to the doctor.

"The body's still relatively warm and rigour is only just stiffening the jaw and neck but hasn't reached the other muscles yet, so not long. Two hours, three at the most."

Jack checked his watch. It was just coming up to eight o' clock. "So between five and six. If this had happened at the end of the month when the clocks changed it would have been light.

Cause of death?"

"Catastrophic blood loss. The carotid artery has been severed. Death would have followed very quickly. Two minutes, three tops."

"And what about the stab wounds to the stomach?" Jack pointed to the blood-soaked shirt.

Fenwick shook his head. "Superficial. None of them look deep enough to be fatal. They could be hesitation wounds but I think rather they were designed to cause pain, not to kill."

"It's a shame he was taken down," Jack said. "I would have liked to have seen the body in situ, so to speak."

"Your man took photographs," Fenwick said. "But if it helps you to visualize it, his arms were raised above his head and a six-inch nail had been hammered through the palms of his hands. Judging from the tearing of the flesh on his palms I'd say he was hanging there for several minutes being tortured before his throat was cut. Of course the autopsy will yield a more accurate picture."

"As will the photographs," Jack said with a shudder.

"Now this *is* interesting." Fenwick leaned closer to the body. He took a pair of tweezers from his bag and started probing the black moustache on the body's top lip. A few moments later he said. "Yes, I thought so." He lifted his hand. Caught between the tweezers' points was something thin black and hairy.

"Fake," Jack said, staring at it.

Fenwick nodded, dropped the false moustache into a polythene bag and returned his attention back to the body's face. "Can I have some more light here," he called to an officer holding a torch. The officer swung the beam down to the dead man's face. Jack glanced at it and took in the details of the corpse; a middle-aged man of Latin extraction judging from the look of the swarthy skin. Fenwick leaned in closer still and the shadow cast by his body obscured Jack's view.

"Curiouser and curiouser," Fenwick muttered as he worked at the face with the tweezers.

Jack moved in to get a closer look at what the doctor was doing. He appeared to be poking the corpse's nose with the point of the tweezers. Finally with an almost exultant cry of,

"Yes, I thought so," Fenwick pulled back and rested on his haunches. He looked up at Jack. "Well, what do you make of this?" he said and brandished the tweezers. Jack stared at them. Caught between the points was a blob of something light brown and fleshy.

"What the hell is that?" he said.

"Nose putty," Fenwick said. "Or mortician's wax." He saw the look of bewilderment on Jack face and smiled. "It's a fake nose, Chief Inspector and, judging from the paleness of the skin beneath it, it looks like your man here is wearing makeup – the theatrical kind."

Jack crouched down beside the body, took a handkerchief from his pocket and started to wipe greasepaint away from the face. A few minutes later he said, "Good God!" and stood upright.

"What is it, guv? Do you recognise him?" said Fuller, who'd been watching the whole procedure with a kind of macabre fascination.

Jack nodded, still staring down at the body. "Yes, Sergeant. I recognise him. In fact I was talking to him just this afternoon. His name is Tony Turner. He's an actor."

"Well, I suppose that would explain the makeup."

"Yes, but not why he was wearing it. Nor does it explain why he was found nailed to a tree with his throat cut," Jack added grimly.

3 - TUESDAY

Jack surveyed the scene bleakly. Several yards away WPC Myra Banks was standing, talking to an elderly man wearing a windcheater and corduroy trousers, holding a equally elderly looking golden retriever on a leather leash.

"I take it that's our dog walker," Jack said to PC Alan Blake who was standing nearby looking a little green around the gills. Blake nodded and swallowed loudly. He was only twenty-two, not long out of Hendon, and this was his first murder scene.

"Are you all right, Constable?" Jack said to him.

The young constable shook his head. "I've never seen anything like it."

"You'll see worse before you're finished. Get off home. Come in tomorrow morning after a good night's sleep."

"Yes, sir." Blake looked suitably relieved. "Thank you, sir," he said as he scuttled away from the crime scene.

"Do you remember your first murder, Eddie?" Jack said, watching the constable's trouser cuffs flapping over the grass as he hurried away.

"It's etched indelibly on my mind. An old woman killed in a block of flats in Stevenage. Robbed for her pension money, her head split open like a ripe melon. I threw up for two days solid." He shuddered.

"There's nothing else I can do here," Jack said. "I'm going to break the news to Turner's wife. Give me the keys and I'll take the Wolseley. Can you get a lift back to the station with one of the others?"

"Don't worry about me. It's a mild night. I'll walk."

"As you like, but talk to the dog walker first. See if he's told us all he knows. Myra!" he called to the WPC. "You're coming with me."

"Where are we going?" Myra said as she settled into the seat beside Jack.

"Up to the Broadway. A house called *Elsinore*. We have to break the news to Tony Turner's wife. It's why I wanted you along…to comfort her while I make a cup of tea."

"Great," Myra said grimly. "*I* could always make the tea."

"Your shoulder is more absorbent than mine," Jack said with a smile.

"I doubt it. But I'll do my best."

"Yes, I know you will." He liked Myra Banks. She was on secondment to CID after a number of years spent in uniform and Jack wanted to make her position permanent. He had the *nose* of a good detective and, from what he'd seen of her so far, he had yet to be disappointed by her talents.

"Well, not exactly a Danish castle," Myra said as they pulled in through the gates. "But impressive nonetheless."

The Turner house was a turn of the century yellow brick mansion, with a red tiled roof and four large picture windows taking up much of the downstairs frontage. Jack pulled up outside the maroon-painted front door and switched off the engine. He took a deep breath and glanced at Myra. "Let's get this done." He opened the driver's door.

The woman who greeted them was plump, elderly with wavy grey hair and rosy-apple cheeks.

"Chief Inspector Callum and Detective Constable Banks to see Mrs Turner," Jack said brandishing his warrant card.

The plump woman peered at the card myopically before opening the door wide. "Please come in and wait in the hall," she said. "I'll tell Lois you're here."

Leaving them standing in the spacious hallway, she disappeared through a doorway to the left of them. Jack looked about, noticing the framed playbills hanging from the striped wallpapered walls. Ahead of them was a wide staircase and on the wall at the top of the stairs was an oil painting in an ornate gilt frame.

"The master of the house," Jack said wryly. "Looking a lot different to when we saw him an hour ago."

Myra followed his line of sight and stared up at the portrait of a handsome man, relaxing on a high-backed chair, dressed casually in blue slacks and a cream shirt, open at the neck to reveal a dark blue silk cravat. The pose was relaxed, legs crossed, hand on his chin, a cigarette caught between his fingers. The artist had deftly caught the blue-grey cigarette smoke eddying up to mingle with the oh-so-carefully-ruffled hair of the sitter, giving Turner the look of a rather stylish vagabond.

Myra opened her mouth to say something and then snapped it shut as a tall, elegantly-dressed woman stepped into the hallway. From her elaborately coiffed honey-blonde hair to the tips of her expensive Italian stilettos, Lois Turner, née Franklin, looked every inch the high-class model she used to be. With a broad smile that lit up her perfectly made up face she walked towards them, hand extended.

"Lois Turner," she said. "Very pleased to meet you."

There was just a hint of an American accent to her voice. Jack shook her hand. "Can we go somewhere and sit down," he said. "I'm afraid I have some very distressing news about your husband."

"About Tony?" Lois said, the poise slipping from her features as if someone had thrown a switch. "What is it?"

"If we can just go somewhere and sit down," Jack said again.

Lois looked flustered. "Yes, yes, of course, come through."

As Jack followed them through another door leading from the hallway he glanced back up the stairs in time to see a young fair-haired girl duck back out of sight behind a wall.

Lois Turner led them through the house to a smallish room, its walls lined with books, interspersed with more framed playbills, these ones looking older than the ones hanging in the entrance hall. Some of the names were familiar to Jack, but he could see from the bemused look on Myra's face that names like Herbert Beerbohm-Tree and Mrs Patrick Campbell meant nothing to her.

"This is Tony's office. Please take a seat," Lois said and indicated an expensive looking settee upholstered in deep red velvet. "Now," she said. "Would you mind telling me what all this is about?" She pulled a hard chair out from under an oak desk and sat down rather primly, demurely crossing her ankles and leaning forward slightly as if wanting to catch every word.

"It's your husband, Mrs Turner," Jack said. "I'm afraid there's been an incident."

"Has he crashed his car again? I keep telling him not to drive so recklessly. Do you know if he'll be home soon?"

Jack held up his hand to cut her off. "I'm afraid it's a lot more serious than that."

The words did not come easily to him but eventually he managed to convey that her husband would not be coming home that night, or any other night for that matter.

When he'd finished speaking a hush settled over the room, broken by Myra who got to her feet and announced she would make a cup of tea.

"That won't be necessary," Lois said, her composure restored. "Hester will make one." She crossed to the desk and pressed a black bell push. A few seconds later the door opened and the plump woman from the hall stepped into the room.

"Tea for our guests, Hester, if you please."

"Of course," Hester said and asked if they wanted milk or lemon.

"My rock," Lois said as the older woman left the room. "I don't know how I would cope if it wasn't for Hester. She keeps me organized, and she's especially good at helping me with Geraldine, my stepdaughter. I can't leave the house you see."

"Yes," Jack said quietly. "I spoke to your husband earlier today. He told me of your problem."

"Ah, my *problem*, yes. I suppose that's one way of putting it." She sat back down on the hard chair. "So, Tony's dead," she mused. "I can see that causing problems, especially for Geraldine. She and I have never got on, and Tony, dear Tony, played the role of peacekeeper throughout our marriage."

Myra leaned forward in her seat. "Forgive me for saying this, Mrs Turner, but you don't seem exactly heartbroken that your husband has been killed."

Lois winced and Jack glared sharply at the young constable. "What WPC Banks means…"

Lois shook herself, cutting him off herself. "I'm sad…of course I'm sad, but I never saw Tony and I making old bones together."

"Have you any idea who might have done this?" Jack said. "Did your husband have any enemies?"

"Would you like me to compile a list?"

"You're saying that your husband had a lot of enemies?"

Lois crossed her ankles again. "Tony was a...how can I put this? Tony was a difficult man. He made enemies as easily as you or I make acquaintances."

"I see," Jack said.

Lois gave a brittle laugh. "I doubt that very much. Go to any theatre in the West End, or any film set in Hertfordshire for that matter, and get the people there to tell you what they thought of Tony Turner. I think you'll find that their answers will make your hair curl."

"And you?" Myra said. "You don't seem that surprised...or even dismayed...that someone's killed him."

"I loved my husband very much...for all his faults," Lois said, and then tears started to flow. She reached into her handbag and took out a handkerchief, dabbing at her eyes and blowing her nose.

Hester came back into the room carrying a tray. She set the tray down on a coffee table and, with an effort, squatted down next to Lois, wrapping a comforting arm around her shoulders.

Lois shrugged her off. "I'm all right, Hester, really. I've just had some very bad news. It's Tony, he's been killed."

"Oh, great Heavens," Hester said. "Is there anything I can do?"

"You can pour the tea," Lois said.

Once the tea was poured into bone china cups, Hester once again left the room.

"There's the question of identification," Jack said. "We need you to identify the body."

Lois sipped her tea and looked at him tearfully over the rim of the cup. "Well, that's not going to happen," Steel was suddenly back in her voice. "You told me that my dear departed husband had appraised you of my situation. I won't leave the house."

"But the law requires that..."

19

"...that a formal identification must be made by the next of kin," Lois said. "Yes, I'm aware of that. Tony's parents are still alive. They're living in Shillington in Bedfordshire. I'm sure they meet your requirements."

"They do but..."

"No ifs, no buts," Lois said forcefully. "If necessary I can get my doctor to write a letter to your boss excusing me. Mark Francombe understands agoraphobia and has helped me a great deal."

"And Mark Francombe's your doctor?" Myra said, jotting the name down in her notebook.

Lois gave her a withering look. "Of course. I can give you his address if you like."

"Thank you," Myra said.

"And I would appreciate that list," Jack said.

"List?"

"Of the people who could wish your husband harm."

With a sigh Lois got to her feet, went across to the desk, opened a drawer, took out a notepad and a Biro and started to scrawl the doctor's address together with a list of names.

"The ice maiden cometh," Myra said when they got back to the car.

"She seemed quite emotional."

"She was play acting. There was nothing until I mentioned that she didn't seem very upset by her husband's death, and then she turned on the waterworks."

"You're a cynic."

"I'm a woman, guv. It takes more than a few crocodile tears to fool me. Do you think she could have had something to do with it?"

"I'm not ruling anything out."

"But you heard her, sir. She can't leave the house."

"She said *won't*, not *can't*," Jack said. "But somehow I can't see her nailing her husband to a tree and cutting his throat in the middle of Norton Common, can you?"

Myra shook her head. "And risk chipping her nail varnish? That manicure must have cost her a packet. So no, I don't think so."

"Check her story with the doctor anyway. Mark Francombe. He's in East Street. The Millbrook surgery."

"I'll call on him on the way in tomorrow." Myra fell silent, staring out at the darkened streets as Jack drove them back through the town. "I wouldn't put it past her to pay someone to kill him though," she said after a while.

"You've got the mind of a detective," Jack said.

"Well, don't tell him. He might want it back."

Jack smiled. "Can I drop you off at home? It's getting late."

She shook her head. "Thanks, but no thanks. Can you take me back to the station? I have to see Chief Superintendent Lane before I go home."

"Do you think he'll still be there at this time of the evening?" Jack said doubtfully.

It's at his request, so he'd better be there."

4 - WEDNESDAY MARCH 18ᵀᴴ 1959

"What do you mean, *she won't identify the body*?" Chief Superintendent Henry Lane said as he paced back and forth in his office.

"Just that," Jack said. "She can't leave the house."

"Well, that just won't do. We need a formal identification."

"She'll get her doctor to write a letter of excuse if we put any pressure on her."

"Excusing her for carrying out her public duty?" Lane said, a vein in his temple bulging ominously as his temper rose. "Never mind her duty as a wife."

"She's agoraphobic, sir," Jack explained patiently. "She suffers from extreme panic attacks if she goes out into the open. Her doctor will confirm that, or so she says. WPC Banks is going to verify that on her way in this morning."

"Never heard such rubbish," Lane muttered and stopped pacing. "Well, what are you going to do about it, Chief Inspector?"

"His parents live in Shillington. I'm going to pay them a visit and see if they'll oblige."

"Yes, do that, and then we can move this investigation onto a more formal footing." Lane sat down at his desk and picked up a pen that was lying on the blotter in front of him. He tapped it against his teeth and put it down again. "Nailed to a tree and tortured. What a way to go," he mused quietly. "Do you think the wife had anything to do with it?"

"I'm not sure," Jack said. "WPC Banks suggested the same thing."

"Bright girl that one. Anything else?"

"Mrs Turner gave me a list of people who might wish her husband harm." Jack took a folded piece of paper from his pocket and laid it on the desk under the chief superintendent's nose. Lane glanced at it and then snatched it up and studied it more closely.

"I've heard of some of the names on here," he said sounding

appalled.

"There's a couple I recognise too."

"Our Mr. Turner could give Mussolini a run for his money in the popularity stakes. Are you going to talk to all of these people?"

"I'm certainly going to try."

"Well, speak to the parents first. See if they can shed any light."

Jack walked to the door. "I'll get over to Shillington."

He drove through the picturesque village of Shillington, tucked just inside the Bedfordshire border. He'd been here some years before when he was looking to make the move from Tottenham in London but had dismissed it as being too rural, too much of a departure from his urban roots.

The Turners lived in a bungalow situated at the blunt end of a cul-de-sac. The surrounding houses looked well appointed, with neatly cut lawns, tidy flowerbeds and clusters of trimmed conifers.

He walked up the gravel path and rang the doorbell, sheltering under the tiled porch from a thin drizzle that had started to fall from a leaden March sky. A tall man with short iron-grey hair and a military bearing opened the door almost immediately. His eyes narrowed as he peered at Jack's warrant card. "You took your time," he said bluntly. "After the Harpy's call I was expecting you last night."

"The Harpy?"

"The Franklin woman."

"Your daughter-in-law?"

"Our daughter-in-law was Polly...the lovely Polly." His voice caught in his throat. "But she was like a real daughter to us in so many ways. The Harpy took her place. She usurped her, damn the woman!"

"I gather that you two don't get on. So why did she telephone you to say that I wanted to see you?"

"My wife took the call. I hardly ever see the Franklin woman, thank God." He extended a hand. "Laurence Turner," he said, stepping to one side. "You'd better come in."

He led Jack inside the bungalow. It was modestly furnished with a three-piece-suite that was probably new just after the First World War, and had seen its own share of battles since then.

"I was hoping to speak to both your wife and yourself," Jack said.

"Jean won't see you. As I said, she took the 'phone call from the Harpy and after that she took to her bed, unable to face the fact that her son, her beloved Anthony, was dead. If she sees you it will make her face the reality of the situation and she's not strong enough for that...not yet anyway."

"Your daughter-in...Lois...told her the reason I wanted to see you?"

"You want me to stare at a body on a slab and confirm that it's my son," Turner said bluntly. "Yes. She told her, and no doubt derived a lot of pleasure in doing so."

"They've taken him to North Herts Hospital. The mortuary there is...well, the staff...know how to handle these things sensitively."

Turner flopped down on one of the armchairs and buried his face in his hands. When he took them away from his face Jack was expecting to see tears moistening the old man's cheeks, but the cheeks were dry and the old man's eyes had lost none of their disdain.

"Don't expect me to grieve, Chief Inspector," Turner said when he noticed Jack's interest. "I'll shed no tears for that one."

"But he *was* your son, and the manner of his death was..."

"He was my son," Turner interrupted, "but he was also an unmitigated shit, and I don't care who knows it. He broke his mother's heart, never visiting her from one year to the next. And as for poor Polly... That girl deserved so much more out of life. When she fell ill and needed her husband at her side she got nothing. While she lay dying my son was off, having it away with that American whore."

There was sheer venom in his voice.

"We have a granddaughter, you know, who we haven't seen since her mother passed away. Can you imagine how much that hurts us?" Turner said, his eyes tearful for the first time.

"I can imagine, sir," Jack said gently.

"Can we go to the hospital now and get this over with?" Turner said, gathering himself.

"I can drive you there."

"Let me go up and see my wife, to tell her I'm going to be out for a while. North Herts Hospital you say?"

Jack nodded.

"Bloody inconvenient," Laurence Turner said sourly.

As they crossed the border back into Hertfordshire, Jack said, "Lois wrote me a list of names of the people who might have wanted to harm your son."

"Did she? May I see it?" Turner said unemotionally.

Jack took a folded sheet of paper from his inside jacket pocket and handed it to him. For a short while there was no sound in the car apart from the steady swish of the windscreen wipers, the thrum of the Wolseley's engine and Turner's slightly stentorian breathing.

"It's quite a short list," Turner said at last. "I can think of at least three more names, not including my own."

"Your son was really *that* unpopular?"

"It's hard to credit isn't it? Tony Turner, star of stage and screen. Loved by the masses, loathed by those who really knew him."

Jack fished in his pocket again, produced a pen and handed it to Turner. "Just add the names to the bottom of the list, if you wouldn't mind. Don't bother to add your own."

"As you wish," the old man said.

"Yes, that's him," Laurence Turner said as the mortuary attendant drew back the sheet to reveal Tony Turner's makeup-free face. "Cover him back up, for God's sake. I don't want to look at him any longer than I have to."

Jack nodded to the attendant. "I'll take you back to the station and arrange for a car to take you home."

"Yes, thank you. Jean will start to panic if I'm gone for too long."

"Of the list I showed you, and the names you added, were there any that stood out as being likely suspects?"

"I'm not going to do your job for you, Chief Inspector," Turner said sharply.

"No, sir, I'm not expecting you to do that. I just wondered if any names jumped out at you."

Turner sighed as he sat down in the passenger seat. "To be quite honest with you, ninety per cent of them mean nothing to me at all. Of the few I recognise only one of them would have the guts to do something like this, and the last I heard he was in a nursing home after suffering a calamitous stroke a couple of years ago, so I don't think he's your man."

"I'll take his name anyway, sir."

"Usher. Thomas Usher, my son's old business partner."

"Your son and Mr. Usher were in business together?"

"If you can call prostitution a business."

"Prostitution?"

"My son chose to call it an escort agency. He and Usher used to employ whores to cater to the baser needs of his so-called show business friends. He was a pimp, Chief Inspector, nothing more, nothing less. He closed down the business shortly after he met the Harpy. I think Usher was very angry about it, Anthony killing the golden goose, so to speak. I knew he harboured a grudge over it. Usher had no show business contacts of his own so he couldn't keep the agency open. He lost a packet from what I heard. And he was a man you wouldn't want to upset."

"Really?"

"Thomas Usher was a gangster pure and simple. He owned several drinking dens in Soho and, if my memory serves me correctly, a night club in the West End, but the name of it escapes me."

"And he's the only one you think would be capable of killing your son?"

"In his heyday he could have killed Tony in the blink of an eye and not given it another thought. But as I say, he's not your

26

man. From what my son told me, the stroke has left him with the mental acumen of a cauliflower."

Jack nodded. "Well, thank you for that. You've been very helpful." He drove the Wolseley smoothly into the station car park. "Right, let's see about getting you a ride home."

"Thomas Usher," Jack said to Eddie Fuller when he entered the squad room. "Have you ever heard of him?"

Fuller shook his head. "The name means nothing to me. Should it?"

"Probably not," Jack said and walked through to the stairs that led up to his office. At the doorway he paused and turned back. "Get on to Division and see what you can dig up on him. He was very active in the South London area a few years ago. A stroke put paid to his criminal ways apparently."

He looked beyond Fuller and watched Myra Banks pinning a glossy page taken from a magazine to the incident board she was compiling.

"Something you want to share with us, Myra?" he called.

"It's a *Knight's Castile* soap advert from an old copy of *Woman's Own*. I found it at my mother's. She has copies of the magazine going back years." She smiled. "It's the only image of Lois Turner I've been able to find so far, but I'm still looking."

Jack went across and peered at the advert.

"It was taken before she made her name as the *Cadence Girl*," Myra said.

The advertisement depicted a young woman smiling into the bathroom mirror while spreading a thick soapy lather on her porcelain cheek. *"Knight's Castile. My secret for soft, soft skin."*

"Do you women believe all that guff?" Jack said.

Myra smiled. "I don't, but you live with three of them. Try asking them."

"Do you have a photograph of our victim?"

"Tony Turner?" She shook her head. "The only one I've been able to find so far is a publicity picture from the 1955

Picturegoer annual, but it's been heavily touched up. She rummaged through a small pile of papers on a desk nearby, pulled out a page and handed it to him.

Jack stared at it. "It makes him look like a waxwork of himself, but I suppose we'll have to make do with this until we get a better shot of him."

"I'll get down to the library later," Myra said. "They have copies of *Spotlight*, the actors' directory, in their reference section. I might be able to get a better image from there."

"Good thinking. See if you can get a better one of his wife as well. One where she's not trying to sell me something."

"That might be easier said than done. Selling herself was how she made her name."

"In more ways than one, if you believe Tony Turner's father. I'll be in my office if you need me."

5 - WEDNESDAY

Strange noises were coming from the rear of the Callum household as Jack stepped in through the front door. There was the sound of a strumming guitar and a clattering rattle, all underpinned by a deep thump, thump, thump.

He stuck his head around the kitchen door. Annie was at the cooker stirring the contents of a large aluminium saucepan with a wooden spoon. "What's the racket?" he said.

Annie turned at the sound of his voice, a smile on her lips. "Your son. Eric has some friends round."

"What are they doing back there? Building a tank?"

"They may as well be." Annie lifted a spoonful of steaming brown liquid from the pot and tasted it gingerly. "Hmm. Perfect. Beef stew. I've just got to make the dumplings. Can you go though and tell Eric he only has three quarters of an hour before I'm ready to serve."

"Is it safe back there?"

She smiled. "You might want to take earplugs with you."

Jack shook his head and wandered through to the back room. He raised his eyebrows at the scene and the noise that greeted him. Eric, his fourteen-year old son, was sitting on a dining chair, a guitar resting on his knee, his head bowed over it. While the fingers of his left hand contorted around the guitar's neck making chord shapes, his right hand strummed the guitar furiously.

Beside him, standing with one foot resting on a scruffy looking tea chest was a thin boy of a similar age dressed in jeans and a plaid shirt open at the neck. Attached to the side of the tea chest was a broom handle. A thin cord snaked up from a hole in the chest and appeared to be tied to the top of the handle. The thin boy had his eyes closed and was pulling back on the broom handle whilst, at the same time, plucked at the thin cord with a leather-gloved hand, making the thumping sound Jack had heard as he'd walked in through the front door.

In the corner was yet another boy, who he recognised as Philip

Langton, son of the local butcher. On his knee was a glass washboard. He had metal thimbles on his fingers and he was moving them quickly them over the corrugated glass of the washboard, making a percussive, rattling sound that jarred the filings in Jack's teeth.

His daughter, Rosie, two years older than Eric and pretty enough to turn heads in the street, got up from the armchair. Eric, still strumming, nodded to her and she started to sing a bouncy skiffle song about a freight train in a voice as clear as a bell. She looked across at Jack and stopped singing halfway through the verse. "Oh, hello, Dad," she said. "What do you think?"

"I didn't know you could sing." Jack raised his voice to make himself heard above the din.

Rosie blushed. "I can't, not really. I'm just helping Eric out. This is his skiffle group."

"So I gathered." Jack stared at his son who grinned back at him. The other boys stopped playing and looked to Jack for signs of approval.

Jack smiled indulgently. "Very good," he said to them and turned to Eric. "Mother asked me to tell you that dinner will be in forty five minutes, so you might want to think about packing this in soon."

Back in the kitchen, he sat down at the kitchen table and poured himself a cup of tea from brown earthenware pot. "Was it really such a good idea letting him have a guitar?"

"You should be pleased he's so enthusiastic," Annie said. "It's just a hobby."

"So is stamp collecting…and it's quieter."

"Don't be such a grouch." Annie came across and kissed the top of his head.

"Rosie's got a set of pipes on her," he said.

"You would have known that if you'd ever managed to get to one of her school concerts."

Annie's comment stung him. "It's work. Crime doesn't stop just to accommodate my social life."

"No, but it would be nice if it did, just once in a while." Annie wrapped her arms around his neck. "I'm not nagging, Jack. I just don't want you to miss out on our children growing up just because people are beastly to each other. I sometimes wonder what's the matter with them all."

"I do that on a daily basis." He changed the subject. "That stew smells marvellous."

"It won't be long." She hugged him briefly and went back to the cooker.

Eddie Fuller pushed open the swing doors of the *Dog and Duck* and made his way to the bar. There were a few of the regulars in there drinking, even this early in the evening. His sometimes girlfriend, Judy Taylor, was pulling pints with her usual aplomb. She looked up as Eddie strolled towards her. "Hello, stranger," she said heavily, weighting her words to show her displeasure. "What are you doing here tonight? Is it business or pleasure?"

"It's always a pleasure to see you, Judy, but tonight it's business."

She shook her head resignedly. "Yes, I thought it might be."

"Actually, I'm meeting someone here."

"Anyone I know?"

"I doubt it. Charlie Somers, my old guvnor, from when I was a DC over at Stevenage. I was his bagman. He went to work for the Met in '53, but we've stayed in touch."

"What will you have while you're waiting?"

"Just a half of bitter. I want to keep a clear head."

Judy took a half-pint glass from the shelf above her head and pulled down on one of the pumps, filling it at a stroke. "There you go." She put the drink down on the towelling bar mat. "Is that your friend?" she said as the doors swung inwards and a middle-aged man wearing a Gabardine raincoat and sporting short, neatly clipped grey hair, pushed into the pub.

Fuller glanced around and threw a salute at the man. "Yes, that's him. You'd better pour a pint of Guinness. I doubt his tastes have changed." He turned to Charlie Somers and called,

"Grab a table, Charlie. I'll bring the drinks over."

Somers took off his raincoat, hung it from a stand in the corner and went across to a small round table under the window. Fuller took the drinks across and settled himself opposite, pushing the Guinness across to the older man. "Thanks for coming," he said.

"Free beer. How could I resist?" Somers picked up the pint and downed half of it with one long gulp. He wiped the creamy froth from his top lip and sat forward. "Now, what is it you wanted to talk to me about that you couldn't say over the 'phone?"

Fuller sipped at his pint. "Thomas Usher."

Somers glared at him and pushed the glass away angrily. "Is that what you dragged me up here for? I thought more of you than that, Eddie." He started to get to his feet.

Fuller stretched out his hand and laid it over the older man's arm. "Simmer down, Charlie, and sit down. Just hear me out."

"About Usher? You have to be kidding me. That bastard effectively put the kybosh on my career...at least he ensured I'd never climb higher in the force than DI, and I was already that when I first joined the Met."

"They say that if you lie down with rats you never get the stink of the sewer off you."

"The inquiry cleared me of any wrongdoing." Somers' glare intensified and for a moment Fuller was concerned that his old boss might thump him.

"But both you and I know that they weren't in possession of all of the facts," he said quickly, trying to mollify him.

It didn't work. "Are you saying I'm dirty, Eddie? Because if that's what you're implying, I'll take your sodding head off."

Fuller held up his hands. "Christ, Charlie, calm down. That's not what I'm saying at all. I know you were never in Usher's pocket, but your connection to him rubbed a lot of people up the wrong way."

Somers' eyes narrowed. "Does your current guvnor know that you're talking to me about this?"

Fuller shook his head. "And I told him I'd never heard of Usher."

"Do you think that was wise? I know Jack Callum's

reputation. Nothing much gets past him. He made Barry Fisher look bloody stupid last year when the superintendent was up here on a case, and Fisher's no fool, believe me. Jack Callum doesn't sound like the type of man you want to cross." Somers relaxed into his seat and picked up his glass again.

"Look, Charlie, Jack's a great boss and I think of him as a friend. He told me to get onto Division and find out all I can about Usher, but you're my friend as well and I wanted to speak to you before I did."

"Well, you don't have to bother Division. I have everything you need to know, up here." He tapped the side of his head. "I suppose you know that Usher's out of the picture now."

Fuller nodded. "So I hear."

"Yeah. A stroke got him. From what I've heard, they've got him stashed away in a nursing home, somewhere in Kent I think it is. He's little more than a vegetable these days. Serves the bastard right." He shifted in his seat and finished his pint. "I'll have another of those."

Fuller picked up the glass and took it across to Judy for a refill.

By the time he took it back to Somers his old boss had lit a briar pipe and was sucking on it, watching two of the locals playing a game of darts.

"Those two couldn't hit a cow's arse with a banjo," he said disparagingly. "I hope they're not in your pub's darts' team."

"They're not. Just having a bit of fun, that's all. I remember you used to be quite handy with the arrows yourself."

"I gave it up when my eyesight started failing. I need glasses just to drive the sodding car these days." He took the Guinness and quaffed another half pint. "So why the sudden interest in Usher? He was never really in your bailiwick."

"No, but his business partner was."

"Usher had lots of business partners. Anyone I know?"

"The actor, Tony Turner. We found him yesterday evening, nailed to a tree, tortured, with his throat cut."

Somers blew out through his lips. "Nasty. I see now why you're asking about Usher. That kind of thing was his stock in trade. Did Turner still have his conkers?"

"Conkers?"

"Conkers, testicles, gonads...*his balls*."

"Yes, I think so."

"It wasn't Usher then. Castration was one of Tommy's chief delights. He made it a kind of trademark; his own personal calling card."

"I think you'd better tell me everything you know about him."

"Do you have your notebook?"

Fuller nodded.

"Let's just hope you have enough pages."

6 - THURSDAY MARCH 19TH 1959

Jack sat at his desk reading through Tony Turner's post mortem report.

"Any surprises?" Fuller said as he came into the office and took a seat at a desk alongside Jack's. Office sharing was Chief Superintendent Henry Lane's latest cost-cutting measure as he struggled with the county council's swingeing cuts to the police budget.

"I don't like it any more than you do, Jack. But needs must…"

Jack noted to himself wryly that Lane himself would not be sharing *his* office with anyone. He had no real problem sharing his space with Eddie Fuller. They worked so closely together that Annie had once joked they were almost joined at the hip.

He looked up at his sergeant. "Pretty much as we expected really. Cause of death was massive blood loss from a severed carotid artery. The wounds to the body were mostly superficial, as Barry Fenwick said, designed to cause maximum pain without being life-threatening."

"So, you think that whoever did this knew what they were doing?"

"I would think so."

"Was Turner castrated?"

Jack flicked over a page. "It doesn't say so here."

"It can't be Usher then."

"What makes you say that? Oh, yes, you spoke to Division, didn't you?"

"Yes…yes I did." Fuller's cheeks flushed slightly. "Castration of his victims was Thomas Usher's signature." He avoided Jack's gaze.

"Well, don't keep me in suspense. What else did you find out?"

"In his day, Usher was a thoroughly nasty piece of work. He built himself a crime empire South of the river that stretched up as far as the West End of London. He had his fingers in many pies, all of them illegal. From prostitution to gambling dens, illegal drinking clubs, large scale smuggling of cigarettes and booze, protection racket, in fact, you name it, if it was against the law and guaranteed to bring in cash then Usher was involved. He was linked to several bank robberies, but never arrested through lack of evidence. It was the same story with the murders. Potential witnesses ended up disappearing in suspicious circumstances, but there was nothing to link Usher directly to any of them.

"Of course, he had his legitimate interests as well. He owned a nightclub in Bloomsbury, *The Purple Flamingo*, and the escort agency he ran with Tony Turner, although the Met were about to look into that when Turner shut it down."

"And you still don't think he's our man?"

"He had a stroke, guv. From what they know, he's not *compos mentis* these days, certainly not in any condition to kill anyone, or even to order someone else to do it for him."

"Which more or less confirms what Laurence Turner told me. I just wanted to check to see if the old man was flannelling me. It seems not. Thanks, Eddie. Good work. I didn't think it was going to be *that* easy."

There was a knock at the door and a uniformed WPC entered the room. It took Jack a few seconds to realize it was Myra Banks.

"Myra? Back in uniform?"

Myra smiled at him tightly. "My secondment to CID ended yesterday, so yes, back in the blues. Orders from Chief Superintendent Lane."

He could tell from the tremor in her voice that she was less than happy about her situation.

"Doctor Francombe confirmed Lois Turner's story, and I've got new images of Tony Turner and his wife." She was holding two black and white photographs, and laid them down on his desk.

Jack glanced at them. "Much better. Are you still in charge of the incident board?"

"Until I'm told otherwise."

He frowned. "Well, that's not going to happen. You'd better take the photos downstairs and pin them up on the board."

"Yes, sir."

"One more thing. What did the chief superintendent say about your application to join CID?"

"He turned it down flat." She was unable to keep the bitterness out of her voice.

"Did he give you a reason?"

She shook her head. "He just said, *not at this time.*"

"Best you leave it to me. I make you no promises, but I'll see what I can do."

"Yes, sir. Thank you, sir."

"Well, that'll be all for the moment."

Myra stiffened to attention. "Yes, sir." Her hand moved slightly at her side.

"Myra, if you salute me I'll have you thrown into one of the cells," Jack said gently.

A smile was playing on her lips as Myra left the office.

"Why the makeup and the false nose?" Fuller said when they were alone once more. He was reading through the post mortem result and finding nothing new.

"That's what's been bothering me. He'd just finished a run at the *Lyric* theatre and the next thing he had lined up was a film in two weeks-time, so he wasn't working on another play, and yet there he was wearing makeup to darken his skin, a false moustache and that bloody wax nose."

"So it was a disguise of some sort."

"Yes, but one that wouldn't bear close scrutiny. It might have convinced those in the front row of the stalls, but close to it would have been fairly obvious." Jack thought for a moment. "But maybe that was the point. It only had to be convincing to someone twenty feet away."

"For what reason?"

Jack scratched his head. "I don't know, Eddie. Maybe we're coming at this the wrong way. Maybe it has nothing to do with his association with criminals like Thomas Usher."

"The acting world?"

Jack reached into his pocket and took out Lois Turner's list and handed it to Fuller. "You and Frank start checking out these names. Look into their backgrounds. See if any of them strike you as likely candidates. There are a couple of fairly well known actors on there, but apart from professional jealousy I can't see any motive for murder. When I met Turner I didn't like him much, and I can see how he could easily get people's backs up, but it's a huge step to take from being annoyed with someone to nailing them to a tree and slitting their throat. I spoke with him about noon on Tuesday and by five o' clock he'd been murdered. We need to find out what he was doing in those hours preceding his death. I think I'm going to talk to the wife again. See if she can shed any light."

"Do you want me to come along?"

Jack shook his head. "No, I'll take Myra with me. She didn't buy any of that loving spouse stuff, in fact she was quite unsympathetic to the woman. We men are soft touches, easily taken in by a few tears. Myra's made of tougher stuff."

"You really like her, don't you?"

"She reminds me of my Joanie, a marshmallow exterior with a steel core at her centre. She'll make a fine detective someday. I just don't know why Lane can't see that." He shook his head again. "I'm going to have a word with him, see if I can't get him to change his mind."

"Good luck with that," Fuller said. "When Frank Lesser complained to him about having to share an office with Trevor Walsh and Harry Grant he threatened to sack him."

"He's under a lot of pressure at the moment what with the cuts in the police budget, and I doubt that the Chief Constable Rix is making life easy for him, setting impossible targets for him just to appease the county council. But I have to try. Myra deserves it. She's worked hard these past six months."

Jack walked into Lane's office. "You turned down Myra Banks' application to join CID."

Lane looked up from his work. "Has knocking gone out of fashion?"

Jack glanced back at the door. "It was open."

"My door is always open," Lane said blithely, "to those who have a genuine grievance."

"But I've worked with Myra Banks day in, day out, for six months now, and I know she's got what it takes to make a damned fine addition to my team."

"Actually, you've had her for a little over eight months. I added another two months to her secondment while I monitored her progress. So you should be counting your blessings. I could have had her back in uniform in January."

"So why now? And why block her application to join CID?"

Lane regarded him steadily for a moment. "Take a seat, Jack."

"It's okay, I'll stand."

"Sit down, Chief Inspector!" Lane's voice rose.

Jack pulled up a hard chair and sat.

"Right." Lane cleared his throat. "Firstly let me say that I don't have to justify my decisions to you, or to anyone else in this station for that matter." He took off his glasses, started cleaning them with a handkerchief and inspected them. "Secondly." He placed the glasses back on the bridge of his nose. "I think Myra Banks is a very fine police constable, but at the moment that's her level. CID? I think not."

Jack opened his mouth to speak but Lane raised a finger to silence him.

"I haven't finished. Please do me the courtesy of listening without interruption."

Jack nodded his acquiescence.

"Very well." Lane leaned forward in his seat. "Do you know how many female CID officers there are in the country, Jack?"

Jack shook his head.

"Less than fifty, and do you know the reason for that?"

"I'd imagine it's not their lack of intelligence or commitment."

"No, it's not. As I said, I've seen Banks work and she's very good at what she does…"

"But?"

"But the truth is, Jack, give her another few years and she will have married and left the force." Lane smiled indulgently, as if he was lecturing a child. "She'll be domiciled in some two up,

39

two down, popping out babies with monotonous regularity, and…" He paused for effect. "And my budget won't stretch to training someone who'll be gone in a blink of an eye."

"And does the Chief Constable agree with that view?"

Lane snorted derisively. "Most senior police officers do, the Chief Constable included."

"So you're telling me that you're willing to sacrifice a valuable member of my team to budgetary restrictions? I see that the budget allowed you to redecorate this office last year."

Lane's eyes narrowed. "Careful, Jack."

"I'm sorry, sir, but I just don't understand your priorities."

Lane held up his hand to stop him. "You don't have to understand them, Jack. That's why *I'm* the Chief Superintendent and you're not. I'm paid to make the difficult decisions. You're paid to follow my orders, and I'm ordering you to drop this now, right now."

Jack stayed silent, he could sense the lecture wasn't finished.

"For your information, the only reason I had my office decorated was because I have a friend in the Rotary Club who runs a painting and decorating business and he had some paint left over from a hotel contract his firm had just completed. He offered to do the work for just the cost of the labour. Take a look around you, Jack. This building is old and in time will need a complete overhaul, either that or it will be pulled down to make way for one of those concrete and glass monstrosities that seem to be popping up all over the country. The decoration of my office was a small step towards getting this building ship shape, and it was well within the maintenance budget. In fact the Chief Constable congratulated me personally about it."

"I'm very pleased for you, sir," Jack said heavily.

Lane got up from his desk, walked around and perched on the edge of it. "Look, Jack, I know you had high hopes for Myra Banks, and I can see why. As I said to you the other day, she's a bright girl, but face facts, the police force is a man's world, always has been, and I can't see that changing, not in my lifetime anyway. Accept my decision for the good of your team. It doesn't need a disgruntled boss just now, not with their workload and all the other changes we've had to accept recently. I need you to rise above the mundane politicking that is going on at the moment. At least until the county council sees sense anyway. Her day will come, one way or another." He went back to his seat and sat down. "How are you getting on with the murder of that actor chap?" He smoothly changed tack.

Jack brought him up to date, all the while resisting the urge to storm out of the room.

"Bloody dinosaur!" he said as he walked back into his office.

Fuller looked up. "It went well with the chief super then."

Jack glowered at him and sat down at him desk, pulling a file from the ever-increasing pile in his in-tray and flipping it open.

He stared at it blankly for a moment before closing it again and slamming it down on the desk, then went across to the coat rack. "I'm going out, to interview Lois Turner, for the second time." He grabbed his coat from the rack and stormed from the office.

7 - THURSDAY

"Myra, get your coat. You're coming with me," Jack barked as he walked into the squad room.

Myra looked up from her desk and hesitated.

"We haven't got all day." Without waiting for her to follow him, he headed out to the car park.

Myra still sat at her desk mouth slightly agape. She had never seen him look so angry.

"I think you'd better get your skates on, love," Andy Brewer, the desk sergeant, said. "Don't keep him waiting."

As if stung, Myra rushed over to grab her coat and hurried after her boss.

She caught up with him in the car park. "Where are we going?" she gasped as she tried to catch her breath.

"To talk to the Turner woman again," Jack said as he unlocked the car door.

"And you want me along?"

He looked at her sharply. "Why shouldn't I? You know the turf. Get in the car."

"Right, sir, Yes, sir." She climbed into the passenger seat. Once she had shut the door, Jack started the car and pulled out of the car park.

Myra watched him as he drove. His face was set in a frown and his mouth was a thin grim line. This wasn't the Jack Callum she was used to seeing and it unnerved her.

"Is everything all right, sir? Only you seem a little put out."

He glanced round at her. "I'm not a *little put out*, Myra. I'm bloody furious. Here we are investigating a savage murder, and the chief superintendent deprives me of one of my best officers."

"He wouldn't budge on my application rejection then."

"No, Myra, he would not, and for that I'm sorry. I raised your hopes and that was wrong of me."

"I didn't want you to stick your neck out, sir. Not on my behalf."

"Well, who the Hell's going to, Myra? Tell me that. Did you know that there are less than fifty women in the CID in the entire country? It's a bloody disgrace and men like Chief Superintendent Lane are largely responsible for that situation."

"Why do you think that is, sir?"

"Backward thinking. A hangover from the time just after the war when the men of this country returned home and women were once again expected to be housewives. Some were happy to do that, to go back to what it was like before the conflict, but others were used to having something more to do with their lives than cleaning the house, looking after the kids, and making sure there was a hot meal on the table when their husbands got in from work. During the war women kept this country going. Some working in factories, others driving lorries or toiling on the land. Without their contribution this country would have ground to a halt. My Annie was one of them, working in a munitions factory, as well running a house and bringing up three small children."

"She doesn't work now though?"

"That's entirely her choice. If she wanted to get a job I certainly wouldn't stand in her way. We're entering a new decade, Myra, and I think it's going to be a time of change. The police force is just one of this county's institutions that is going to have to rethink the role of women within its ranks."

"You seem very passionate about it."

"I live in a house with three very strong women," Jack said ruefully. "They keep me in my place." He flashed Myra a smile. "Lecture over."

"Don't mind me. It's good to know there's men like you on our side. It gives me hope."

"If there's nothing else, Myra, there's always hope."

Myra was silent for a while. "How do you intend to deal with Lois Turner this time?"

"I don't intend to deal with her." He paused and gave her a knowing smile. "You will, as you seem to have her measure. I'll give you an idea of what we need to find out, and this time I want to speak to the daughter as well. You didn't see her last time, but she was there."

43

"Oh, she was there, sir. Pretty little thing, blonde hair."

"That's Geraldine. You saw her?"

Myra nodded. "She was on the stairs when we arrived, but she ducked out of sight when she realized I'd clocked her."

"Yes, I saw her as well. She's pretty highly strung, apparently."

"You've met her before then?"

Jack explained his encounter with Geraldine Turner at the school.

"Why would she say such a thing?" Myra said. "Killing her brother. That's pretty macabre, even for a teenage girl going through puberty."

"That's what I thought, though it has a whole new resonance in light of what happened to her father. That family just aren't right."

"And you're going to try to find out what makes them tick?"

Jack nodded. "And open their closets to see if I can't shake out a few skeletons."

Myra smiled. "I almost pity Lois Turner. *Almost.*"

For the rest of the drive to *Elsinore*, Jack primed Myra for the interview. Lane couldn't see her worth, but he certainly could.

"Chief Inspector Callum to see Mrs Turner," Jack said to Hester, in case she had forgotten who he was.

"Yes, of course." The plump woman pushed the door open wide for them to enter. "I'll fetch her for you. Come in."

They stood in the hallway, listening to someone playing the piano somewhere in the house. *A Chopin* étude, Jack thought, *and a pretty decent attempt.*

It was a few minutes before Lois Turner finally made an appearance. The Chopin carried on as Lois sashayed down the hall towards then, stumbling in her high heels. When she reached them it was obvious from her glazed eyes and the smell of whisky on her breath that she'd been drinking.

"Hello, Chief Inspector. What can I do for you this time?" She was slurring her words.

"A few more questions," Jack said.

She again led them towards Turner's office. She glanced back over her shoulder, blinked twice, refocused, and made a beckoning motion with her arm. "Come through."

"Actually, Constable Banks has the questions. I'd like a word with your step-daughter."

Lois gazed at him as if he were speaking a foreign language. She blinked again. "Geraldine? What do... Oh, never mind. Hester, show the chief inspector through to the conservatory."

Hester stepped forward. "This way, sir."

Jack turned to Myra. "You go with Mrs Turner."

Myra grimaced. "Certainly, sir."

Jack followed Hester through to the back of the house.

The conservatory was much more than a sun lounge. It was four times the size of Turner's office, took up the entire back of the house, and was furnished with chintz upholstered bamboo furniture. Ferns in large terracotta pots were spaced out underneath wide picture windows, the floor was laid to tiles that looked Italian and expensive, and in the centre of the room was a full-sized concert grand piano.

The slight figure of Geraldine Turner was seated at the piano, her head bowed as her fingers moved effortlessly over the keys.

"Geraldine," Hester said loudly over the Chopin. "There's someone here to see you."

Gerry's fingers stopped mid-arpeggio and she glanced round at Jack.

"Oh, hello."

"Hello, Gerry." He turned to Hester who was moving towards the door. "If you could stay."

"What? Oh, yes, all right." She went across to one of the bamboo chairs and sat, folding her arms.

He sat down next to Geraldine on the piano stool. "You play very well."

"I know," Geraldine Turner said without a hint of conceit. "My ambition is to go to the Royal College of Music to study composition. Of course, that's probably all going to change now."

"Yes, yes, of course. Look, shall we sit in comfort?" He indicated the bamboo sofa.

Geraldine shrugged. "Okay."

Jack went across to the sofa sat down again. Geraldine joined him, curling her legs underneath her.

He caught the disapproving look on Hester's face, but the woman said nothing. She just edged forward in her seat in case she should miss anything.

"I'm sorry about your father, Gerry," Jack said.

Geraldine gave a non-committal shrug.

"When he brought you home on Tuesday, he went out again in the afternoon."

She nodded.

"Do you have any idea where he was going?"

"He was meeting someone in town." Geraldine's bright, open face showed no trace of guile.

"Do you know who?"

"He didn't say. When we got back on Tuesday I came straight in here to practice and he went upstairs. I didn't see him again." She bit her lip, wanting to cry but forcing herself not to.

"Not at all? Not even as he left the house?"

"She told you," Hester said. "She didn't see him again after she came in here."

"Thank you, Mrs…"

"Gough. Hester Gough."

"Well, thank you, Mrs Gough, but I'd like Gerry to answer for herself if you don't mind."

"Her name is Geraldine," Hester said tartly.

"I prefer Gerry," Geraldine said, glaring at the woman.

Jack tried again. "So you didn't see him again. Did he tell you who he was going to meet?"

"We weren't talking by the time we got home. We had an argument in the car. That was why I came straight in here. I had to get out of his way."

"Did you argue often?"

Hester Gough cleared her throat, loudly.

Jack asked the question again.

"We never used to argue at all when mum was alive. It's only

46

since *she* came to live with us."

"You mean your stepmother?"

Geraldine looked at him, a contemptuous look in her eyes. "Who do you think?"

"I take it she and you don't always see eye to eye."

"Try never. You've seen what she's like. If she isn't drunk, she's drugged up to the eyeballs."

"Geraldine! That's enough!" Hester Gough was on her feet. "I'll not sit here and listen to you say such horrible things about your mother."

"She's *not* my mother!" Geraldine's voice rose to a shout. "She's just dad's wife. My r*eal* mother died."

Jack took her hand and squeezed it comfortingly. "Okay, Gerry, calm down. I'm sure Mrs Gough didn't…"

"It's not *Mrs* Gough. It's *Miss*," Geraldine said. "Ask her about *her* relationship with my stepmother. Her *darling Lois*."

Hester moved towards her. "Not another word, you ungrateful child. If it wasn't for you your brother would still be alive."

"Now that's enough!" Jack sprang to his feet, putting himself between Hester and Geraldine who was cowering slightly on the sofa, her eyes brimming with tears.

Jack put his arm around Hester's shoulders and with some effort guided her towards the door and out of the room.

"Would you mind explaining that last comment you made to her?" he said.

Hester was red in the face and breathing loudly. "It was that little bitch with her constant demands and her temper tantrums that brought about Lois's miscarriage."

"You can't blame a thirteen-year old girl for that." Jack was fighting down his own temper.

"That's what her father said. Always giving in to her. Letting her have everything she wanted. He was a weak, weak man. I just don't know what Lois saw in him."

Jack looked up to see Myra walking toward them. "Is the interview over?"

"Apparently." Myra smiled. "She passed out on the settee."

Hester pulled away from Jack. "Is Lois all right?" she said, her voice rising in panic.

47

"She will be once she sleeps it off," Myra said.

Hester glared and pushed past her. "I think you'd better leave." She hurried away to tend to her mistress.

Myra watched her as she bustled away. "What now?"

"Come through to the conservatory and meet Gerry. I think you'll like her. She's got spark, a bit like you really."

8 - THURSDAY

He led Myra through to the conservatory. Geraldine had returned to the piano and was lazily practicing scales. "Gerry, I'd like you to meet Myra Banks. Myra, Miss Geraldine Turner. Known to her friends as Gerry."

"Hello, Gerry," Myra said, stepping forward and sticking out her hand.

Geraldine shook it enthusiastically. "Are you police too, like Mr. Callum?"

"Yes," Myra said. "But I'm only a lowly WPC."

"I saw you," Geraldine said. "The other night."

"Yes, and I saw you too. You should have come and said hello."

"I was trying to hide." Geraldine blushed.

"Yes, I thought you were."

"I was trying to hear what was going on," she said. "Did she really pass out on you?"

Myra smiled. "Sparko. Out like a light."

Geraldine giggled. "Serves her right. She's been drinking all morning."

"Are you going to be all right?" Jack said, "only Miss Gough made it quite clear she wants us to leave."

"I'll be fine. Hester will be preoccupied with Lois. She won't even notice what I'm doing."

"And what *will* you do?" Myra said.

"What I always do. I'll amuse myself."

"If you're sure." Jack frowned.

Geraldine gave him an old-fashioned look. "I'm not a child, Mr. Callum."

"Well, take care," he said and reached into his pocket. He took a card from his pocket, scribbled down two telephone numbers and handed the card to her. "If you need me during the day call the top number. The bottom number is my home. I'm available night or day."

Geraldine took the card and stared at it. "Thank you, You

49

know, you're not so bad…for a copper."

"I try," Jack said. "I try."

Eddie Fuller walked into the office DS Frank Lesser was sharing with two detective constables, Trevor Walsh and Harry Grant. Lesser looked round as Fuller entered the room. A T-shaped dressing was covering Lesser's nose and there was bruising around his eyes. "Christ, Frank, what happened to you? You look like just gone fifteen rounds with Rocky Marciano."

"Bad night at the *Seymour Hall*," Lesser said. "Lincoln put me in with a kid from Stepney whose only wrestling experience was in the booth at Southend. The bloody fool tried a dropkick. He'd never done one before and thought it was easy, but he missed my chest completely and the heel of his boot broke my nose. Blood everywhere. The referee had no choice but to stop the match and award it to the kid on a technical knockout. Technical knockout, my arse! Technical cock up, more like. You wait 'til I see Paul bloody Lincoln. Putting me in with amateurs!"

"At least you kept your mask on," Harry Grant said. "He didn't blow your cover."

Lesser had been moonlighting as a professional wrestler for the last five years, fighting under a mask and a *nom de guerre*, as the *Black Phantom*. So far most of his superior officers, apart from the ever-astute DCI Callum, seemed unaware of his extra-curricular activities, but that situation could be about to change, all thanks to a spotty teenager from Stepney who thought he was going to be the *next big thing*. If he ever had the misfortune to fight him again Lesser would show the boy the error of his ways.

"Wasn't Lincoln watching last night?" Grant said.

Lesser shook his head. "No, he was probably at the 2 I's. That bloody Soho coffee bar seems to take up all his time since he bought the lease from the Irani brothers back in '56. That, and bloody rock and roll. Wrestling is taking a back seat with him at the moment. I can't remember when *Dr Death* last fought." *Dr Death* was wrestling promoter Paul Lincoln's alter ego, another masked man, and one much more successful than Lesser's *Black Phantom.*

"Can you still work?" Fuller said.

"I'll be out of the ring for the next three weeks, until this nose mends."

"I was talking about police work."

"Oh, yes. I can still do that."

"Well cast your eyes over this." Fuller handed Lesser the list Jack had given him. "The guv wants us to check out the names on here in connection with the Tony Turner murder."

"Where did he get this from? There are some names on here I recognise."

"From Turner's old lady. It's a list of people who might have had it in for him."

"Fred Tozer's name is on here. He's a bloody dancer isn't he?"

"Not in the same league as Fred Astaire," Fuller said, "but yes, he's another hoofer."

"And Betsy Maclaren? I've seen her in a film, a musical I think it was."

This produced a hoot of laughter from Harry Grant and Trevor Walsh. Even Fuller was smiling.

"What?" Lesser's voice sounded slightly hurt. "I *like* musicals."

"And is the *Black Phantom* planning a song and dance routine during his next bout?" Walsh said.

Lesser glared at him. "Shut up and get on with your work."

"Seriously," Fuller said. "We should divide this list up and work out who is going to check out who."

Lesser sat forward in his seat. "Bloody hell! Thomas Usher's name is on here. I heard about him when I was working at Camden, and I don't fancy going anywhere near him. He's a mean bastard."

"Not anymore," Fuller said. "He had a stroke. I doubt he could even tie his own shoelaces these days, so don't worry about him. The guv has already discounted him. I meant to cross him off the list."

"That will make our lives a lot easier, and a lot safer."

"Yes, it will." Fuller took back the list and laid it flat on the desk. "Right, let's start breaking this down."

"Wasn't there an inquiry about Usher's relationship with some Met officers a couple of years ago?" Lesser said. "Your old guvnor Charlie Somers was involved wasn't he?"

A look of alarm flashed across Fuller's face. "You knew about that?"

"I remember reading something about it in *Police Gazette*."

Fuller started to feel sick. Jack Callum read the *Police Gazette*, regularly.

"Was that wise?" Myra said as they drove away. "Giving her your home number?"

"She needs someone, Myra."

"I agree. But why you?"

"Because I owe her. Did you get any information out of Lois before she passed out?"

"Not much. She was pretty incoherent. She confirmed that her husband went out in the afternoon, but she couldn't say where he went. Apparently she was in bed with a headache. I suspect she was nursing a hangover."

"Gerry confirms that. According to her he was going out to meet someone, but she didn't know whom. Did Lois say what car he was driving?"

"A maroon *Singer Gazelle Coupe de Ville*."

"So, a convertible. That shouldn't be too hard to find in Letchworth. Get on to the registration office at the council and see if you can't get a licence plate number. I'll put a call out when I get back to the station and get the beat bobbies onto it. I wouldn't have thought it would be too far away from Norton Common."

"They've found the car," Eddie Fuller said.

Jack looked up. "That was quick. Where?"

"Letchworth train station."

"Right. Let's get over there."

Thirty minutes later they were driving into the car park of Letchworth station. A lone police constable was standing guard over the pristine maroon convertible. He saluted as Jack approached. "Have you touched it at all?"

"No, sir," the PC replied. "I was just passing when it caught my eye, sitting over here in the corner. Couldn't believe my luck really. I'd only been told to keep an eye out for it as I was leaving to go on my beat."

"Well, good work." Jack earned himself another salute. He turned to Fuller. "Right, let's take a look at this. Can we get the boot open?"

"We have the keys we found in Turner's pocket."

"Well, what are you waiting for? Get the bloody thing open."

Fuller put the key in the lock and twisted. There was a satisfying click and the boot lid sprung open a fraction.

Jack looked inside, reached in and took out a wooden box about twelve inches square, with a hinged lid. "Now, what do we have here?" He put the box on the ground and lifted the lid.

"What is it?" Fuller was looking over Jack's shoulder at the rows of bottles, tubes and boxes stacked neatly in compartments within the box. Jack removed one of the tubes and unscrewed the cap, squeezing the tube slightly and watching a pinkish cream ease out from the open end. "Makeup, of the theatrical kind. This is Turner's makeup kit."

The inner tray of the box lifted out. Beneath it were skeins of crepe hair and a tin of mortician's wax.

"So he comes to the station, parks his car here and, while he waits for the person he's meeting to arrive, he uses the time to disguise himself with a false nose and moustache, and to darken his skin with greasepaint." Fuller shook his head. "It seems a bit elaborate to me especially as the disguise wasn't that convincing."

Jack nodded in agreement. "The question is who was he here to meet? Check the inside of the car for fingerprints and get them to the lab as quickly as possible. We may just get lucky."

"Not if it's anything like the crime scene on the Common. Not a fingerprint or a footprint. Nothing."

"Then it's time for our luck to turn."

"I wish I had your confidence."

"Call it blind faith," Jack smiled and walked back to his car.

9 - THURSDAY

When Jack walked into the bedroom that night, Annie was sitting up in bed, her nose buried in a magazine. He took off his dressing gown and climbed into bed beside her with a yawn.

"Long day?" she said.

He glanced round at the alarm clock on the bedside table. The luminous hands were pointing to eleven o'clock. "I'm ready for my bed." He yawned again. "I'm bushed."

Annie put down her magazine. "I was speaking with Rosie earlier."

Jack adjusted his reading glasses and turned his newspaper to the sports pages. "And?"

"Mrs Painter is looking for someone to work in the baker's a couple of mornings a week."

"As well as Rosie?"

Rosie had been working at Painter's, the baker's for just over a year now. It was undemanding work but she seemed happy enough with it.

"Yes. Gladys Newton, who's been with them for years, has handed in her notice. Apparently her husband has just retired and she wants them to spend more time together."

"How does this affect Rosie?"

"It doesn't. Not directly."

"I see,' Jack said, but clearly didn't. He went back to his newspaper.

Annie took a sip from her cocoa. "I was thinking of popping along to see Mrs Painter tomorrow and putting my name down."

Jack glanced round at her. "For what?"

Annie raised her eyes skywards. "Jack, are you being deliberately obtuse? For a job, what else?"

Jack lowered his newspaper. "A *job*? I thought you were happy at home."

"I am, Jack…at least I was."

"What's changed?

She let out a long sigh. "I'm starting to feel redundant."

Jack said nothing but continued to stare at her. Eventually he took her hand and said, "Elaborate."

"Well, for years now I've kept house, raised our children I've looked after my gorgeous husband, and I've been happy to do so. It's been a labour of love and I've enjoyed every minute of it…well, mostly."

"So what's changed?"

"Nothing." She shook her head. "And everything. Eric's getting older and if he's not rehearsing with his friends then he's down at St Mary's youth club. Rosie is at work all day. I thought that, when Joanie came back to us, I would at least have something to occupy myself with, but now she's got this job with Avril so it means I'm going to be kicking around the house all day on my own, with no one to talk to until you all get home in the evening. There's only so much housework a girl can do, you know?"

"Phew! It seems like you've given this some thought."

"You wouldn't mind would you, Jack? It's only four mornings a week."

"You said it was a *couple*."

"Well, it's four…but I wouldn't be working Saturdays."

"I should hope not."

"So may I go along there and put my name down?"

Jack opened his mouth to answer when the telephone in the hall started to ring. "Damn! Who's calling at this time of night?" Cursing, he threw back the bedclothes. "I'd better get that before it wakes the whole house." His feet found his slippers and he padded out of the room.

Annie sighed and muttered, "Saved by the bell, Jack."

"Chief Inspector Callum," a querulous voice on the other end of the line said.

"Yes?"

"It's Hester Gough…from *Elsinore*."

After she demanded they leave the house Hester Gough was the last person he expected to be calling him. "What can I do for you, Miss Gough?"

It sounded as if she was crying. "I'm sorry to call you so late, but I'm at my wits end." She drew in a ragged breath. "It's Geraldine...she's gone," she said and Jack could hear her sobbing into the mouthpiece of the telephone.

"All right, calm yourself, Miss Gough. What do you mean, *she's gone?*"

"Just that. I took her cocoa up to her about half an hour ago, but she wasn't in her room. I spent the next twenty minutes searching the house, but there was no sign of her, so I went back to her room and realised that the window was wide open and the bed was still made. I fear something terrible has happened to her."

"How did you get this number, Miss Gough?" Jack said thoughtfully.

"I found it. There was a card on her dressing table and it had your name and number on it."

"Right. Don't touch anything else. Go and make yourself a cup of strong sweet tea. I'll be with you shortly."

"Where are you going?" Annie said as Jack rushed into the bedroom, tore off his dressing gown and started pulling on his trousers.

As he dressed he told her briefly what the phone call had been about.

"That's awful." Annie bit her lip pensively. "Of course, you must go round there."

"You try to get to sleep." He pecked her on the cheek. "I'll be back just as soon as I can. I'll try not to wake you when I come in." He rushed to the door, stopped on the landing and stuck his head back into the room. "We'll continue our conversation in the morning." And then he was gone.

Annie listened to the car start up and ease smoothly away from the kerb, and then she picked up her magazine and started leafing blindly through the pages, her mind miles away, thinking about abducted teenage girls. Finally, she reached over, turned out the bedside lamp and stared up at the ceiling until sleep eventually claimed her.

Hester was waiting just outside *Elsinore's* front door as Jack pulled up on the drive. She came down the steps to greet him as he stepped out of the car. "Thank you so much for coming. I really didn't know what else to do."

"You did the right thing by calling me. Has Mrs Turner been informed?"

Hester shook her head. "Lois took some sleeping tablets at about nine. She's still fast asleep."

"Very well. Can you take me up and show me Gerry's room?"

"This way," Hester said and led him into the house.

Geraldine's room was big for a bedroom, with a large oak wardrobe, a glass-topped dressing table and a king-sized bed. Floral curtains billowed fitfully in the breeze that blew in from the open sash window. The other window in the room was shut. On the walls were framed pictures of Geraldine's heroes. Mozart, Chopin, Artur Rubenstein shared wall space with French jazz pianist, Jacques Loussier. Geraldine obviously had eclectic tastes.

"How did she seem this evening?" Jack said.

"Perfectly fine. I really didn't see much of her, to be honest. She was practicing in the conservatory until dinner, and then she went up to her room, and I didn't see her again."

"She didn't seem upset or distressed? She has, after all, just lost her father."

"As I say, she seemed fine, but Geraldine's a very secretive child. Keeps herself very much to herself."

Apart from when she's telling a perfect stranger that she'd killed her brother, Jack thought, but said nothing. "May I use the phone? I should call this through to the station."

"And now we wait," Jack said after making the call. "They're sending a team along. Did you make that tea?"

"Yes." Hester's tears had returned and she was dabbing at her eyes with an embroidered handkerchief. "Come through to the kitchen." She led him through to the back of the house.

A large pine refectory table dominated the room. Against one wall was a huge American-style refrigerator, and set into the chimney wall was a cream *Aga*. A kettle sat between the two hot plates. Hester moved it onto the boiling plate. "It just has to boil again."

Jack sat down at the kitchen table. "Geraldine came to speak to me after I gave a talk at her school. She told me that she'd killed her brother."

Hester clucked her tongue. "Foolish girl," she said dismissively.

"Only I noticed that you said a similar thing to her yourself when we were here, in reference to Mrs Turner's miscarriage."

Hester turned away and made a great play of pouring boiling water into a large brown teapot

"Miss Gough?" Jack said, determined not to let the woman off the hook. "You do realise the damaging effect a comment like the one you made can have on a young mind?"

"Nonsense." Hester bridled. "That girl's savvy enough to know I didn't mean anything by it."

Jack glared at her. "I think it was a totally irresponsible thing for you to say."

"When I want advice on how to talk to children, Chief Inspector, I ask for it. Until I do I'll thank you to keep your opinions to yourself." The frail, tearful Hester Gough had disappeared to be replaced by a hard, no-nonsense woman who was not at all intimidated by his presence. "All I want you to do is to find the girl before her mother wakes up and realises she's not here."

So that's it, Jack thought. *She's more worried about Lois Turner's disapproval than Gerry's safety.*

"We'll do all we can to find her."

"Good" Hester poured the tea. "That's good."

Twenty minutes later two police cars pulled up on the drive next to Jack's and half a dozen policemen stepped out. Two uniformed and four plain clothed officers approached the house to be met at the door by Jack.

"Hello, sir. We got here as soon as we could," DI Alan Healy said as he shook Jack's hand. "What's the story? We were told it's a missing girl."

"Geraldine Turner, thirteen. Went missing from her home some time this evening."

"Abduction or runaway?"

"That's what you're here to find out," Jack said. "I'm hoping it's the latter. The former doesn't bear thinking about."

"Then best we get started straight away. Do you want me to take point on this?"

Jack rubbed his eyes. "I'd rather you did. Your mind will be sharper than mine. I've been up since six o'clock this morning. Come inside and I'll give you what I know."

It didn't take long to bring the team up to date. When the rest of them had dispersed to various parts of the house and garden to begin their investigation Healy hung behind in the kitchen. "If I were you, sir," he said to Jack. "I'd get off home and let us take it from here."

Jack liked Alan Healy. He was only in his mid-thirties but had proved himself a fine detective, cracking some very high-profile cases wide open with his thoroughness and dogged attention to detail. "If anything turns up then call straight away. If you don't find anything then call me before you clock off in the morning."

"Hopefully I'll have some good news before then."

"Fingers crossed."

"Before you go, sir, what's the story with the old girl?"

"Her name's Hester Gough. She's a kind of housekeeper-cum-nursemaid to Geraldine *and* her mother Lois."

"Is the mother around?"

"In bed asleep, apparently. Knocked out on sleeping pills, so she won't be much help to you. And watch out for Hester Gough," he added quietly as he walked out to the front of the house. "She's more concerned about having Lois upset than genuinely worried about Geraldine. She couldn't really give two hoots about the girl. So take everything she may tell you with a very large pinch of salt." He looked up at the night sky.

A thin drizzle had just started to fall, dampening the earth outside and beading on the bonnet of his car. "Sometimes God doesn't make our job any easier."

"He likes us to work for our money," Healy said grimly as he pulled up the collar of his raincoat.

10 FRIDAY MARCH 20TH 1959

"What time did you get back last night?" Annie said as Jack walked into the kitchen.

He corrected her. "It was one in the morning. You were sound asleep."

She poured him a cup of tea and set it down on the table. "Did she turn up?"

Jack shook his head. "I left Alan Healy in charge. He was going to 'phone if she did."

"Try not to worry."

"She's thirteen, Annie. A child, younger than Eric."

She sat down at the table next to him and took his hand in hers, squeezing it. "There's nothing you could have done, Jack."

"Knowing that doesn't make it any easier."

"I know, pet. I know. Let me make you some breakfast. Toast?"

He squeezed her hand and nodded. Annie stood and went across to the larder, taking out half a loaf. She cut off a doorstep and slipped it under the grill. Soon the kitchen was filled with an appetizing aroma of toasting bread.

The smell jogged his memory of last night's conversation. "I think you should go and see Barbara Painter."

Annie glanced round at him. "Are you sure?"

"I'm sure. It'll do you good to get out of the house for a few mornings a week."

"And the extra money will come in handy."

"I'm sure it will. But it's *your* money, to do with whatever you like."

"I'll save it. For a holiday perhaps, or maybe I'll renew my wardrobe. Having Joanie here has made me realise how drab I've got. I feel like I've been letting myself go."

"You still look beautiful to me."

"Take off those rose-tinted glasses and put on your real ones." She smiled at him as she buttered his toast. "Maybe I'll ask Joanie to do my hair for me," she added thoughtfully as she put the plate down next to his cup. "There again I could always use the money to rent a television."

He looked round at her sharply. "We don't need a television."

"Not according to Rosie and Eric. They're starting to feel deprived."

"Deprived?" He could scarcely believe what he was hearing.

"Yes, *deprived*. Eric feels like he's being left out of conversations at school, because all the other boys talk about is what they watched on the television the night before, and Rosie tells me that people are coming into the baker's asking her if she saw this or that, and she can't answer them."

"We have the wireless. What do we need a television for?"

"I've just told you."

"And you're willing to spend your hard-earned money on a whim of our children?"

"If necessary."

"Ye Gods! It will be the end of family life as we know it."

"Don't exaggerate."

"You'll see, but as I said, it's *your* money." Jack bit into his slice of toast as the telephone started to ring. "That will be Healy." He dropped the toast back onto his plate and went to answer it.

Annie followed him out of the kitchen and stood in the doorway as he spoke.

"Any news?" she said as he put down the receiver.

He blew through his teeth. "No sign of her."

Her face fell.

"But there's no sign that there was anyone else in her room either, so it doesn't look like she was taken."

"That's good isn't it?" she said hopefully.

"In one way, yes. But it still means we've got a teenage girl out there somewhere, and we don't know where to start looking for her."

"DI Healy left this for you this morning, sir." Desk Sergeant Andy Brewer handed Jack a colour photograph of Geraldine Turner as he walked into the police station.

"Thanks, Andy."

"And this arrived for you this morning." He handed Jack a large white envelope.

Jack stared at it, turning it over in his had. Apart from DCI CALLUM printed across the front in bold capitals, the envelope was blank. There was no stamp so it had obviously been delivered by hand.

He said as much to Brewer.

"Yes," the desk sergeant said. "I noticed that, but it was in the box with all the other post, so whoever dropped it in must have got up early to do so because the postman usually comes at about eight, and it was there at the bottom of the pile."

Jack tore open the flap and looked inside. The envelope contained another photograph and a folded piece of paper. He rolled the envelope into a tube and slipped it into his pocket, and then he took the photograph of Geraldine Turner through to the squad room and pinned it to the board next to the photo of her father.

"Right, gather round." He called to the other officers in the room. "This is Geraldine Turner," he said to the semi-circle of expectant faces. "Some time during yesterday evening she disappeared from her house on the Broadway."

"Was she taken?" Frank Lesser said.

"I don't know. DI Healy was leading the investigation last night and his team could find no indication that anyone broke into the house and took her. But her bedroom window was wide open."

"So, do you think she might have run away?" Lesser said.

"It's a possibility. Her home life isn't what you could call harmonious."

"But her bedroom is on the first floor," Myra said.

"I know," Jack said. "Her room is at the back of the house, but underneath her window is a trellis that supports a wisteria. She could have climbed down that."

"She didn't strike me as the tomboy type."

"Nor me, but desperate people are capable of desperate acts."

"Surely if she climbed down to the ground she would have left her footprints at the base of the wisteria," Lesser said.

"Maybe she did, but when I left there last night it had started to rain. Healy's men couldn't find a trace of any footprints."

"Of course, she could have just walked out through the front door," Myra said. "I doubt Miss Gough would have noticed."

"And Lois Turner was drugged up to her eyes on sleeping pills. Either way, she's gone and it's down to us to find her. Frank, she has grandparents who live in Shillington. Get over there and have a chat with them, but before you do, I'll see you in my office. Myra, get down to Dispatch and see if anyone's called in to say they've seen a young girl walking the streets in the middle of the night."

"That's a bit of a long shot," Fuller said doubtfully.

"Yes, Eddie, it is, but it's worth trying. You never know, some public-spirited resident might have seen her and reported it. The rest of you get out there with your ears to the ground. Use your contacts, your snouts, your friends if necessary. I want her found."

The officers stood staring at him.

He sighed in exasperation. "I mean now. Not next week."

Suddenly the room sprang into life and there was a rush to the door.

Jack turned back to the incident board and stared the photograph of the smiling girl with the blonde corkscrew hair. When he spoke it was almost a whisper. "Where are you, Gerry? Where the hell are you?"

"Nothing's been reported," Myra said.

"Well, Sergeant Fuller said it would be a long shot. Myra, if you were a young girl, running away from home, where would you go?"

"If I had no family nearby, then probably to a friend's house. Somewhere I felt safe, I suppose."

"Then go along to the school. Have a word with Geraldine's friends, if she has any, and see if any of them have heard from her."

"Yes, guv. What school does she go to?"

"Hatfield County. You can walk it from here."

"I know, sir. I went there myself. Is Mrs Arnold still the head?"

"Yes, she's still there."

"The old trout. I couldn't stand her, and she didn't like me much either."

"Use your charm, Myra. You know how to do that, don't you?"

Myra smiled. "I'll do my best."

"Oh, I'm sure you will, Myra

Lesser was standing outside his office when Jack got up there. "Come in, Frank."

Lesser followed him into to the office. Eddie Fuller was seated at a desk tucked into the chimneybreast alcove.

"Eddie, go and get yourself a cup of tea."

"Pardon?" Fuller glanced round, saw Lesser standing there, and got to his feet. "Yes, right," he said and left the room.

"Take a seat, Frank."

Lesser dropped into the seat Fuller had just vacated.

Jack sat down at his desk. "Right, tell me how you got the broken nose?"

"I walked into a door, sir."

"Really? A door? Or an opponent's boot?"

Lesser flushed and stared down at his shoes. "The latter," he mumbled.

Jack nodded. "I thought so."

"He was green, sir. Just a kid…"

Jack raised his hand to silence him. "Spare me the details, Frank."

"How *did* you know I was wrestling?"

"Frank, I'm a detective. You know damn well I've been aware of it almost from the beginning. You didn't honestly think you could keep it a secret from me, did you? Besides, I've *seen* you wrestle as the Black Phantom. I took my son Eric to one of your shows. He thought you were pretty good."

"Don't you mind?"

"As long as it doesn't interfere with your job, why should I? I

66

dare say you're one of the fittest officers in the Hertfordshire Constabulary, and it's nice to know you can handle yourself should the need ever arise. I know and I indulge it, but I don't think Chief Superintendant Lane would view it with the same tolerance, and with this injury you're on perilously thin ice. He's bound to ask me how you picked up the broken nose, and he's canny enough to see through your excuse that you walked into a door."

Colour spread to Lesser's cheeks.

"So, if he asks, I'll tell him that you picked it up in the line of duty. An altercation with a drunk, or something like that."

"Why would you go out on a limb for me, sir?"

"Because I'm a bloody fool, Frank. No, actually, I think you're a very good DS and I don't want to lose you from the team. WPC Banks has been sent back to uniform and she won't be replaced. We've got a murder and a missing girl on the books, as well as all our other cases, cases that are going to have to take a back seat for now. I can't be another man down."

"Yes, sir. Thank you, sir."

"Just try to be a little more careful in future." He scribbled down Laurence Turner's address on a piece of paper and handed it across to him. "And just remember, this man has just lost his son and you're there to tell him his granddaughter is missing, so tread lightly."

Lesser took the note and nodded. He paused at the office door and looked back. "Who was I fighting, sir, when you brought you son?"

"A rather large chap. Hunter was it? It was at the *Granada*, Edmonton, spring last year."

"*Rebel Ray*, yeah, he's a good worker. Took him down in the fifth round. It was meant to be the fourth, but I messed up the suplex and nearly brained myself in the process, so he carried me for another round until he could make the pin fall look convincing."

Jack smiled indulgently. "Now, get yourself over to Shillington."

Relieved, Lesser walked to the door.

It was only after Lesser had gone that Jack remembered the

envelope in his pocket. He opened it and tipped it up. The photograph and folded paper slipped out onto the desk blotter. He unfolded the paper. It was a note that said simply, *I hope this is useful*. It wasn't signed.

He picked up the photograph. It was a black and white print of a boxing match audience. Taken from the other side of the ring and shot through the boxers' legs, it plainly showed the men sitting in the front row. One of them he recognised instantly as Tony Turner.

Turner was leaning back in his seat, a fat cigar clamped between his teeth. Jack scanned the faces of his neighbours but failed to recognise any of them. At the same time the photograph was vaguely familiar to him and started bells ringing at the back of his mind.

He flipped the photograph over. Neatly printed on the back was – *From L to R. Simon Docherty, Thomas Usher, Tony Turner, Det. Insp. Charles Somers*.

In the right-hand corner was a small blue printed stamp: *Property of J Talbot & Son, Photographers*.

Jack turned the photograph again and studied the other faces. Simon Docherty looked to be in his late-thirties, conventionally handsome, with fair hair styled in a crew cut. Charles Somers was older, with a rugged face and short grey hair, but Jack's eyes were drawn to Thomas Usher. With his swarthy skin, slightly hooked nose and moustache, he looked continental. He stared at it for a full minute before his mind made the connection. He reached for Turner's file in his In-tray.

He opened it and flicked through it until he came to the crime scene photos.

Tony Turner in full theatrical makeup, hanging from a tree, his throat a red slash. He placed it on the desk next to the boxing shot. The likeness between Thomas Usher and the deceased Tony Turner was unmistakable.

It was obvious now who Turner had been impersonating.

11 - FRIDAY

"Take a look at this," Jack said as Fuller came back into the office.

Fuller came across and stared over his boss's shoulder. "What am I meant to be looking at?"

Jack jabbed his finger at Thomas Usher's face. "The resemblance between him and this." He moved his finger across to indicate Tony Turner's made up face.

Fuller looked closer. "Could be twins. Who's the one at ringside?"

Jack jabbed at the photograph with his index finger. "Thomas Usher. That's Tony Turner just two seats away from him, and isn't that your old boss, Charlie Somers?"

Fuller's gaze followed Jack's finger as it moved across to hover underneath Charlie Somers' face. He took a breath. "Yes, that's Charlie all right."

"When were you going to tell me that he knew both Thomas Usher and Tony Turner, Eddie?"

"I didn't know, Jack," Fuller lied. "I've never seen this photo before."

Jack stared at him for a long moment, and then slipped the photograph and note back into the envelope, left the office and trotted downstairs to the front desk.

"Andy, did you see who dropped this off? You normally get here before the post arrives?" Jack handed the desk sergeant the envelope.

Brewer shook his head. "I heard the postman deliver the letters, and I'd checked the box when I first got in and it was empty.'

"So sometime between you checking the letter box and the postman coming, someone hand-delivered this. You say you didn't see who that person was?"

Brewer shook his head.

"And yet you were at the desk all the time, with a clear view of the front door."

"I saw nothing." Brewer said defensively. "I swear."

Jack frowned. "I don't like mysteries. Someone stuck this through the door, Andy. Did you leave the desk at any time, to answer a call of nature perhaps?" He looked down at the enamel mug on the desk, cold tea grouts at the bottom.

Brewer followed his gaze. "Well, I left the desk for a second, to make myself a cup of tea."

"Then that was probably when he came and dropped it off."

"I'm sorry, sir." Brewer avoided Jack's eyes.

"Don't trouble yourself, Sergeant."

"Yes, sir, but even so…"

"I said, don't trouble yourself. It's not the end of the world. In fact it could prove fortuitous."

"Yes, sir, Very good, sir."

Jack went back up to his office.

"Did Andy see who left the envelope? Fuller said as he walked back in.

Jack shook his head. "He was out the back making tea." He took the note from the envelope and handed it across the desk to Fuller who scanned it quickly.

"Look carefully," he said. "Do you recognise the writing?"

Fuller recognised Charlie Somers' neat and precise printing immediately but shook his head. "No. It means nothing to me."

"Well, someone's trying to help us, Eddie, and whoever it is thinks there's a link between Tony Turner's death and Thomas Usher. Perhaps I was too hasty in dismissing Usher from the crease. I think we need to look into him a little more deeply."

"If you say so, guv. Where do we start?"

The bell affixed to the door jangled as Annie walked into Painters. Rosie stepped out from behind the counter and hugged her mother. "You came then," she said. "I wasn't sure dad would let you."

"He was fine about it…in his usual grumpy old bear kind of way. Is Mrs Painter in?"

"Out the back." Rosie jerked her thumb in the direction of the door behind the counter. "I said you were coming in, so she's expecting you."

Annie gripped her daughter's hand. "Why do I feel so nervous? It's a part-time job at the local baker's. It's not as if I'm running for government or something, but I've got butterflies."

"Just go in and see her, Mum. She doesn't bite."

Annie patted down a flyaway strand of hair and took a deep breath. "Right." She walked towards the door. "Wish me luck. Here goes nothing."

"Do you still see Charlie Somers?" Jack said

Fuller took a breath. He was wishing now he had come clean with Jack in the first place. Covering up was becoming awkward and he hated the deceit. "On occasion."

"Well, make a point of catching up with him. Find out what he knows about Turner and Usher."

"Yes, guv. Will do."

"And do it sooner rather than later."

"I'll see if he's free tonight. I can pop over and see him."

"I thought you told me that he'd moved to London."

"He joined the Met, but he still lives in Stevenage. It won't take long to drive out to see him."

"Well do that if he's free to see you." Jack slipped the photo out again. "Simon Docherty. Do we know anything about him?"

"I don't recognise him, and the name means nothing," Fuller said, truthfully this time.

"I'll pop down and check with Bob Lock, see if he has anything on him. While I'm doing that, track down the photographer, Talbot, or his son for that matter, and find out where and when this photograph was taken."

Sergeant Bob Lock had run the Welwyn and Hatfield collator's office years before Jack transferred to Hertfordshire, and was the best collator he had ever worked with. His office was lined almost from floor to ceiling with wooden filing cabinets crammed with files covering crimes in the area for over four decades, and other assorted information that made the detectives' work easier. Lock had an almost photographic memory and an uncanny ability to recall case details, often without needing to check through the files.

He was sitting at his desk in the crowded office, eating a cheese and pickle sandwich. He put down the sandwich and dabbed his lips with a handkerchief. "Chief Inspector. What brings you down to my dungeon?"

Lock was getting close to retirement age but with his pale skin, almost white hair and rheumy eyes he looked a lot older, but, as Jack knew only too well, looks could be deceptive. Bob Lock's mind was as sharp and as incisive as a surgeon's scalpel.

"Simon Docherty, Bob. Does the name mean anything to you?"

Lock closed his eyes and leaned back in his chair as he rolled the name around in his mind. "Simon Docherty. American lawyer. Harvard educated and as crooked as they come."

"You know him, just like that?"

"Know thine enemy, Chief Inspector. I shouldn't need to tell you that."

"You've come across him before then."

Lock sat forward in his seat. "His name has floated across my desk from time to time. The Met have a file on him that makes for some interesting reading."

Jack sat down at the desk. "Anything you'd like to share?"

"Nothing specific. I could go through the files, but that would take some time. From what I remember he first appeared on our shores just after the war, got his qualifications to practice law over here a few years later, and started to build a reputation as brief to some of the underworld's biggest movers and shakers."

"Was Thomas Usher on his client list?"

Lock's eyes narrowed. "Usher? Taking a trip down memory lane, sir. Only Thomas Usher has been off the scene for a while."

"I heard he'd had a stroke."

Lock chuckled. "Yes, I heard that one too."

"So it's not true?"

Lock shrugged. "It could be, for all I know. There were so many stories circulating about that one back then it's hard to know where fiction ends and fact takes over."

"You have your doubts about the stroke then?"

"All I know for sure is that Usher disappeared from public life a while back and, so far, hasn't resurfaced. It was about the time when Scotland Yard were turning their attention to Soho's gangland, so, personally, I don't think it was a coincidence."

"Do you know if Usher was one of Docherty's clients?"

"That's one I can't answer with any degree of certainty, but I wouldn't be at all surprised."

"I have a photograph of the two of them together at a boxing match, look." Jack handed him the photo.

Lock stared at it for a moment and then flipped it over to read the names on the back. "Well, it speaks volumes, but proves nothing, I'm afraid."

"Well? How did you get on?" Rosie said to her mother.

"She said I'd been out of the circulation, stuck at home, for too long to have the job."

Rosie grabbed her mother's arm. "Mum, you're kidding. That's outrageous. The old..."

Annie laughed. "No, I *am* kidding. I start Monday."

"Seriously?"

"Yes, seriously. Barbara's lovely. We were chatting for ages, and not just about the job. Did you know she was a fan of Frank Sinatra?"

"No, but I knew *you* were."

"Well, so is she. She went to see him at the *London Palladium* when he came over here in 1950. And he sang *Nancy*. That's always been one of my favourites. Dad was going to take me to that one, but something came up at work so we never made it. I was *so* disappointed."

"Ancient history."

"Don't." Annie chided her. "Imagine it was one of the boys you like to listen to, that Cliff Richards for instance."

"His name's Cliff *Richard* and it's totally different. Cliff's *dreamy*."

"And so is Frank, in my eyes anyway. So it's just the same for me as it is for you."

"I suppose," Rosie said. "I don't think dad would agree though."

"Your dad's got different tastes in music to me. It wouldn't do if we all liked the same thing."

Rosie quickly bored of the musical comparisons. She and her mother would never agree. Sometimes her mother could be so *square*. "So, are you going to walk to work with me on Monday?"

"If you don't mind. I'm sure Joanie can get Eric his breakfast."

"Eric can get his own breakfast, the lazy little bugger."

"Rosie! Language!"

"Get used to it, Mum. We're work colleagues now."

Annie rolled her eyes. "Perhaps this wasn't such a good idea after all."

Rosie grinned at her. "Don't be daft. We'll have fun. Besides, you ought to hear Mrs Painter if her sausage rolls don't turn out just so. She could make a navvy blush."

"Are you telling tales, Rosie Callum?" Barbara Painter emerged from the back room to check the till. "See you Monday, Annie. Bright and early."

Annie smiled at her. "Yes, see you then, Barbara." The butterflies had gone now, to be replaced by a flutter of excitement. *New beginnings*, she thought.

12 - FRIDAY

Frank Lesser pulled up outside the Turner's bungalow.

"Is your husband in?" he said to the frail, grey-haired woman who answered the door.

She peered up at him through a pair of rimless spectacles, drinking in Lesser's battered face and not liking what she saw. She took a step back, her hand on the door, ready to pull it shut. "Who wants to know?" she said.

Lesser produced his warrant card and held it out for her to see. "Detective Sergeant Lesser, Welwyn and Hatfield CID," he said.

"Oh, you're a policeman." The woman stared at his bandaged broken nose. "You don't look much like one."

"Your husband?" Lesser persisted.

"My husband is out. I'm Jean Turner. How may I help you?"

"May I come in?"

"I suppose so." She opened the door a little wider to allow him to enter.

Lesser sat down on the threadbare armchair. "You have a granddaughter, Geraldine?"

"Yes, I do."

"Have you had any contact with her in the last twenty-four hours?"

"I haven't had any contact with her in the last twenty-four *months*, Sergeant," Jean Turner said pointedly. "Not since my son…" Her voice trailed off and tears filled her eyes. She took a handkerchief from the pocket of her housecoat and wiped them away, "I'm sorry." She blew her nose. "It's been so difficult since I learned of Anthony's…" The tears started to flow freely.

An elderly man walked into the room from the back of the house. "What's the meaning of this? Who are you, coming here and upsetting my wife?"

Lesser got to his feet. "I'm sorry, sir. I take it you're Laurence Turner. Only your wife said you were out."

Turner glared at him. "And so I was. Out, in the garden."

"DS Lesser." Frank Lesser held out his hand. "I actually came to see you, sir. It's about your granddaughter."

Turner ignored the proffered hand. "What, about my granddaughter?"

"She's missing, sir. Disappeared from her home last night. We have teams out searching for her."

"Geraldine? Missing?" The old man narrowed his eyes suspiciously.

"I was wondering if she'd contacted you recently."

Laurence Turner sat down on the settee next to his wife, resting a comforting hand on her knee. "Go and lie down, Jean. I'll take it from here."

Jean Turner stood up, smiled at her husband tearfully, and gripped his hand in both of hers. "Would you, dear? I don't think I can cope with any more bad news." Dabbing at her eyes, she left the room.

Lesser listened to her heavy tread as she walked up the stairs. "I'm sorry, sir. I didn't mean to upset her."

Turner wheeled on him. "Understand this, Sergeant. The last few days have been very difficult for us. Difficult and deeply upsetting, especially for my wife. She's not a strong woman. You march in here in your size twelve's, looking like something out of an Edward G Robinson gangster film, scaring her half to death. I'm not surprised she's upset."

"I'm sorry, sir. I had to come, to ask you if you'd seen or heard from your granddaughter."

Turner glared at him. "Well, the answer to your question, Sergeant, is no. Geraldine hasn't been in touch with us for months."

"Aren't you concerned, sir, that something might have happened to her?"

"Damn your impertinence, man!" Turner said hotly. "Of course I'm concerned about my granddaughter, but if she's gone missing then surely it's up to you and your men to find her. You should be out there now, looking for her, not harassing an elderly couple in their own home."

Lesser looked down at his feet. "Yes, sir. I'm sorry. Perhaps

I'd better leave."

"Perhaps you had. And be good enough to contact me as soon as you find her."

"Yes, of course." Lesser headed to the door.

Once back in his car he sat back in his seat and blew through his teeth. For an old man, Laurence Turner was a formidable opponent. He'd rather face six rounds with *Dr Death* than go through that again.

Standing outside the headmistress's door, waiting to see Cynthia Arnold, brought back some uncomfortable memories for Myra Banks. She had managed to clash with the woman the very first day she started at Hatfield County and the ensuing years had done nothing to build bridges. Detentions were an almost weekly event and the headmistress had made it very clear that she could see no bright lights in Myra's future. It was going to be odd now, going back to see her old nemesis, knowing that despite the woman's gloomy predictions, she had managed to make something of herself.

Cynthia Arnold sat up straight in her chair as Myra entered the office. "Ah, it *is* you. I did wonder, when Sandra announced that WPC Myra Banks was here to see me, if it was the same Myra Banks who led me such a merry dance a few years ago. I had heard that you'd joined the police force and I must say I was sceptical, but now I see I was mistaken. How is that line of work progressing for you?"

Myra caught the sneering tone in the woman's voice and bridled, but sat there clenching her fist, her fingernails digging into the fleshy part of her hand.

"It's progressing well, Mrs Arnold," Myra said tightly. "It's been suggested that I join the CID," she added for effect, not elaborating about her application being turned down.

"Yes. I always saw you connected to the criminal world in some way or the other."

Bitch! Myra thought, but smiled.

"I'm here to ask for your help, Mrs Arnold. My boss, DCI Callum..."

"Oh, a charming man," Cynthia interrupted. "And so helpful."

"Yes. Well, DCI Callum suggested I come to speak with you about Geraldine Turner."

"Her again." Cynthia rubbed her forehead wearily. "You realise she hasn't come in to school today?"

"No. Ma'am. Geraldine is missing. We think she might have run away from home."

"But that's terrible. Her poor father."

"Her father was killed Tuesday evening." Myra watched with guilty satisfaction as shock bleached the older woman's face.

"Killed?" Cynthia screwed up her eyes and laid her palm across them. "That's awful. Positively dreadful." When she took her hand away from her eyes she was glaring at Myra, angry at her for bringing such terrible news to her door.

"Which is why DCI Callum wanted me to come and see you, to see if you could help us in our inquiries."

Cynthia looked affronted. "I really don't see how *I* can help you. You'd be as well to go back to the chief inspector and tell him that I...'

Myra held up a hand to stem her flow. "Just that, you're her headmistress and you may be able to tell me the names of Geraldine's friends, here at County."

Some of the indignation seemed to drain away from Cynthia Arnold and she sagged slightly in her seat as if the fight had suddenly left her. "I know she's very tight with Sally Wilson," she said. "They take music together. I think Geraldine's helping her with her piano studies. There's Sally, and Phyllis Mayhew. Thick as thieves those three are. I don't think they have a lot of time for anyone else in the school."

"And are Sally and Phyllis in school today?"

"I believe I saw them in assembly this morning, but you'll have to check with their form mistress, Mrs Rosser, to be certain."

"I remember Mrs Rosser," Myra said. *Another bitch.*

"Then you'll remember where her form room is."

Myra got to her feet. "Yes, I do. Thank you for your help."

"She'll either be there or..." She glanced at her wristwatch. "Or you'll find her in the domestic science block. Do you even know where that is? From what I remember, you were never a regular attendee of the cookery classes."

Myra summoned up her most charming smile. "No, I always hated cookery, and I still do, but I remember where the block is though." Without another word she walked out of the office.

Fuller pulled up outside the shop in the Holloway Road. The sign above the shop read *J Talbot and Son, Photographers*. In the window were several easels holding framed wedding photographs and formal snaps of contented-looking families, dressed in their Sunday best, wearing tight smiles as they posed for posterity.

As he drew closer to the window he realised the photographs were faded in their frames and dust had gathered around the feet of the easels. The dust extended to the floor of the window display where it formed a grey carpet, dotted with the bodies of dead flies and wasps, their desiccated husks adding a patina of decay and neglect to the ancient display.

He pushed open the door. A dust-covered brass bell above his head alerted the owner to the fact that he might have a customer.

The inside of the shop echoed the window display. Along one wall was a long, dusty, glass-topped counter and in the corner was a metal magazine rack containing old, dog-eared copies of amateur photography magazines with browning pages.

The old man who shuffled out from behind a bead curtain at the back of the shop was dressed in stained khaki trousers with threadbare knees, and a dark green cardigan that hung on his thin frame like a mouldy sack. On his feet were a pair of tan carpet slippers with zips up the front of them and holes in the toes. He peered at him through a pair of pebble glasses and rubbed a hand across the stubble on his chin. "Can I help you?" he said in a voice that sounded out of practice.

"Mr Talbot?"

"Eh? You'll have to speak up. The battery in my hearing aid has gone."

"Mr Talbot," Fuller said loudly. "I was wondering if you could take a look at this photo and tell me when it was taken."

He produced the rolled-up envelope from his pocket, tipped out the boxing photograph and laid it out on the counter.

The old man leaned forward and adjusted the glasses on the end of his nose. He stared at the photograph for a few seconds and then shook his head. "Not one of mine."

"But it has your stamp on the back."

The old man picked up the photograph with arthritic fingers and turned it over, bringing it up close to his eyes to read the blue lettering of the stamp. "It says J Talbot and Son."

"Yes," Fuller said patiently. "That's why I'm here."

"Well, I didn't take it," the old man said. "This is my son's work."

"Ah, I see. Would it be possible to have a word with your son then?"

The look in the old man's eyes became inscrutable. "Yes, you can speak to him...if you get along to Highgate cemetery and take a medium with you."

"Your son's dead?"

The old man nodded sharply. "Eighteen months ago. Walked out in front of a bus, the bloody fool. They had to scrape his body off the road."

Fuller looked hard at Talbot senior and saw tears misting the old man's eyes. He softened his voice. "I see. So you've no idea when he took this."

"Before he died."

"I gathered as much, but have you any idea when and where it was taken?"

"Looks like a boxing match."

"Have you any idea where the venue might be?"

"The York Hall, Bethnal Green, I should imagine. Benny used to photograph all the fights there."

"Benny being your son?"

The old man nodded. "It was his passion, had been since I first got him into photography. As I said, he was a bloody fool. Weddings and portraiture, that's where the money is in this game, bread and butter shots, not taking snaps at sporting events on the off chance of selling them to the newspapers. That's a mug's game. Mind you he did manage to get rid of this one."

"Really, he sold it? To where?"

"The *Police Gazette* of all places. The bloody *Police Gazette*! I remember when he sold it, two weeks before he died. He was crowing so loudly about it, mind you they only paid him pennies for it. 'That's not going to make your fortune,' I told him, but did he listen? Did he hell. He wouldn't listen to his old man. He was always on the lookout for what he called *the money shot*. The one photograph that the newspapers would pay him a fortune for. That's how he got himself killed, trying to snap someone as they came out of the *Purple Flamingo* in Tottenham Court Road. Stepped into the road to get a better angle and a bus hit him. Bloody fool!" The old man slapped his palm down on the counter. "You don't get hit by buses at weddings."

"No. I should imagine not."

"I lost heart in the business when Benny passed." He rubbed his palm over his face, squeezing the bridge of his nose with his thumb and forefinger. "I don't know. You spend your life building something up. Something to pass on to your nearest and dearest, and then in a split second it all goes to hell under the wheels of a number 29 bus."

Fuller left the old man to his bitter memories and headed back to the station.

13 - FRIDAY

If Edith Rosser had been more put out by Myra's presence in her classroom then she would have had difficulty expressing it to any great effect on her sour-featured face. As it was, she stood up in front of the class and said, "Phyllis Mayhew and Sally Wilson, please come down here to the front of the class."

Myra watched as two of the girls put their books away in almost identical satchels, stood up from their desks and moved down the aisle to the front of the classroom.

"Right," Mrs Rosser said as they assembled uncertainly at the front. "Please go to the staffroom with WPC Banks. She has some questions for you."

Myra smiled tightly at her old domestic science teacher. "Thank you, Mrs Rosser. I'll try not to keep them too long."

Whether or not it was the girls' first time in the out-of-bounds staffroom Myra couldn't say for sure but, judging from their wide-eyed expressions as they entered their teachers' inner sanctum, she guessed it was.

"Okay, girls. Take a seat and make yourself comfortable."

There were a dozen matching leatherette armchairs in the room and several low coffee tables, complete with used coffee cups, and each with their own overflowing ashtray. In fact the whole room stank of old coffee and stale cigarette smoke.

Sally Wilson wrinkled her nose in mild disgust and took a seat by an open window. The less confident Phyllis Mayhew vacillated for a few moments before plumping for an armchair alongside her school friend. She sat down, hugging her satchel to her chest as if for protection, and looked up at Myra with an apprehensive expression on her rather plain, moon face.

"It's okay, girls. You're not in any trouble." Myra reassured them.

Phyllis exhaled her relief noisily while Sally, an altogether more attractive girl with curly red hair and freckles, stared out of the window, a *couldn't-give-a-damn* look in her green eyes.

Myra took a position at the front of the room, turned to them and cleared her throat to make sure she had their attention. "Geraldine Turner. She's not in school today. Have either of you any idea where she might be?"

Phyllis was quick to shake her head. Sally just continued to stare out of the window.

"Sally?" Myra said.

"I haven't seen her since afternoon break yesterday." The girl took a long time to answer and, when she finally responded to Myra's question it was in a bored voice.

"And you, Phyllis?" The girl looked close to tears. "Have you seen Geraldine since yesterday?"

Phyllis closed her eyes tightly and shook her head vehemently.

"So neither of you have any idea at all where Geraldine might be today?"

"Erm…" Phyllis started, but Sally rounded on her.

"Sshh, Phyll! We promised!" Her friend hissed the words at her angrily.

"Okay." Myra clapped her hands together. "*Pax, fainites*. I don't want you two to fall out over this…and I'm sure Geraldine wouldn't want that either."

"Her name's *Gerry*, and she swore us to secrecy," Sally said.

"I wasn't going to say anything, Sal." A tear ran down Phyllis's cheek and she looked wretched.

Sally glared at her.

"All right, Phyllis," Myra said gently. "You can go back to your class,"

Uncertainly, Phyllis got to her feet and, still hugging her school bag, hurried to the door.

Sally stood as well.

"Not you, Sally," Myra said in a stern voice. "Please sit down."

Sally glared at Myra, but she sat back in the chair and again directed her gaze out through the window.

Myra waited until they were alone in the room, then went and sat in the seat that Phyllis had vacated. "Gerry's not in any trouble, Sally. I want you to understand that. It's just that we're all worried about her."

Sally blinked hard, twice.

"If you tell me what you know, you won't get into any trouble either."

"But Gerry will know I told you," Sally said. "And she made me promise."

"You care about Gerry, don't you?"

Sally nodded.

"Then you'll be helping her, really you will."

Sally continued to stare out through the window but tears were welling in her eyes.

You're nowhere near as tough as you think you are, Myra thought.

"They beat her, you know," Sally said suddenly.

Myra looked at her sharply. "Who beats her? Her parents?"

"Her stepmother and the old bag who lives with them during the week."

"Hester Gough?"

Sally nodded. "She's the worst. She hates Gerry, and Gerry hates her."

Myra took a breath. "I see."

Sally shook her head. "No, you don't. You have no idea how awful it is for Gerry, living in that house."

"Then tell me, and tell me where she's gone. Will you do that?"

"She threatened to break Gerry's fingers!" Tears were running freely down Sally Wilson's cheeks now. She nodded her head slowly. "I'll tell."

"Threatened to break her fingers?" Jack said, shocked. "What kind of people are we dealing with here?"

"Not the type I'd want on my Christmas card list," Myra said.

"Nor mine. Break her fingers! Music, *the piano* is everything to that child."

"So you can see why she ran away."

"Oh, yes, I see. Only too well. Did this Sally Wilson have any idea where Gerry might have gone?"

Myra shook her head. "Gerry wouldn't tell her. Only that it was somewhere safe."

Jack sat back in his chair and rubbed his chin. "The poor girl was probably scared out of her wits."

"They used to beat her on a regular basis as well." Myra could empathise with Gerry, coming as she did from a family with a violent drunken father and a weak and ineffectual mother. Myra's teenage years were blighted by the uncertainty of where the next blow or slap would come from. In her mind, it was what drove her on to become a policewoman. It was a need to right injustice and bring to book those who preyed on the weakness of others.

"Is DS Lesser back from seeing the grandparents?" Jack said.

"He'd just got in as I came up."

"Then send him up to see me. Let's see if he's had any luck. Hopefully Gerry won't be missing for much longer."

"What are you going to do about Hester Gough and Lois Turner, sir?"

Jack looked at her grimly. "Oh, I'll deal with those two. In my own time, and in my own way."

"How did you get on, Frank?"

Lesser grinned "Old man Turner's a bit fierce. Sent me away with a flea in my ear."

"Did he indeed? Sit down and tell me what was said."

Lesser pulled a chair up to the desk and sat.

"Did he seem upset that his granddaughter was missing?"

"Not especially," Lesser said. "He seemed more concerned with getting me out of the house and back on the streets to look for her."

"What about Mrs Turner? Did you get to see her?"

"Bit of a wet weekend that one."

"But you saw her, which is more than I managed. Did *she* seem upset? If it were my granddaughter and I'd just been told she was missing, just days after my son was murdered, I think I'd be frantic with worry, maybe even a little hysterical."

"You, guv?"

"My only granddaughter has gone, for all I know, taken by the same person who's just killed my son? Yes, sergeant, I think I'd be pretty hysterical."

"Well, she was crying, but I wouldn't have called it that extreme. I might just have told her that her dog had run away."

Jack scratched the back of his neck. "I'm going to go and see them myself."

"You think they may be lying about having some contact with her?"

"Through their teeth, Sergeant. In fact I wouldn't be at all surprised if Gerry Turner was with them in the house all the time you were there. She might have been in one of the other rooms."

"I should have checked."

"My fault. I told you to tread lightly. You didn't want to upset them further. Gerry told her school friend that she was going to go somewhere safe. Where could be safer than with her grandparents?"

"Then why didn't the Turners say something? They must know that we're expending a lot of man hours in the search for their granddaughter."

"They probably think we'd just ship Gerry back to her stepmother and Miss Gough. They'd go out on a limb to protect her from that, if Gerry told them what her life was like with those two bitches. Leave it with me, Frank. I'll drive over there again once I've spoken to Eddie. He's up in Islington checking out a lead for me. He should be back any time."

"Stepped out under a bus?" Jack said.

"Apparently." Fuller crossed his legs under the desk. "He was snapping someone either going into or coming out of the *Purple Flamingo* nightclub on the Tottenham Court Road. Stepped into the road to get a better angle and wham!" He clapped his hands together, "Goodnight Vienna."

"So let me get this straight. Benny Talbot sells a picture of Thomas Usher and his cronies at a boxing match to the *Police*

Gazette, and two weeks later he falls under a bus outside Usher's nightclub. Is it just me, or does that sound like an unlikely coincidence?"

"When you put it like that."

"How else would you put it, Eddie? Those are the facts." Jack got up and took his raincoat from the stand. "Have you contacted your old guvnor?"

"Yes, first thing. I'm going to drive over to see him this evening."

"Well, there's another thing you can ask him. Did the Met look into the circumstances surrounding Benny Talbot's *accident*? Because, to my mind, this stinks like a haddock left out in the sun for a month."

"I'll check with him." Fuller watched his boss walk out of the office and then leaned back in his seat and closed his eyes. *Charlie, what the hell are you up to?* Fuller thought.

Jack almost made it out of the front door before being hailed by Andy Brewer. "Sir?"

Jack stopped with his hand on the door handle and looked back at the desk. "What is it, Sergeant?"

"Gentleman to see you, sir," Brewer nodded towards a youngish man sitting on the bench, under the public information signs on the wall.

Taking Brewer's nod as his cue, the man got to his feet. He was pencil thin, with stringy black hair and a protruding Adam's apple. On the bridge of a hooked nose he wore a pair of thick, rimless glasses. As he spoke his Adam's apple bobbed up and down. "Chief Inspector Callum? Neil Clarke, *News of the World*."

A reporter, Jack thought. *That's all I need.*

"It's about the Tony Turner murder."

"Then I'm afraid you're going to have to make an appointment to see Chief Superintendent Lane. He deals with all the press reports issued from this station. Sergeant Brewer here should have told you that." He shot a withering look at Andy Brewer who had just developed an acute interest in a pile of missing pet forms on the desk.

"Ah." Clarke adjusted his glasses, pushing them back on the bridge of his nose with his finger and peered at Jack. "I've just seen your chief superintendent, sir. He told me to wait here to have a word with you, as you are, 'in charge of the investigation'. His words, not mine."

Thank you, Henry, Jack thought. Chief Superintendent Henry Lane rarely missed an opportunity to get his name in the papers, so why was he passing the buck now? Perhaps had it been the *Sunday Times* and not scandal sheet, he'd have been keener to give a quote.

"Perhaps you can answer a few of my questions? Superintendent Lane gave me the outline of the case, the bread and butter so to speak, but I need you to supply the meat for the sandwich."

Meat? Sandwiches? Jack thought. *What the hell is he talking about?*

"I'm sorry, Mr. Clarke. I really haven't got time for this. You need to make an appointment to see me. There's somewhere I need to be." He looked at his watch pointedly and moved towards the door. Clarke moved as well, keeping up with him, step for step.

"Yes," he said. "I'll make an appointment. Just one thing before you dash off though. Bearing in mind Mr. Turner's past relationship with Thomas Usher, would you say there is a connection between his murder and the historic gang rivalry between Usher and Albert Klein?"

Jack looked at the reporter uncomprehendingly for second, and then shook his head. "I'm not at liberty to discuss the details of our investigation."

"Would that be a 'No comment' then?"

Jack glared at him. "Yes, Mr, Clarke, it would."

Clarke gave him an obsequious smile. "Thank you, Chief Inspector. That will be all for now. I'll call up and make that appointment." With that he pushed past Jack out of the station, letting the doors swing shut behind him.

"Why have I got the feeling I've just been stitched up?" Jack said to Brewer.

Brewer smiled. "Because you just gave him the golden answer. 'No comment'. Which, for a reporter, is like being handed the keys to the kingdom. He's free now to write any kind of speculative nonsense he likes. Do you read the *News of the World*, sir?"

"I wouldn't let that *rag* through the letter box."

"Shame, because if you did you'd realise that speculation and innuendo are their stock in trade. I think they invented the motto, *never let the facts get in the way of a good story*."

Jack shook his head. "Marvellous. Absolutely bloody marvellous."

14 - FRIDAY

"Chief Inspector, twice in one day? To what do I owe this dubious honour?" Bob Lock said.

"Was Thomas Usher involved in some kind of turf war with a chap called Albert Klein?"

Lock considered the question for a moment. "You might call it that. At his height Usher had the South pretty much sewn up, from the Thames down to the coast. Albert Klein has North of the river, almost as far up as Watford."

"Why haven't I heard about Klein before? Why does it take a hack working for the gutter press to tell me something I should already know and be on top of?"

Lock smiled. "I call it the *Hertfordshire effect*. Once you get out of London to live in this pleasant part of the world, the grimy world of urban crime just passes you by."

Jack shook his head. "I'm slipping, Bob. I should know what's going on in other parts of the country, especially London."

Lock shook his head. "No, sir, not really. There's more than enough crime here up here to deal with, without importing more in from the smoke."

"But *you've* heard of this Klein chap?"

"The way my mind works is both a blessing and a curse. I get the chance to read everything that comes across my desk and ninety per cent of it doesn't concern us at the Hertfordshire Constabulary at all, what does affect us I pass on. The rest of it goes on file but, because I've read it, it lodges here." He tapped the side of his head. "And I have the devil's own job of getting rid of it."

"Well, dig out everything you have on file about Usher and Albert Klein. I'll be out for a couple of hours, so have it all on my desk for when I return."

"Your wish is my command."

"Do genies live in dungeons?"

"Apparently, this one does," Lock said with a rueful smile.

Jack pulled up outside the Turner's bungalow and sat, with his engine off, watching the windows, looking for movement from within. The bungalow had heavy net curtains but after about five minutes he saw what he was expecting to see. He got out of the car and walked up the path. At the front door he pressed the doorbell and rapped on the door with his fist for good measure.

Laurence Turner opened the door and when he saw it was Jack, his face folded into a furious frown. "You again."

"I just want to talk to her, Mr. Turner."

"I don't know what you're talking about." Turner blustered but his face flushed.

"I think you do. Now, we could stand out here in the street and have a slanging match, or you can invite me inside so that I can talk to Geraldine."

Suddenly all the bluster went out of him and Turner's shoulders sagged, making him look a good ten years older. He pulled the door open wide and stood aside to allow Jack entry into the house.

"Who is it, pet?" Jean Turner called from the living room. Her face fell as Jack walked into the room. Geraldine was curled on the settee, her legs folded under her as she leafed through a magazine. She too looked up at Jack and her face froze in the expression of a startled deer.

"I'm not going back," she said.

Jack smiled at her kindly. "And no one's suggesting that you should. I just had to satisfy myself that you're all right."

"She's better now she's here." Jean Turner gathered herself, ready to pounce to protect her granddaughter.

"We can't send her back to that house," Laurence Turner said in a more reasonable tone than he had adopted at the front door.

Jack walked across to an armchair. "May we sit down?"

"As you wish." Turner planted his bony frame on a hard chair by the dining table.

Jack settled himself on a chair opposite the girl. "You gave us quite a scare, Gerry."

A look of regret flashed across the teenager's eyes. "I just couldn't stay there. Hester said she would break my fingers."

"Yes. I'll be having words with Miss Gough." He turned to Turner. "May I use your 'phone. I need to let my people know that Geraldine is safe."

Fear flashed in Geraldine's eyes and she grabbed her grandmother's hand.

"Gerry, It's okay. No one's going to take you away from here. I can see you're in a much better place."

"Thank you," Jean Turner said to him, gratitude in her eyes.

"But I must call this in. My chief superintendent will have my guts if I don't."

"The telephone is out in the hall. This way." Turner led Jack out of the room and closed the door behind them. Once out in the hall he turned to Jack, his voice low. "You can't guarantee that Geraldine won't be taken away from us."

"No, I can't. But I'll do my level best to see that Geraldine is settled with you. I can't see her stepmother putting up too much of a fight, can you?"

Laurence Turner smiled tightly. "I think not."

"Well. You look like the cat that got all the cream," Annie said as Jack walked in that evening.

He told her what had happened at Laurence and Jean Turner's bungalow.

"Jack that's wonderful news."

"All we have to do now is find out who killed Gerry's father." He picked up an overstuffed leather briefcase.

"What's in there?"

"Homework." He put the briefcase down on the kitchen table. "I asked Bob Lock to give me all he had on two villains I'm investigating. I wasn't expecting this much."

"It looks like they've been busy."

"And then some. I think I'd best take this through to the back room, then I can spread it all out on the table and go through it." He hefted the case again.

"Don't you want to know how I got on today, with Barbara

Painter?"

Jack looked at her vaguely for a moment, and then remembered. "Yes, sorry, the job at the bakers."

"I got it." Annie grinned. "I start on Monday."

"That's wonderful. Congratulations. Well done."

"Okay, okay." Annie put up her hands. "Don't overdo it."

"But I'm pleased for you."

"Are you, Jack? Really?"

He dropped the briefcase to the floor and wrapped his arms around her waist, pulling her close. "Really," he said close to her ear and kissed her cheek.

Annie swivelled her head until she reached his mouth. Planting her fingers in his hair she forced his lips against hers, kissing him passionately. When she finally broke the kiss he said, "Hey, you should get a job every day."

"Thank you." She snuggled her face into his chest. "I love you, Jack Callum."

"Never mind that, woman. Where's my dinner?" He pulled her tighter into him.

"In the oven." She pushed him away and gave him a playful slap.

"Ouch! I am famished by the way. I haven't eaten since breakfast."

"Patience, darling. All things come, etcetera, etcetera. By the way, on the way back from *Painters*, I called in at *Howards*, the electrical store in town. You know the one on the corner of Station Road."

"I know it."

"They'll let us have a set for eight shillings a week. Both channels, BBC and ITV, a fifteen-inch screen."

"Is that good?"

"It's wonderful. If you go in there in the morning and countersign the rental agreement, they'll deliver it on Monday."

"That quickly, eh?"

Annie nodded her head excitedly.

"Hold on a moment. Before you get carried away, we'll both be at work on Monday. There'll be nobody here to let them in."

"Joanie will be here. Avril doesn't need her until later in the

93

week."

Jack shook his head. "Well, that's that then. The end of civilization as we know it."

"Oh, shut up, you old bear, and kiss me again."

So he did.

"'allo, Eddie," Francoise Somers said in her delicious French accent and kissed the air either side of Fuller's cheeks. "Charles is in the games room. Come through."

Francoise, Charlie Somers' wife, was a slim beauty, who wore her light brown hair poker-straight and cut into a blunt fringe that just grazed her eyebrows. She had large brown eyes and a retroussé nose over a full-lipped and, Fuller thought, very kissable mouth.

How a grizzled old reprobate like Somers ended up married to such a beauty was one of life's enduring mysteries.

Fuller went through to the back of the house, guided by the clacking of snooker balls as they crashed into each other.

Somers was leaning over the baize, his hand forming a bridge on which to rest his cue as he attempted a difficult cut into the centre pocket. The table was a third full-size and had a slate bed, but Fuller could see the beads of perspiration on the older man's brow as he leaned on the table and strained to make the shot.

"A dollar a frame," Somers said. "Fancy it?"

Fuller laid two half crowns on the edge of the table. "Why not?"

"Go and grab yourself a cue while I frame up."

The snooker cues were kept in a purpose-built rack in the corner of the large games room. He took one out and peered down its length, checking to see if it was true. Satisfied, he walked back to the table and picked up the chalk hanging from a length of string tied to the top corner pocket.

"You can break," Charlie said, taking the blue chalk from him and screwing it against the tip of his own cue.

Fuller positioned the cue ball and lined up the shot. With a flourish he struck the cue ball and sent it rolling down the table to graze the end ball of the triangle of reds. The white cue ball spun away, hit the side cushion, bouncing onto the cushion at the far end of the table, where its momentum sent it back up the table towards him. It rolled to a stop just under the top cushion.

"Hmm" Somers said. "Not bad. Have you been practicing?"

"The result of a misspent youth."

"Well, let's see what I can do with this." Somers bent to take the shot.

"Why did you send the photo to my guvnor, Charlie?" Fuller said as Somers drew back his cue. Somers glanced up at him and struck the cue ball down the table, where it cannoned into the pack of reds and sent the balls spinning across the baize.

"I thought it might help him." Somers glared at the number of balls he'd inadvertently knocked into potable positions.

"Well, it's certainly got him thinking." Fuller bent to pot his first of four red balls. "Did the Met investigate the death of the bloke who took the photograph, Benny Talbot?"

"From what I remember, he fell under a bus on the Tottenham Court Road," Charlie said.

"Yes, a number 29 to be exact, but did he have any help?"

"Do you mean was he pushed?"

"Yes."

"There were several witnesses who saw him fall."

"Credible witnesses?"

"I wasn't personally involved in the investigation, but I believe so. It was deemed an accident, nothing more, nothing less."

Fuller missed an easy black into the corner pocket, and Somers came back to the table.

"You know Jack Callum's not going to let the photograph go," Fuller said.

Somers glanced round at him. "Are you deliberately trying to put me off my stroke?"

"My five bob looks safe from where I'm standing."

15 - FRIDAY

The door to the room opened and Francoise walked in carrying a tray containing a coffee jug and cups.

Eddie Fuller found it hard to drag his eyes away from her as she moved effortlessly around the room and deposited the tray on a coffee table in the corner. She gave the wooden and brass scoreboard a glance. "Who's winning?"

"He is," Somers said sourly.

Francoise smiled at Fuller and lit up the room. "Well done, Eddie. Charles hates to lose, and doesn't very often."

She pronounced her husband's name the French way, making it sound both endearing and incredibly sexy.

"You're a lucky so and so," Fuller said when Francoise had left the room.

"And don't think I'm not aware of it. I count my blessings every day."

"How did you two get together?"

Somers smiled. "That was all thanks to Tommy Usher. She used to work for him?"

"As what?"

"As a whore, Eddie. She was nothing more than a common prostitute. Of course Usher always described his girls as *escorts*."

"A rose by any other name is…"

Somers smiled. "Still a rose. Yes, I know. We'd been seeing each other, in a professional capacity and, believe it or not, we fell in love. She told Tommy, fearing that he'd be furious, that he might even stripe her, but he was as nice as pie about it and gave us his blessing. I suppose he figured he had a detective inspector in his pocket, and if it only cost him the services of a whore then it was worth it. I told the inquiry about it. So that's not one of the skeletons rattling around in my closet."

"You mean there are others?"

"Oh, plenty. But none that I'd lose any sleep over. So let Chief Inspector Callum do his worst, or his best. As I said before, the inquiry cleared me of any wrongdoing."

"And as *I* said before, they weren't in possession of all the facts."

Somers potted an easy black and rested his fists on the table. "Listen, Eddie, I like you, so I won't take what you say as personal, but what you saw, or think you saw, when you were my bagman, is open to many interpretations. I was working to get Tommy Usher off the streets, and I would have succeeded if God hadn't intervened before I could make an arrest."

"The stroke you mean."

"Yes, the bloody stroke. Once he had that, his people spirited him away to a private sanatorium, first in Switzerland, from there, to Brussels. We lost track of him when they moved him to Germany."

"And you believe now he's back in the country, living in a nursing home, in the South of England?"

"Yes, Kent, like I said."

"But it's just an assumption. You don't know that for certain."

Somers shook his head. "No, but it would make sense. He always had strong family links to that part of the word."

"So did you pursue it further?"

"I did, but by the time I heard he was back in the country, the investigation had gone cold and my superiors weren't keen on reopening it. The Chief Constable was of the opinion that the Met had ploughed enough money into bringing Usher down without much success. I think general thinking was that God had done their work for them. Usher was out of their hair without the need of a costly investigation and an even more costly trial. I suppose, as far as they were concerned, having Usher confined to a private nursing home was as good as having him in prison, without it costing the taxpayer a penny."

"So everybody wins," Fuller said.

Somers glared at him. "No, Eddie, nobody wins. What about justice? Where is the justice for the poor bastards Usher maimed, and for the ordinary people whose livelihoods were ruined and whose families he destroyed by his crimes? What about them? I joined the force to fight for people like them, the little people, and to see that thugs like Usher got what was coming to them." There was passion in his voice.

"So that's why you sent my guvnor the photograph. You're hoping Jack Callum may reopen the case and get the result you wanted but could never have."

Somers nodded and cracked the pink ball into the centre pocket. "That's a dollar you owe me." He grinned in triumph.

Fuller slid the two half-crowns across to him. "Why Jack?"

"Because he's not part of the Met, so not tied by their hidebound thinking and, if he's half the copper I've heard he is, he should have no trouble getting a result against Tommy Usher."

"You hate Usher *that* much?"

Somers poured coffee into a tiny cup. "Listen, Eddie, the only good thing to come from my time spent in Usher's company was Francoise. Everything else sits on my soul like an indelible stain that no amount of scrubbing will remove. Another frame?"

Fuller sighed. "Might as well, though I'd forgotten how good you are."

"The police Southern area snooker champion, or had you forgotten that too?"

Fuller shook his head ruefully. "Go on then, you old rogue, frame them up."

He sipped from his cup and nodded approvingly. Francoise certainly made good coffee. "Has anyone seen Usher since he had the stroke?"

Somers shook his head. "Nobody from my team."

"Are you sure he actually had one, a stroke I mean?"

"There were witnesses."

"Credible ones, like the ones who witnessed Benny Talbot falling under a bus?" Fuller said as he watched Somers break.

"What are you implying, Eddie?"

"Could Usher have faked it, just to get the Met off his back?"

Somers watched the cue ball roll back into baulk and gave a satisfied nod. "I must admit, that's what I thought, initially. It was all too bloody convenient, but eventually we heard, from reliable sources, that the stroke was genuine. A doctor from

Barts' hospital, where the bastard was treated, spoke to my Sergeant, Bill Sampson, and told him that it was touch and go for Usher for seventy-two hours, and the doctor had no reason to lie. That, and the fact that Tommy Usher's firm suddenly dropped off our radar, almost as if they had stopped trading."

"Has another firm stepped in to fill the vacuum? Blast!" Fuller cursed as the cue ball cannoned off the black and dropped into the corner pocket.

"Careless. Seven points to me." Somers adjusted the scoreboard. "You need to concentrate, Eddie."

"I know. The underworld, like nature, abhors a vacuum. I would have thought they'd have been queuing up to fill Usher's shoes."

Somers shook his head. "The Richardson gang came sniffing around about a month after it happened, and we had them in the frame for a couple of post office jobs, but we never made anything stick and, after a few weeks, they dropped out of the picture again."

"So, since Usher's stroke, the South's been crime free?"

Somers laughed and potted a red, followed by a blue, and then another red. "Don't be so bloody naïve. There're still as many incidents, thieving, assaults, and the brothels are still making money. If anything, they've seen business increase since Usher left the scene, but there hasn't been any significant gang related crime."

"Don't you find that odd?"

Somers rested the end of his cue on the floor. "Frankly, Eddie, yes I do, but my superiors take a different view. They don't believe in looking a gift horse in the proverbial. As I said, there's still a lot of villainy out there on the streets but, overall, the crime figures have fallen, so my bosses are cock-a-hoop. They're toasting their success, the bloody fools."

Fuller drained his coffee cup, poured himself another, and watched Somers build a break of thirty-five. "According to Bob Lock, our collator, Jack is looking into Albert Klein. Do you know anything about him?"

Somers looked at him askance. "Mr. Callum is a busy boy, isn't he? First Usher, now Klein, what's he trying to do, wipe out crime in the whole country?"

"Klein's name came up and Jack's following it up. I haven't spoken to him about it yet. I wanted to have your thoughts first."

Somers finished the break with a missed black that rattled in the jaws of the pocket. "Damn! Eddie, are you sure you want to do this?"

"Do what?"

"Do you want to keep going behind your boss's back? If I were Callum and I learned my sergeant had been consulting with his old DI, I'd string you up by your nuts and let the vultures have you for breakfast."

"I'm just trying to be a good detective." Fuller was stung by his old mentor's criticism.

"Yes, I realize that. But, there are ways and means. If Jack Callum wants my help, he can come to me off his own bat." He leaned over the table and attempted a difficult canon, missed it and swore again. "Divided loyalties, Eddie. Never a good thing in our line of work."

"I never thought of it like that."

"Bollocks, you didn't. Remember, *I know you*, Eddie. I know what a bloody good copper you are. And I know how bloody ambitious you are too. How old were you when you made detective sergeant? The youngest DS in the South, weren't you?"

"Maybe."

"You know damned well you were. So don't be bloody coy about it."

Fuller avoided his old guvnor's penetrating gaze. "This isn't about me."

"Isn't it?"

Eddie Fuller shook his head.

"Well, try telling that to Jack Callum if our recent conversations ever come to light."

"Jack *told* me to come and see you, to find out what you knew about Usher and Tony Turner."

"Something you have significantly failed to do," Somers said. "You haven't mentioned Turner once since you got here."

"I was working my way round to it."

"Via Albert Klein," Somers said archly. He rested his cue against the table and put his hands on his hips. "Let's stop pissing around, shall we? Just tell me what you want from me and what your guvnor wants, and let's see where that gets us." He walked to the door and opened it. "Francoise? More coffee please, angel. And when you come back in can you bring that bottle of brandy and two glasses from the lounge."

Fuller listened to the French beauty's muffled response, leaned over the snooker table and sunk a red into the centre pocket.

After another five shillings had found their way into Charlie Somers' pocket, the two men sat together on the old, but comfortable, sofa in the corner of the room, the snooker match abandoned.

"Tony Turner was nothing more than a thrill-seeker and a hanger-on. I think he liked to associate himself with criminals. You see it a lot with theatricals. They see it almost as a duty, as if it somehow adds to their credibility. Personally, I've always found it rather pathetic. Tommy Usher embraced it, but that was Tommy, always looking for an angle he could use and, with Tony Turner's show business connections, he struck gold. So he kept the poor sod around, stroking his ego and mining his contacts for new business opportunities. There was also the matter of the cachet he got from being seen in the press with a famous actor. It lent him a certain respectability. Of course it all turned to shit when Turner met that awful Franklin woman and married her."

"You knew Turner's wife, Lois?"

Somers grimaced. "I met her a few times. She's a hideous woman; a lush, and a few saucers short of a tea service, if you want my opinion, but Turner was besotted by her. He thought the sun shone out of her *derriere*. Carrying on with her while his poor wife lay dying of cancer in hospital, the bastard!" Somers shuddered.

"And Albert Klein?"

"A different proposition altogether. He's an old school villain.

101

Jewish and devout in his faith, attends the synagogue every Sabbath, takes time off from his criminal activities during the Yiddish festivals. But he's a vicious, nasty piece of work and as crooked as they come."

"Worse than Usher?"

"In some ways, yes. He runs North London like his own private fiefdom, and woe betide any who challenge his position, as the twins from Bethnal Green found when they tried to muscle in on his protection rackets in their area. Klein sent them packing, back to Vallence Road with their tails stuck firmly between their legs."

Somers took a mouthful of brandy, swilling the smooth liquor over his tongue, before swallowing it with a contented sigh. "They'll have him in the end though. They're mad and dangerous, Reggie and Ronnie, the both of them. Genuine psychopaths. At one time there was talk of Klein and Usher joining forces to consolidate their hold over London, but their cultural differences caused too much conflict. I can't ever imagine Tommy Usher taking time off for religious holidays. Not when there's bent money to be made and, for all their similarities, the two of them also had fundamental differences when it came to business."

"Such as?"

"Well, drugs were the main one. Klein gets a significant portion of his income from trafficking and dealing in drugs, dope and amphetamines mainly, cocaine and heroin for those who can afford it. It was one area Tommy Usher steered clear of with a passion. He lost his younger brother, Cyril, to a heroin overdose just after the war. After that he wouldn't have any truck with them. He had an almost pathological hatred of them, and Klein was never going to sacrifice a significant proportion of his income just to climb into bed with him, so the unholy union never happened and the antagonism between them continued."

"Do you think Klein could be involved in Tony Turner's death?"

"To the best of my knowledge they never actually met, at least, I wasn't around if they did. Why would you think that?"

"Because when Turner was found dead, he was made up to look like Tommy Usher, complete with false moustache and fake nose."

Somers eyes widened. "Really? Well, I'm blowed." He drained his glass. "But I can't see Klein's fingerprints on it. He and Usher didn't get on, sure, but there was a mutual admiration there. And they both respected the North/South divide. If Callum's going down that route with his investigation, I think he'll hit a brick wall. Honour amongst thieves and all that crap. Another frame before you go?"

"To give me a chance to win my money back?"

"Don't be silly, Eddie," Somers said with a sly smile.

16 - SATURDAY MARCH 21ST 1959

As Jack carried the stepladder along the landing he heard the alarm clock sounding off its shrill bell in Rosie's room. She had an early start at the baker's this morning. He set the ladder under the loft hatch and started to climb to release the catch.

"Couldn't you sleep, Dad?" Rosie yawned as she came out of her bedroom, hair awry and rubbing the sleep from her eyes as she opened the door to the bathroom.

"Just looking for something." Jack released the catch and let the hatch swing down,

"Is mum awake?"

Jack shook his head and put his finger to his lips. "It's only you and me so far, and we'll try to keep it that way for another hour at least."

"Quiet as a mouse," she whispered and tiptoed into the bathroom.

Jack hoisted himself into the loft and found the light switch, flicking it on and watching as the 100 watt bulb cast its light over the neatly ordered stacks of boxes, old suitcases and cartons containing rolls of wallpaper and Christmas decorations. The loft was as well ordered as his garden shed. A place for everything and everything in its place, and he had no trouble locating the large suitcase containing back-issues of the *Police Gazette* stretching back in time to 1950.

He unfolded a dusty card table onto the loft boards, and then erected a small canvas camping chair. He opened the case, set it down on the table and started going through the old periodicals, starting with the most recent and slowly working his way through the back-issues.

Thirty minutes later he found the edition he'd been searching for. He flattened it out on the table. Taking up a third of the page was a reproduction of the boxing photograph he'd been sent. Above the photograph the headline read, *Senior Officer cleared of Corruption Charges*. The three-column story went on to report how detective inspector Charles Somers had been exonerated by an inquiry into police corruption. It charted his relationship with certain gangland figures of whom Thomas Usher was but one.

The piece ended with the Police Commissioner praising Inspector Somers for his diligent work in gathering intelligence on organized crime in the capital.

Jack stared at the photograph, at the names printed underneath it, hoping to discover the reason why he'd been sent the boxing shot but, apart from a feeling that one of the other characters, Simon Docherty, looked vaguely familiar, there was nothing more to be gleaned.

He stared hard at Docherty's face. He was sure he had never crossed paths with him before, but the man's face was nagging at something locked in the back of his mind, but refusing to fully reveal itself.

From down below he could hear stirrings coming from his bedroom. Annie was awake and moving about the room.

Rolling up the copy of the Gazette, he stuffed it into the pocket of his cardigan and put the suitcase away. He turned off the light and lowered himself out of the loft in time to see his wife emerging from the bedroom. Annie looked up at him and yawned as he started to descend. "I thought I heard someone moving about up there. I guessed it'd be you."

"Sorry. I didn't mean to wake you."

"Don't worry, you didn't. The milkman stole that honour from you with his bloody whistling. But once I was awake I heard the noises from up there and for a moment I thought we had rats, then I realised you weren't in bed. What have you been doing?"

"Looking for something." He tugged the Police Gazette from his pocket and held it aloft. "I found it."

"Good. What time did you turn in last night? I didn't hear you come up."

"After one." Jack closed the loft hatch and shut up the stepladder.

Annie shook her head. "I'm thinking candles and burning them at both ends?"

"You worry too much." He pecked her on the cheek.

"Well, someone's got to. Eggs for breakfast?"

He glanced at his watch and shook his head. "Just tea and toast for me. I'll have to get a move on if you want me to drop in at *Howards* about that television before I go to the station."

"How did your meeting with Charlie Somers go?" Jack asked when Eddie Fuller came into the office.

"It cost me fifteen bob." Fuller sat down at his desk heavily.

"How come?"

"Snooker. The old bugger took me to the cleaners."

"Serves you right. Did he shed any light on Usher's relationship with Tony Turner?"

"Oh, yes," Fuller said, and spent the next thirty minutes recapping his conversation with his old guvnor.

"And what did he have to say about Benny Talbot and his argument with the number 29?"

"The Met treated it as an accident."

Jack was silent for a moment. Eventually he leaned forward in his seat. "What happened to the camera?"

Fuller looked at him quizzically.

"Benny Talbot's camera. Who was he trying to photograph when he met with his *accident*?"

"I didn't ask, and I doubt that Charlie would know. It wasn't his case."

"Shame. I'd like to see that roll of film."

"Why?

Jack shrugged. "I'm not sure really. It's just an idle thought buzzing around my brain at the moment." He picked up his mug of station tea and took a swig, shuddered and set it down again. "Bloody awful. Who makes this stuff? What about Albert Klein? Did Charlie have anything to say about him?"

"He's a North London villain and devout Jew, who respects the Sabbath and observes all the religious holidays…"

"And is good to his mother, no doubt. Any history between him and Usher that Turner might have fallen foul of?"

"Charlie can't recall Klein and Turner ever meeting."

Jack sighed. "Round and round in circles," he said, almost to himself. "Well, let's see what Frank comes up with. He's working his way through his half of the list Lois Turner gave us. I believe he's up in the West End today, trying to speak to that dancer chappie."

"Fred Tozer."

"Yes, him. It'll probably be another dead end, but who knows?"

Frank Lesser stood in the wings of the *Carlton* theatre, watching the colourful and athletic dance routine play out on the stage. Fred Tozer stood out from the rest of the twenty-strong troupe, not only because he was centre stage, but also for something Tozer had that set him apart from the rest. *Charisma.* Lesser had seen it before in the wrestling ring. Some performers had it and could have the crowd eating out of their hand, others didn't and would remain lower to middle card throughout their careers.

Tozer had it in spades, which was probably the reason that it was *his* name up in lights, above the title of the revue.

The tap routine ended and an assistant threw Tozer a towel for him to wipe the sweat from his freely perspiring face. Then the assistant spoke quietly into the dancer's ear and pointed towards Lesser standing in the wings.

Still wiping the rivulets of perspiration from his face Tozer walked towards him, calling back over his shoulder to the troupe. "Take five! And then we go again, from the top."

A susurration of groans rippled across the stage.

"Are you Lester?" he said.

"*Lesser*, sir. Detective sergeant, Welwyn and Hatfield Police."

Tozer's eyes narrowed. "Bit out of your jurisdiction, Sergeant, aren't you?"

"It concerns an incident that happened in our area a few days ago. Can we go somewhere and talk? I have a few questions."

Tozer regarded him quizzically for a few moments and then shrugged. "Very well. We can talk in my dressing room." He walked past Lesser. "This way."

Lesser followed him through the maze of narrow walkways that constituted the backstage area of the theatre, until they came to a corridor with a door at the end. The door had a star affixed to it. Tozer opened it and held the door open for Lesser to enter.

Tozer sat down at a dressing table that had a large mirror surrounded by small light bulbs. They showed up the fine age-lines wrinkling Tozer's face that hadn't been apparent before. He was still a good-looking man, with almost symmetrical features, a finely chiselled nose above lips that could be called voluptuous. His body was lean and toned and the muscles of his legs were clearly defined under the sheer nylon of his black tights. He wouldn't have looked out of place in a wrestling ring, Lesser thought.

"Grab a seat." Tozer pointed to a wooden chair standing in the corner.

Lesser grabbed it and set it down a yard away from the man.

"So, what do you want to ask me about?"

"Tony Turner," Lesser said, and watched a cloud spread over Tozer's face.

"He's dead. There were a couple of paragraphs in *The Stage*. It said his death was being treated as suspicious and the police…" He slapped his forehead. "That's why you're here, isn't it?"

Lesser nodded.

"Well, I didn't kill him, if that's what you think."

"Why should I think that, sir?"

Tozer shook his head. "God knows, it's not as if I didn't have reason to, but no, Sergeant, I'm not your man."

"Glad to hear it." Lesser produced his notebook from his pocket. "Can you tell me where you were last Tuesday afternoon, the 17th?"

"Yes. Here."

"And do you have any witnesses who can corroborate that?"

Tozer smiled. "Yes. About five hundred of them in fact. We give a matinee performance on Tuesdays."

Lesser smiled indulgently and jotted it down in his notebook. "What time did the show end?"

"It runs from two-thirty 'til five, with a fifteen-minute intermission."

"And you were on stage all that time, apart from the intermission of course?"

"Come to the show, Sergeant, and you can see for yourself what a demanding performance it is."

"Perhaps I will," Lesser said, with no intention of ever doing so.

Further conversation was halted as the dressing room door was thrown open violently. It crashed against the wall and a short, bald man stormed into the room.

"There you are, you bastard!" he yelled at Tozer, ran across the room and yanked the dancer out of his seat. "I ought to smash your bleedin' face in."

Lesser sprang to his feet and within seconds had the fat man pinned against the wall, his arm forced up between his shoulder blades. The fat man yelped. "Here, what's your game?" Tears sprang to his eyes as Lesser applied more pressure to his arm.

Fred Tozer stood there, a look of wry amusement on his face. "It's all right, Sergeant. You can let him go."

Lesser looked at him uncertainly.

"Really. Julian's bark is far worse than his bite."

"You know this man, sir."

Tozer chuckled. "Yes, more's the pity. I've known him all my life. Detective Sergeant Lesser, may I introduce you to Mr. Julian Tozer, my brother."

"Your brother?" Lesser released the fat man and held him at arm's length, all the while looking him up and down, searching for a hint of familial resemblance, and finding none.

"Yes," Tozer said ironically. "The likeness is astonishing, isn't it?" He turned to his brother. "Calm down, Julian. You'll give yourself another coronary."

Julian Tozer was breathing heavily, and his face was red and puffy. Lesser pulled up the chair and placed it behind Julian's knees. "I'd sit down, sir, if I were you."

Julian Tozer was wheezing but he gave Lesser a filthy look and flopped down into the chair. "Are you here to arrest him?"

"Not today," Lesser said.

"Well, you should. He's a bloody thief."

Lesser raised his eyebrows and turned towards Fred Tozer. "Something I should know about, sir?"

"Ignore him, Sergeant. Julian's just upset because our recently departed mother favoured me in her will and left the rest of her money to a donkey sanctuary in Dorset."

Lesser shook his head. "None of my concern, sir. If you don't mind me asking though, what did you have against Tony Turner?"

"The man was a welsher, Sergeant. He owed me several hundred pounds. I helped him out when his career was on the skids, more fool me."

"And he never paid you back?"

"Not a brass farthing, the bastard, and it's not as if he didn't have it."

"Serves you bloody well right," Julian Tozer said to his brother venomously.

"Be quiet, Julian," Fred Tozer snapped. "Will there be anything else, Sergeant?"

"No. I think I've taken up enough of your time."

"Are you a boxer, Sergeant? You certainly seem to know how to handle yourself, and judging from your face…"

"A wrestler, sir."

"Ah, so that's why you seemed so at ease backstage in a theatre. Most people who come back here always seem a little bit, well, awestruck for want of a better word, but you seem very comfortable in the environment."

Lesser nodded. "Yes, you could say that." The nether regions of theatres held no mystery for him. Many of his bouts were held in run-down provincial theatres. To him it was just a place to pick up another wage packet.

Lesser excused himself and headed off to another theatre, this one in Shaftesbury Avenue, where Betsy Maclaren was appearing in a Noel Coward play.

17 - SATURDAY

An hour later he was sitting in another dressing room. This one was cramped and cluttered and lacking a star on the door. Betsy Maclaren's star had been fading of late, along with her ingénue status and her *girl-next-door* looks.

She sat opposite Lesser, a pink *Sobranie* cocktail cigarette clutched between nicotine-stained fingers. "Polly Turner was my best friend," she said. "We trained at Webber Douglas and graduated together. I was bridesmaid at her and Turner's wedding, for Christ's sake."

"So you must have taken her death very badly."

"I cried for weeks." Betsy paused. "But I was crying for Polly for a long time *before* her death, once I learned what that piece of scum Turner was doing. Polly was a lovely girl, one of life's little gems. We shared a flat in Ladbroke Grove when we were first starting out. She was twice the actress I am, but so modest and self-effacing. For that bastard to betray their marriage vows and start sleeping with that…that bitch, Lois Franklin, was one of the cruellest things I have ever witnessed."

Lesser could see that the affair had hit Betsy Maclaren hard. Tears were welling in her eyes and she was torturing a silk handkerchief, twisting it tightly around her fingers. "I had no idea that Polly Turner was an actress too."

"That was how they met. She was Eliza to his Professor Higgins in Bristol rep. He was far too young for the part, of course, but Polly's interpretation of Eliza secured glowing praise from the critics and made the play a success. It was the worst part she could have taken."

"Oh?"

"She fell in love with her leading man," She sighed and wearily ran a hand through her hair. "The worst of all theatrical clichés really, and after that, convinced *he* was going to be the major star, she put her own career on the back burner, especially after Geraldine was born, focussing all her efforts into making her conviction come to fruition." She took a savage draw on the

Sobranie and ground it out in an already overflowing ashtray.

"You seem very bitter about it."

"You could say that. To think what Polly sacrificed for that pig." She shuddered. "I hope one day the gods catch up with him and condemn him to the hell he so richly deserves."

"You haven't heard?"

"Heard what?"

"Tony Turner was murdered last Tuesday evening."

The news seemed to jolt her in her seat.

"Murdered? Tony?"

Lesser nodded. Betsy reached for another *Sobranie*, powder blue this time, and stuck it between her lips, lighting it with a match from a box on the dressing table. She drew a lungful of the smoke in one long pull, and blew it out through clenched teeth.

"Good. Murdered you say? I hope the little worm suffered."

"Where were you Tuesday afternoon?"

Betsy Maclaren's mouth dropped open and the cigarette fell from her lips, hitting the floor and rolling underneath her chair. "You don't think I killed him, do you?"

"You seem to have had a lot of animosity towards him."

"I did. I think you could almost say that I hated his guts, and I'm delighted, absolutely delighted, he's dead, but no, not last Tuesday. I was here all afternoon rehearsing. Twenty or so people saw me and will back me up." Her chin tilted up defiantly, as if daring Lesser to doubt her. "Do I look like a murderer to you?"

"Crippen didn't look much like a murderer, but he was."

Betsy glared at him. "Don't take offence, Sergeant, but I'm going to tell you to piss off now."

Lesser stared back at the diminutive Betsy Maclaren, with her blonde curls and blue, doe-eyes, mildly shocked by the coarseness of her language. He got to his feet. "I'll check your alibi before I go."

"Yes, do that," she said coldly, and turned her back on him, smoking furiously.

"Bloody theatricals!" Frank Lesser said as he walked into Jack's office later that afternoon.

"What are you moaning about, Frank? You're almost one of them yourself," Fuller said from his desk.

"Watch it, son. I'm a sportsman and an athlete."

Fuller gave a fake yawn. "If you say so, Frank."

"I bloody do." Lesser moved towards Fuller with his fingers balling into fists.

"That's enough, you two!" Jack said loudly. "Save your squabbles for the bloody playground. Sergeant Lesser, would you mind sitting down and telling me what you found out today?"

Still shooting daggers at Eddie Fuller with his eyes. Lesser pulled a chair up to Jack's desk and sat down.

"Two suspects questioned, both with alibis for Tuesday afternoon."

"So, a trip to London's West End wasted?"

"Not really, sir. I found out that Tony Turner was a bit of a shit."

"We knew that already," Fuller said.

Jack glared at him. "Be quiet, Eddie. And let Frank continue."

"Thank you, sir. As I was saying, Tony Turner was a...'

"Yes. I think that's well established now." Jack cut him off. "And you don't think either Fred Tozer or Betsy Maclaren could be responsible for the murder?"

"Of the two of them, only Tozer would have the strength to pull it off. He's a trained dancer, athletic and well-muscled. But his alibi is rock solid. Betsy Maclaren is about five foot four and probably only seven-stone soaking wet. Again, a strong alibi, and she was unaware Turner was dead. It came as quite a shock to her."

"She's a bloody actress, Frank," Fuller said. "She could have been putting on a performance for your benefit."

"Sir?" Lesser turned to Jack.

Jack glared at Fuller again. "Button it, Eddie. I think Frank's more than capable of recognising when someone is telling the truth."

"Thank you, sir." Lesser smiled slyly at Fuller.

"Type out your report and have it on my desk by three o'clock," Jack said to him. "Eddie, how are you getting on tracking the name's on your list?" he said as Lesser went back to his own office, to the laborious task of typing up his notes.

"I've got an appointment with Michael Lewin later this afternoon."

"Who's Lewin?"

"He's the last name on the list. An architect. How he connects to Turner I've yet to find out."

"Well, let me know as soon as you do. Are you coming round to give Eric his guitar lesson later?"

Fuller shook his head. "No. He got Bert Weedon's *Play in a Day* book from the library last week."

"Bert Weedon's written a book?"

"Have you heard of him?"

Jack chuckled. "I remember him when he used to play with Ted Heath and Mantovani. Well, I suppose Eric can't go far wrong if he's leaning that kind of music."

"Well, just to warn you, he's discovering rock and roll as well. He'll be asking for an electric guitar and an amplifier soon."

"Good God, he's only just got your old one."

Fuller shrugged. "That's how these things work. My first instrument was a banjo and I'd graduated to the guitar within six months, and got a better one two weeks later. Anyway, Eric reckons he doesn't need me anymore. Still, I suppose it will save you five bob a week."

"More for you to lose on your snooker matches with Charlie Somers."

"You have to be kidding. I learned a hard lesson playing that old devil. He's good."

"Southern area champion for three years running, from what I hear."

"You knew that?"

"I knew it, like I knew it was Somers you went to for information, when I specifically told you to contact Division," Jack said with a wry smile.

Fuller blushed. "You knew that too?"

Jack nodded. "Oh, yes."

"And you don't mind?"

"Only that you didn't tell me what you were up to. I need to be able to trust my sergeants, Eddie."

"You *can* trust me, Jack."

"Actually, I applaud your use of initiative. I would have done the same thing."

"So you're not annoyed?"

"Bloody furious, but only because I didn't think of it first. Just keep me in the picture in future, yes?"

"Yes," Fuller said.

"You found Talbot, the photographer, in Islington, right?"

"On the Holloway Road."

"Then that's where I'll be this afternoon. I'm going to pay him a visit myself."

"Is there any point?"

"You used your initiative, Eddie, this is me using mine."

It wasn't easy to park on the Holloway Road. Saturday shoppers were out in force, and those that had driven into town had parked their cars close to the shops, but Jack squeezed his Morris Oxford into a space between a blue Hillman Minx and a Bedford van.

The old man behind the counter looked up as Jack entered the shop, glanced at him briefly and then went back to polishing a camera lens with a soft cloth. He looked up again as Jack spoke. "Mr. Talbot?"

"Jacob Talbot, yes," he said.

Jack introduced himself. "You spoke with my sergeant yesterday," he said. "I was sorry to learn about your son."

Talbot said nothing but put down the camera on the glass-topped counter.

"I was wondering about his camera," Jack said.

"What about it?"

"What happened to it, after the accident?"

"The bus ran over that too. Shame. It was a *Leica M3*. It cost him an arm and a leg, and ended up costing him a whole lot more."

"Yes." Jack looked at the old man sympathetically. "Was the film recovered?"

Talbot shook his head. "The camera was crushed, the film ruined. I've got the bits if you want to see them. The police gave me a brown paper bag with Benny's effects in it. Want to see?"

Jack shook his head. "That won't be necessary."

"Then why are you asking?"

"I was just wondering who he was taking photos of when he died. You told my sergeant the accident happened outside *The Purple Flamingo* nightclub."

"That's right, on the Tottenham Court Road. Benny was always hanging around there in the evenings when he wasn't at the boxing, though what he was trying to achieve I'll never know. Getting snaps of people coming and going. I suppose there's a market for that sort of thing in some of the murkier sections of the press, but I don't think he ever made much out of it."

Jack went across and looked through the grubby glass counter at the array of cameras and lenses that were steadily gathering dust of the shelves. "I don't suppose Benny kept hold of the photos he took?"

Jacob Talbot laughed. "Are you kidding me? Benny never threw anything away. He called them his legacy, though who he was preserving them for I'll never know. Certainly not for me."

"You still have them?"

The old man nodded. "Didn't seem right somehow to just throw them away. I suppose I'll have to one day. I'm selling the shop and whoever takes it over isn't going to want them."

"Could I see them?"

"All of them?" the old man said incredulously. "There're hundreds of them."

"Well, maybe the ones taken in his last six months or so. I take it he had some kind of filing system."

"Oh yes, he had that all right." Talbot came around the counter and walked to the front door, locking it and flipping the sign over from *open* to *closed.*

"I don't want to interfere with your business."

Talbot gave a bitter laugh. "What bloody business? You're

116

the first person to come in here today." He shuffled back behind the counter and pushed a curtain to one side, revealing a wooden staircase. He beckoned Jack forwards. "Come through. He kept them up here."

Jack followed him up the stairs. At the top there was a landing with several doors leading from it. Talbot opened the third one along. "In here." He pushed the door wide to allow Jack to enter.

As he followed Jack into the room Talbot leaned in through the doorway and flicked down a Bakelite switch.

"My son's legacy." The light from a single bulb hanging from a twisted flex in the middle of the room cast a milky glow over the boxes arranged on shelves that covered three of the walls from floor to ceiling. In the centre of the room stood a drop-leaf table and a wheel-backed chair. On the table was a desk lamp with an articulated neck and lying on the lamp's heavy base was a four-inch magnifying glass with a brass handle. "He spent a lot of his time up here. Either in here or the darkroom next door, when he should have been downstairs with me in the shop."

Jack stared at the stacks of boxes. Each box had a date of the year they were taken neatly printed on them in heavy black ink.

Talbot, in turn, was staring at him. "The last year is on the shelf to your right."

Jack crossed to the shelf, located a box labelled 1958, slid it out and took it back to the table.

"Switch on the lamp. You'll strain your eyes otherwise."

"Yes, of course." Jack pressed the switch on the lamp and opened the box, groaning inwardly when he saw the hundreds of photographs contained within. He sat down on the hard wooden chair and began to take the photos out, spreading them on the table.

"I'll leave you to it then. You obviously know what you're looking for."

Jack glanced around at him. "Yes, fine. I'll come down when I've finished."

The old man inclined his head and pulled the door shut. Jack listened to Talbot's heavy tread on the stairs as he went back downstairs. This could take hours, he thought. He picked up the magnifying glass and began the search for familiar faces among the many hundreds Benny Talbot had snapped.

18 - SATURDAY

Lewin and Stern, Architects, occupied a modern office in the centre of Welwyn Garden City. Eddie Fuller walked in through the glass door and found himself in a spacious foyer dominated by a large model of a modern town centre rendered in white cardboard. Fuller stared at it for a long moment before deciding that it was not a place he'd like to live. "Bloody rabbit warren," he muttered under his breath.

"May I help you?" a female voice sounded at his elbow. He turned at the sound of the voice and found himself face to face with a young and very attractive blonde woman. Dressed in an elegant navy-blue suit over a crisp white blouse, secured at the collar by a delicate cameo brooch she looked as if she had just stepped from the pages of *Vogue* magazine. Her hair was cut in a chic pageboy, curling under just above her collar and finished with a blunt fringe that hovered half an inch above clear blue smiling eyes.

"Yes," Fuller said, returning the smile. "Detective Sergeant Fuller. I telephoned and made an appointment to see Mr. Lewin."

The young woman checked her wristwatch. "You're very prompt, Sergeant Fuller."

"I try to be."

She pointed to a pair of leather and chrome easy chairs set either side of a large potted plant. "Take a seat. I'll tell Michael you're here." She flashed him another smile and disappeared through one of the two oak-panelled doors leading off from the foyer.

Fuller had barely settled himself in the comfortable chair before she was back.

"He'll see you now." The smile had gone from her eyes and her demeanour had chilled slightly. She said nothing more as Fuller got to his feet and crossed the carpeted floor to the door she had left open.

Michael Lewin was a rakish-looking man in his mid-thirties

who was seated on a high stool at a large, modern drawing board. His hair was curly and flopped over one eye. He brushed it back impatiently with his hand and fixed Fuller with an appraising stare. "You're not what I was expecting." His face was thin and pointed, and had a couple of days' worth of stubble darkening his chin, giving him an unkempt appearance.

"Really?" Fuller said, uncertain how to respond.

"I thought you'd be older, dressed in tweeds with size twelve brogues. You look more like a teddy boy, not like a policeman at all."

Lewin had an arrogant, slightly sarcastic tone in his public-school voice that Fuller found hard to warm to. He smiled at the architect blandly. "We come in all shapes and sizes."

Lewin slid off the high stool, walked across to a desk and sat down behind it. "Pull up a chair, and then you can tell me why you want to see me. I hope this won't take long. I'm rather busy."

Fuller dragged a chair from the wall and sat facing Lewin across the desk. "Anthony Turner. I believe you were acquainted with him."

"Were? You said *were acquainted* with him. Has something happened to him?"

"He was killed Tuesday evening, sir." Fuller watched Lewin closely, trying to gauge his reaction.

The shock that registered on Michael Lewin's face seemed genuine enough. "Tony's dead?" he gasped incredulously.

Fuller nodded.

"Good God! How?"

"He was murdered."

"Oh my Christ!"

"Did you know him well, sir?"

Lewin averted his eyes, swallowed loudly and nodded his head.

"How well?"

"We shared digs when we were at Birmingham rep when we were in our late teens." Lewin kept swallowing loudly, struggling to get his emotions under control.

"So you two were friends."

"Very good friends." Lewin opened the desk drawer and took out a packet of cigarettes. He took one from the pack and stuck it between his lips, lighting it with a match, striking the red-tipped Swan Vesta on the desk. His hands were shaking as he took the cigarette from his mouth and blew smoke in a thin stream into the air.

"And you had no reason to kill him?"

Lewin shot forward in his seat his hands planted flat on the desk, fingernails digging into the wood. "How dare you?" His eyes were blazing with fury. "I could never hurt Tony. How dare you even suggest that I could?"

Fuller held up his hands. "Then perhaps I've been misinformed."

"Yes, you bloody have. Tony Turner was like a brother to me. We started out together, appeared in rep together."

"You were an actor then?"

Lewin nodded. "Not much of one, I'll grant you. I didn't have a tenth of Tony's talent. I had the basics, but he carried me through our time together in the theatre, always supportive, always encouraging me, up until the time that I realised that acting was an art I was never going to excel at. When he got the call from the Rank Organization it was a turning point, not only in his career but also in our relationship. He nearly didn't take up their offer. I had to force his hand." He was gazing at a spot a few inches away from his face, lost in the past.

"And how did you manage that?"

Fuller's question brought him back to the moment. He seemed to shake himself. "By quitting the business and moving out of our digs, coming back up here and retraining. I'd always had an aptitude for design at school. I was pretty good at technical drawing, so it seemed an obvious choice to make."

"So there was no ill feeling when you made the decision to quit acting?"

Lewin shook his head. "No, none at all. I came back here to Welwyn and Tony went on to be groomed by Rank and the rest, as they say, is history. Why on earth would someone kill him?"

"That's what we're trying to find out. Did you stay in touch with him when you left the acting profession?"

Lewin had drifted into reverie again. "What...yes. Birthdays, Christmas, that sort of thing, but we moved in different circles. Our paths rarely crossed, despite us both living in Hertfordshire, a stone's throw from each other."

"When did you last see him?"

Lewin winced, as if stung by the memory. "At Christmas actually. Last Christmas. He invited me to spend a few days with him at *Elsinore*."

"And you haven't seen him since December?"

"No." Lewin ground out the cigarette in the glass ashtray on the desk and lit another. "It wasn't an altogether successful reunion and I was in no rush to have a repeat performance."

"Why was that?"

"I hadn't seen him for a few years. I'm afraid I'd let things drift somewhat. When we had last met he was married to Polly. I knew her from our days at Birmingham and we used to get along famously. She was a lovely girl. Lois, his new wife, was a different kettle of fish; brash, loud, and a bloody Yank. I clashed with her throughout the holiday. I didn't like her and she certainly didn't like me. I think she saw me as some kind of threat to her domestic bliss. A ghost from Tony's past, if you like, and she made it very plain that I wasn't welcome at *Elsinore*."

"How did he seem to you when you last saw him?"

"What do you mean?"

"Did he seem troubled, bothered about anything?"

Lewin leaned back in his chair and thought for a moment. "He seemed different," he said at last. "But bear in mind it had been a few years since I'd last seen him and people do tend to change over time. He'd been through a lot dealing with Polly's illness and then her death, and of course he had Geraldine to bring up, by himself. That couldn't have been easy." Lewin paused and took a long pull on his cigarette. "But for all that, there was something about him that I'd never seen before." Another drag on the cigarette. "I suppose you could call it melancholia."

"And how did this *melancholia* show itself?"

"It was Boxing Day morning. He suggested we go for a walk, to get some country air into our lungs. To be quite honest it was a good excuse to get out of the house and away from Lois and her blasted brother who was also spending the holiday with them and was just as obnoxious as his sister. Tony asked Geraldine to come along, but she had a piano exam coming up and wanted to spend the time practicing, so it was just him and me."

Fuller nodded, encouraging him to proceed.

"I had visited *Elsinore* a number of times in the past when he'd first bought the place with Polly, and we'd walked the surrounding countryside on many an occasion. We set off on what had become an established route across the fields, mostly keeping to the paths that ran along the side of them. There had been a frost that morning so the mud had frozen. That route also took us through a farm. 'Squashed Rat Farm' Tony had Christened it. They farmed cereal crops there. Vermin was a problem and a number of the rodents lost their lives under the wheels of tractors and the like.

"Sure enough we were walking past the grain silos when Tony pointed down at a frozen puddle. Caught in the ice was the flattened body of a rat, preserved like a fly in amber. 'See that, Mikey,' he said. He'd called me Mikey from the moment I first knew him. 'See that, Mikey. That's a pretty good approximation of how I feel at the moment.' I tried to joke him out of it, of course. I knew Tony could lean towards the melodramatic sometimes, he was an actor after all, but there was a darkness to his mood that no amount of bantering from me could lift. In the end I gave up trying and we walked home pretty much in silence.

"I didn't hang around when we got back to *Elsinore*. Lois and her brother had started on the eggnog and cherry brandy at breakfast that morning and by the time we got back to the house they were both three sheets to the wind and I could tell Lois was spoiling for a fight, so I invented a maiden aunt that I'd promised to spend the Boxing Day with, made my excuses and left.

"And that was the last time I saw him." Lewin lapsed into silence. There were tears in his eyes and he had reverted to staring blankly into space as doleful memories played behind his eyes.

Fuller decided to leave the man to his misery and stood up. "Just one more thing before I go. Can you account for your whereabouts Tuesday afternoon?"

Lewin looked at him. "Eh? What?"

"Tuesday afternoon?"

"I was here." The arrogance in his voice was a thing of the past. The news of Tony Turner's death had shaken him badly. "Sally will confirm that. Have a word with her on your way out."

"Yes. I'll do that." But he knew that Sally, the receptionist, would confirm the alibi. Michael Lewin did not kill Tony Turner. Fuller was as sure of that as he'd been about anything in his life.

19 - SATURDAY

Jack clasped his fingers behind his neck and stretched. He had just finished going through his third box of photographs and so far they had yielded nothing useful. He put the lid on the box and slid it back on the shelf, taking another down and returning to the table.

As soon as he opened this one he realised his luck had changed for the better. These were all shots taken at night on the Tottenham Court Road, showing the comings and goings at *The Purple Flamingo* nightclub. Familiar faces started to appear in the photographs. There were a couple he recognised from his rare jaunts to the cinema. Douglas Fairbanks Junior was one face that was instantly familiar, Judy Garland another. There were faces from the world of politics and sport. He was pretty sure one of them was the boxer Freddie Mills, but his eyes were hidden behind dark glasses so he couldn't be sure.

There was one face though that was instantly recognisable. A hooked nose over a pencil-thin moustache, and dark eyes set in a rugged, swarthy face. Thomas Usher. Usher owned the club so his presence there wasn't that surprising. Unlike the identity of the blonde woman who was hanging on his arm as he left the club.

He put the picture to one side and continued to rifle through the pictures and within twenty minutes had a large pile of 10 x 8 inch black and white photographs that were of special interest and required closer scrutiny under brighter lights than the one in Talbot's room.

"I'd like to take these with me," Jack said to Talbot as he walked back into the shop.

"Take the bloody lot with you. They're no damned use to me. I told you I'm selling up."

"I wouldn't deprive you of your son's legacy. Just these will be fine for now. They'll help with a case I'm currently investigating."

"What do you make of these?" Jack dropped the sheaf of photographs down onto Fuller's desk.

Fuller scooped up the photos, leaned back in his chair and started leafing through them. He came to the one showing Thomas Usher leaving the club with the pretty blonde hanging on his arm. "That's Lois Turner."

"Yes, that's what I thought. Obviously taken before the onset of her agoraphobia."

"Do you know when exactly?"

"It came from a box of photos marked 1957. I can't be more precise than that, but it must have been before Usher had his stroke."

"She was married to Tony Turner then. Do you think she was carrying on with Usher?"

"A picture paints a thousand words, as they say. But we can't be sure. All I know is that we'll have to dig a little deeper into Lois Turner's background. See what other skeletons we can unearth."

"When do you want me to start?"

Jack shook his head. "Not this time, Eddie. I'm putting Myra on it. She seems to have a nose for this kind of thing."

"But she's not a detective."

"She is in all but name, and more's the pity, but just because she's uniform now it doesn't mean I can't utilise her services."

"The chief super will have kittens when he finds out you're going against his orders."

"Which is why I won't be telling him. Will you?"

Fuller made a cupping motion across his lips with his hand. "Speak no evil, hear no evil, see no evil, that's me."

"Have a word with the others. Make sure they know, but tell them to keep it to themselves. Take a look at the rest of the photos and tell me what you see."

Fuller started flicking through the photographs once more. "There're a lot of famous people in these."

"Ignore them and look at some of the other faces." He took

126

the boxing photograph from the file and dropped it onto Fuller's desk. "See if you can spot any of these?"

After a while Fuller said, "Well Tony Turner seems to be a frequent visitor, as does this bloke." He pointed to a face emerging from the club.

"Simon Docherty, yes. Keep looking, there's an interesting one of him with Lois Turner coming up."

Fuller carried on flicking through the photographs. "This one? It looks like he's holding hands with her. Quite a girl our Lois, isn't she? Who is Simon Docherty?"

"According to Bob Lock, Mr. Docherty is an American lawyer who retrained to practice law over here. It seems he's represented many a low life, Usher included."

"American, you say? Lois Turner is a Yank. Perhaps he was her lawyer back in the United States."

"That's a possibility I want you to look into. In fact I want to know everything there is to know about our Mr. Docherty."

"These ones speak volumes." Fuller laid three prints down on the desk.

It was a sequence of shots featuring Thomas Usher. The first had Usher leaving the club with Lois Turner. The second had Usher and Turner in the background as two heavy-set men in suits moved in front of them. In the third photo one of the men was moving across the road, his face a twisted mask of aggression, one of his hands balled into a fist, the other reaching out to block the shot as he came towards the camera.

"Looks like Benny Talbot finally got under someone's skin, doesn't it?" Jack said.

"This bloke looks intent on shutting Benny down. I wonder if that includes throwing him under a bus."

"These photos were some of the last he took. Some ime after he took and developed them he went under the wheels of the number 29."

"Is *The Purple Flamingo* club still there?"

"Yes, it's still there, but I don't know who owns it now."

"But it has no connection to Thomas Usher?"

"Not according to Bob Lock. As far as he knows the place changed hands a year or so back."

"After Usher's stroke."

Jack nodded. "So it would seem. We need to find out who's been looking after Thomas Usher's business interests since he had the stroke. Who, for instance, was behind moving him abroad, and who is paying for the nursing home he's at now."

"You think it might be Simon Docherty?"

"I wouldn't be a bit surprised," Jack said. "Not surprised at all."

"I'm going to have to start charging you rent, sir," Bob Lock said.

"I have some photos I'd like you to take a look at."

Lock looked up from his desk and took the sheaf of photographs and started leafing through them.

"Do you see anyone you recognise?"

"Well, that there is Douglas Fairbanks Junior."

"Ignore the film stars. Focus on the other faces."

Lock smiled and carried on flicking through. "Well, there's Tommy Usher. Hardly surprising seeing as it's *his* club."

He reached the shot of the thug with the fist and the hand out to stop the photograph being taken. "And that's Jimmy Dymond. I'd know his ugly mug anywhere."

"Who's Jimmy Dymond?" Jack said.

"Tommy Usher's muscle. His enforcer. A nasty piece of work and someone the Met has been after for years."

"And they haven't been successful?"

Lock shook his head. "No. He's a slippery one our Jimmy. He's been arrested more times than I've had cups of tea, but he always seems to wriggle out of the charges. Witnesses either change their stories completely or vanish off the face of the earth. I think he either scares them into silence or persuades them to take a holiday, or worse."

"And I should imagine that if Usher's paying, Dymond has a very good lawyer."

"Speaking of whom." Lock started flicking back through the photos. He took one from the pile and laid it down on the desk for Jack to see. "Simon Docherty, Usher's brief."

"Yes, I recognised him from the boxing photograph."

"Yes, I'm sure you did… but look who he's talking with."

Jack picked up the photograph, took it across to the light bulb hanging from the ceiling and peered at it. He shook his head. "The face means nothing to me."

"Well, I suppose it wouldn't really. But that is Isaac Gold, Albert Klein's right-hand man."

"So why would Usher's brief be deep in conversation with one of the head men of a rival firm?"

Lock shrugged. "Search me. But you must admit it's a bit rum. The way they are standing, in the shadows, off the main thoroughfare, hunched in that doorway, it's almost as if they're trying not to be seen together."

"And then along comes Benny Talbot and takes their photo. 'Say cheese, boys.' It's hardly going to make him popular is it?"

"You're thinking that Talbot may have had some help falling under the bus. But the witnesses…"

"As you said earlier, witnesses can be coerced or threatened into changing their stories."

"So, what? Are you delving into Benny Talbot's death now?"

Jack shook his head. "No, I have enough on my plate with Turner's murder. The Talbot case is closed and besides, it's outside of my jurisdiction. The boys down in Met land won't thank me for raking over their closed cases. The last time I had contact with officers from that part of the world didn't exactly earn me many bouquets, or house points for that matter."

"So why the interest?"

"Because the more I swim through the murky waters of London's underworld, the more another secret or unlikely coincidence floats to the surface. There's a connection, I'm sure, between Tony Turner's murder and the human flotsam and jetsam I'm seeing in these photographs. I just haven't found it yet."

"Well, good luck with that. Many before you have tried and failed to get to the bottom of that particular pool."

Jack looked at the old collator bleakly. "It never gets any easier, does it, Bob?"

"You wouldn't want it any other way, sir, would you?"

Jack smiled. "I suppose not. But catching a break every once in a while would be nice."

"So would Christmas coming along once a week, but it's never likely to happen is it?"

Jack nodded. "Wise words."

"Look, leave these with me. Give me a day or so to go through them and compare the faces with those I have on file. I might get a match."

"That would be good."

"Not that I'm promising anything mind, but you never know. I might get lucky."

Jack picked out a few of the prints, rolled them up and slipped them into his pocket. "I'll take the ones of the people we've already identified, but I'll leave you the rest to go through at your leisure. Work your magic, Bob."

"Who do you think I am, David bloody Nixon?"

Jack looked at him blankly.

"He's a conjurer, on the telly. Oh, I forgot, you still live in the dark ages. Still listening to the wireless for your evening's entertainment."

"Not for much longer, apparently."

"Did you manage to call in at Howard's this morning, about the television?" Annie said almost as soon as he walked into the house that evening.

Annie was sitting at the kitchen table with Joan, Rosie and Eric, all of them regarding him with expectant faces.

"Do you mind if I take my coat off first before subjecting me to the third degree?"

"I'll pour you a cuppa," Joan said.

"I'll fetch your slippers," said Eric, haring out of the kitchen.

"Do you want your pipe, Dad?" Rosie asked.

"Ye Gods!" Jack shrugged himself out of his overcoat and took it through to the hallway to hang it up. Once hung, he returned to the kitchen, sat down at the table and took a mouthful of tea. Eric came back to the kitchen and dropped the slippers at his feet. Jack bent to untie his laces and took off his shoes, flexing his toes before sliding them into the soft leather of the slippers.

"Pipe, Dad?" Rosie handed him the briar.

"What about you, Annie? What can I expect? A massage, perhaps? Or maybe peeling me some grapes for dessert?"

"I'll scrub your back when you next take a bath if you like." She smiled. "Well? Did you call into Howard's?"

Jack chuckled. "Yes, I called in there. The television will be here first thing Monday morning. Can you be here to let it in, Joanie?"

"She'll be here, Dad," Eric said.

"I was asking your sister."

"Of course I'll let them in," Joan said. "I've already cleared a space for it in the sitting room."

Jack's eyes widened. "Phew! You didn't waste any time, did you? What would you have done if I hadn't gone in there this morning?"

"I knew you wouldn't let us down," Joanie said.

"You never let us down, Dad," Rosie echoed her older sister.

Jack shook his head. "You all think I'm a pushover."

Annie got to her feet and wrapped her arms around his neck, kissing the top of his head. "We *know* you're a pushover, darling, but you're *our* pushover and we love you dearly."

"Food, woman." Jack leaned into her embrace. "I need my dinner."

"Coming right up, oh lord and master." Annie skipped away to the cooker.

20 - SUNDAY MARCH 22ND 1959

"There's someone here to see you, Dad," Rosie said sticking her head inside the greenhouse door.

Jack glanced around at the sound of her voice, taking his attention away from the begonia leaf he was cutting ready for propagation, and nicking his finger with the blade. "Damn!" He stuck the injured digit in his mouth and sucked away the blood. "Who is it?"

"He didn't say. He just asked me to give you this." She handed him a folded up page from a newspaper.

Jack took it from her and spread it out on the potting table. It was a page from today's *News of the World*.

The headline read, "TONY TURNER AND HIS SCANDALOUS UNDERWORD LINKS."

Jack briefly scanned the half-page that followed. There was mention of Thomas Usher and Lois Turner, along with inset photograph of Lois as the *Cadence Girl*, and a head shot of Turner taken from a theatre programme. As he read down he saw his own name. "Chief Inspector Callum, of Welwyn and Hatfield CID said, 'We have no comment to make regarding these allegations.'"

"This man at the door, is he about thirty, thin-faced, with thick glasses and a protruding Adam's apple?" Which pretty much described Neil Clarke, the reporter who had visited him at the station on Friday, and whose by-line graced this piece of scurrilous so-called journalism

"No. He's much older, about your age. He's got red cheeks and his breath smells of drink."

"Okay, I'll come in." Jack set the knife down on the potting table and followed Rosie into the house, still sucking his finger.

"Can I help you?" he said to the familiar-looking middle-aged man standing on the doorstep.

Charles Somers smiled and stuck out his hand. "DI Charles Somers. Eddie Fuller's old boss. You can call me Charlie."

Jack took the proffered hand and shook it once. "You seem to have a flair for the dramatic. You could have just given Rosie your name instead of using the rubbish printed in that rag of a newspaper to get my attention. It would have worked just as well. Better in fact. I thought you might have been that reporter chap again, back for another *no comment*."

"But I wasn't sure it *would* get your attention. I don't know what Eddie has told you about me, and my input into your case. So I thought it was time we met face to face."

"He's told me enough. You could have gone through official channels and come to the station, *during working hours*," he added pointedly. "I would have seen you there."

"You and everyone else, including the cleaner. I wanted our meeting to be a little more circumspect. It isn't official."

"Yes, I'm beginning to realise that." Jack nodded slowly. "Then I suppose you won't want to be seen hanging around on my doorstep. You'd better come in." He opened the door wide. "Come through to the front room. We won't be disturbed." Jack ushered him inside and led him along the hall.

In the front room Eric was sitting upright on one of the two armchairs, his head bowed, strumming his guitar, a book open at a page of sheet music and chord charts open on the arm of the chair.

"Can you take your practice upstairs to your room, son?"

"I *was* up there." Eric sounded disgruntled. "Joanie told me to come downstairs. She's lying down, says she has a headache." There was scepticism in his voice. "It's amazing how many headaches people seem to have in this house since I bought this guitar."

"Well, that must tell you something." Jack smiled indulgently. "Now hop it." He jerked his thumb at the door.

Grumbling, Eric grabbed his guitar by the neck and left the room.

"Bright lad," Somers said when they were alone. "How old?"

"Fourteen. Sees himself as the next Tommy Steele."

"And why not? If it can happen for a cockney sailor like Steele, it can happen for your lad, and it didn't sound too bad from where I was standing."

"It seems like any kid with a penny worth of musical talent

can make a record these days."

"You're not a fan of skiffle and rock and roll, then?"

"You didn't come here on a Sunday morning to discuss my tastes in music."

Somers smiled. "I can see why you're a detective," he said wryly.

"Take a seat." Jack pointed at the armchair recently vacated by his son. "And then you can tell me the real reason for your visit. Tea?"

Somers' smile widened. "Unless you have something stronger."

"Tea it is then. Sugar and milk?"

"Milk, no sugar."

"Right. I'll be back in a moment. There're magazines in the rack. Help yourself."

"Who's your guest, Jack?" Annie said as she sat at the kitchen table peeling potatoes for dinner.

"Eddie's old governor from his spell at Stevenage. Charlie Somers."

"And what's he doing here, on a Sunday?"

Jack poured boiling water into a brown earthenware pot. "I'll know that once I've made the tea and gone back to the front room. Tell the kids that we're not to be disturbed."

"No worries there. Rosie's just gone out for a walk. Eric's gone upstairs in a huff, and Joanie's lying down with…"

"With a headache. Yes, I know. Is she all right?"

"One too many *Babychams* last night."

"Serves her right then." Jack put cups, saucers, the teapot and a milk jug on a tray and carried it through to the front room.

When he re-entered the room he found Somers sitting in armchair, legs crossed, reading the article about himself in the *Police Gazette*. Jack had been perusing it the evening before and had left it in the magazine rack.

"If you hadn't been aware I was coming to see you, I'd have

assumed you'd left this here deliberately."

"I'm not that devious. I was looking at it last night before I went to bed."

"So, what do you think?"

"About the article, or the facts?"

"Both."

Jack sat down on the sofa and poured the tea. "It read like a fair account. Whether it's true or not I can't say. I wasn't involved. Met business, and I left that behind me a long time ago."

"Do you miss it?"

"Not at all. We have enough crime up here in Hertfordshire to keep me busy."

"Is there anything about London you *do* miss?"

"Tottenham Hotspur. I used to go to every home match, work permitting and, when they weren't playing at home, I used to go to see the reserves play. Watching the *up and comers*."

"And the *over the hillers*."

"Them too but, whoever was playing, you usually saw a good game." He handed Somers his tea. "Why have you come to see me, Charlie? Not to discuss football I'd guess."

"Tommy Usher. The photo I sent obviously prompted you to dig a little deeper. Hence…" He raised the *Police Gazette*.

"Why did you drop it off anonymously?"

"I wasn't sure how much Eddie had told you about my involvement and I didn't want to get the lad into trouble with you. He's a good'un is Eddie. He'll go far. I thought that when he first came to work for me."

"I agree. But not when he goes behind my back. Then I could happily throttle him."

"Don't be too hard on the lad. He was using his initiative. He knew of my relationship with Usher and exploited it."

"Agreed. Do you think Usher could have been involved with Turner's murder?"

"No." Somers shook his head. "In his heyday, yes, most definitely, but not now, not since…"

"Not since the stroke." Jack finished for him. "The oh-so-convenient stroke."

"You seem sceptical."

"I am."

"There's no need to be. I have it on good authority that the stroke was real enough."

"So why do you want to talk to me about him?"

Somers uncrossed his legs and sat forward in the armchair. "Usher's firm was large, packed with dozens of South London's lowlifes. Has it occurred to you that it could be a member of the firm who's behind Turner's death?" He paused and swallowed the last of his tea. "When Usher was rendered incapable and couldn't continue, there was a brief period, a couple of months, of jockeying for position. People trying to step into his shoes but, ultimately, it came to nothing, and the entire firm imploded, all the members scattering like fleas being sprayed with DDT. Good news for us, of course, but over the last few months we've seen factions starting to emerge. Members of the old firm are coming together again to carry on their nefarious ways. The only thing they lack is a figurehead, a leader to drag all the disparate parties under one banner again."

Jack frowned. "So, what has that got to do with Tony Turner?"

"I understand that Turner was made up to bear a striking resemblance to Tommy Usher. Perhaps he was being used as a kind of totem, designed to unite the troops."

Jack shook his head doubtfully. "It's a novel theory, Charlie, but I saw Turner after his death. His disguise may have been effective on the London stage, but it wouldn't pass muster under close scrutiny."

"I'm sure there's a connection to Usher somewhere along the line. I feel it in my water. It has his mucky fingerprints all over it." Somers voice betrayed a trace of bitterness in his voice.

"Only it hasn't. Not literally anyway. The murder scene was remarkably clean, even down to the nail they used to pin him to the tree. Not a print, not even a smudged one. Everything was wiped down, to get rid of any evidence. You want Usher to be involved because you hate him, don't you?"

Somers sagged back into his seat. "With a passion."

"And you want me to start investigating Usher, because

you've lost the faith of your superiors, am I right?"

"I heard from Brian Fisher that you were bloody good at your job. A pain in the backside and insubordinate, but bloody good at what you do."

"Generous of him." Jack frowned. He still had a nasty taste in his mouth from his last encounter with Scotland Yard's Chief Superintendent Brian Fisher.

"I want you to dig deep into Usher's organization and expose it for the rats' nest it truly is. I'm taking retirement at the end of this year and it would close a very unpleasant, if not final, chapter of my largely unremarkable career."

Jack looked at Somers steadily. He felt quite sorry for the man and Somers theory about the Usher's firm might have some validity, but he had enough of his own battles to fight, without taking on anyone else's.

He stood abruptly and went out to the hall to retrieve his briefcase from the hallstand. Returning to the room he snapped the catch and took out the sheaf of Benny Talbot's photographs. Flipping through them, he peeled one from the pile and handed it to Somers. "Taken outside *The Purple Flamingo*. Recognise them?"

Somers shifted in his seat and peered at the photo. He digested it for a moment. "That's Simon Docherty."

"And the other chap?"

Somers angled the photograph into the light coming from the window. "Unless I'm mistaken, that's Isaac Gold. What the hell's Docherty doing with Gold? You wouldn't expect to see the two of them sharing a pavement, or anything else for that matter. Two men, both in deep with their respective bosses, passing the time of day outside a nightclub owned by one of the said bosses."

"From their attitude, they seem to be doing more than *passing the time of day*."

Somers bit his bottom lip pensively. "I knew Simon Docherty quite well. He was always dancing around Tommy Usher like a trained monkey, offering titbits of legal advice whether Tommy asked for them or not. I thought he was an irritating little sod, but I never said as much. I knew that Usher liked him and I didn't want to upset the apple cart."

"And Isaac Gold?"

"I've met him a couple of times but don't know him well. He has a reputation for cleverness and for being about as ruthless as Albert Klein himself when push comes to shove." Somers eyed the sheaf of photographs in Jack's hand. "Have you got any more gems like this?"

Jack handed him the photos. "Take a look. More tea?"

"If I'm not outstaying my welcome."

"I'll put the kettle on."

21 - MONDAY MARCH 23RD 1959

"Your old governor came to see me yesterday," Jack said as he slid into the car's passenger seat beside Eddie Fuller.

"Charlie Somers came to your house?" Alarm was flashing in Fuller's eyes but he had it quickly under control as he started the engine and eased into the traffic. "Why?"

"Don't look so nervous, Eddie. He had only good things to say about you."

Fuller gave an audible sigh of relief.

"Apart from the fact that you're a lousy snooker player. It seems you start well but can't keep it up."

"Cheek! But I know what he means. I'm impatient to get to the end of the frame and so I take risks."

"Sometimes it's a good thing. I've been accused of that myself."

"So what did he want?"

"Resolution. As far as he's concerned, the Thomas Usher business is not finished. He took the whole internal inquiry thing very badly. He feels his superiors hung him out to dry."

"I tend to agree with him." Fuller indicated and turned left onto a leafy street. "They tasked him to do a job, to get close to Usher, to monitor his criminal activities, and when he started getting results, those same superiors deemed that he was too close to the action and branded him a dirty copper." Fuller scowled angrily. "Charlie Somers has more integrity in his little finger than they have between them. Granted, he sometimes skirted the borders of legality, but he never once crossed the line, and quite a number of Usher's gang went down for long stretches thanks to his willingness to put himself in the firing line." By the time Fuller finished speaking he was gripping the wheel tightly, his knuckles white.

Jack attempted to calm his sergeant. "Okay, Eddie, simmer down. If it means anything, I liked him. He reminded me of me."

Fuller nodded his head in agreement. "You remind me of him

as well."

"But, I'm not convinced there's a direct link to Thomas Usher and the murder of Tony Turner. I think it would be quite wrong to blinker ourselves at the moment. We still have a number of avenues we need to check out first. When we get in, tell Myra to come up to my office."

They swung into the police station car park. "You can tell her yourself. There she is." He nodded towards the far side of the car park. "Just getting out of that car."

Jack looked across the car park to a dark green Morris Minor that appeared to have limped into work. In between grey patches of body filler, rust peppered the bodywork, and the offside wing was dented.

"Is that car roadworthy, Officer?" Jack said as he approached her.

Myra Banks glanced round at him and grimaced. "Please don't say anything." She sighed. "It was my dad's. He gave it to me when I passed my test last November. It's taken me until now to get it on the road and to pluck up the courage to drive it. I only picked it up from the garage on Saturday. They did something to the timing. It wouldn't be *my* choice for a first car, but you know what they say about never looking a gift horse in the mouth?"

"I also know the one that says beware of Greeks bearing gifts. He's not Greek, is he, your dad?"

"Welsh actually." Myra grinned. "Was there something you wanted, sir?"

"Yes, Myra, there is. Come up to my office. I have a job for you."

"I want you to find out everything you can about Lois Turner *née* Franklin," Jack said to Myra when they were seated in his office.

"Everything?"

"Everything. There's more to that woman than meets the eye, and see if you can find out from her doctor when this condition of hers, the agoraphobia, started." He handed her the

140

photograph of Lois leaving *The Purple Flamingo* on the arm of Thomas Usher. "That was taken almost eighteen months ago, so obviously being out and about didn't bother her too much then."

Myra stared at the picture. "But that means she was married to Tony Turner, and she and Usher look like they are more than just friends here."

"Exactly, and that's another thing I want you to find out. How solid was their marriage. Go and have a chat with Hester Gough at *Elsinore*. Have a quiet word with their neighbours and anybody else, for that matter, who might have known them."

"Will do. But I wouldn't bank on me getting anything out of Lois's doctor. When I spoke to Francombe on Wednesday he was reluctant to tell me anything at all, claiming doctor/patient privilege."

"Well, do what you can. You have a way of winkling things out of people."

Myra tilted her head to one side. "Should I take that as a compliment?"

"I should. God knows they don't come along very often. When they do, you have to grab them with both hands."

"I need to interview Albert Klein," Jack said as he stepped into Bob Lock's grotto.

"Why don't you send for him?"

Jack shook his head. "I want it to be a less formal meeting."

"Visit him at home then. He has a house in Hampstead. Bishops Avenue. Quite a pile, or so I'm led to believe."

Jack simply held out his hand. He didn't need to ask if Lock had the address. Of course he would.

Lock pulled out a sheet of paper from a small untidy pile perched on the edge of the desk and scribbled down the address. "Do you know it?" He handed Jack the slip of paper.

"I know Hampstead. I shouldn't have too much trouble tracking it down."

Back in his office he told Fuller that he would be out for the rest of the morning.

LEN MAYNARD

"Do you need me?"

Jack automatically shook his head and then stopped. "On second thoughts, yes, come along. I don't know what my reception will be like, so it won't do any harm if two of us turn up on his doorstep."

The drive to Hampstead in Monday morning traffic was incident-free and, fifty minutes later Fuller swung the Wolseley in through the gates of the Bishops Avenue house.

"And they say crime doesn't pay," Fuller said, taking in the verdant lawns, the stately poplar trees and the huge detached house built from yellow brick with a green tiled roof. "There's probably a swimming pool in the back garden."

"I wouldn't be at all surprised. It looks like we've got a welcoming committee."

Fuller followed Jack's gaze. The front door of the house had opened and three men stood in the doorway, one slightly ahead of the other two. Fuller recognized the man standing alone as Isaac Gold. The other two were both heavy-set and had hard, brutal faces. Sensing potential trouble Fuller took out his warrant card and brandished it as he took a step towards them. "Detective Sergeant Fuller. This is Chief Inspector Callum. We'd like to see Albert Klein."

Gold stepped lightly down the two stone steps that led up to the front door. He studied Fuller's warrant card intently for a few seconds. "Hampstead is a little outside your jurisdiction, isn't it?" He had a mellifluous, almost singsong voice that contrasted sharply with his narrow eyes and menacing gaze.

Jack stepped forward and showed the man his warrant card. "We'd like to speak with Mr. Klein regarding one of our cases." Jack smiled benignly. "For background information only."

Gold turned his attention to Jack, studied the card and appraised him. Judging from the look on his face he didn't seem that impressed with what he was appraising. Finally he bowed his head slightly. "I'll ascertain whether Mr. Klein will be able to see you." With that he spun on his heel and went back inside, leaving Jack and Fuller to continue their staring contest with the

142

two thugs. Moments later he returned.

"Mr. Klein has agreed to see you." There was an edge of resentment in his voice that he failed to disguise. "You have ten minutes. Follow me." He turned sharply and led them into the house.

The interior of Albert Klein's house was every bit as impressive as the exterior. The walls of the entrance hall were covered in a deep red, embossed wall covering, hung with framed watercolours of hunting scenes. The doors leading off from it were oak, polished to a rich lustre, and the carpet that covered the floor looked expensive. *Probably Persian*, Jack thought as the followed Isaac Gold across the hall to an open door on the far side.

The door gave onto a huge room with a glass roof, the walls given over to expansive picture windows that maximized the light bleeding from the overcast sky outside. "There's your pool," Jack said quietly to Fuller as they entered.

Their footsteps echoed on white ceramic tiles that surrounded a large swimming pool. There was a heat haze shimmering above the blue-toned water and they stood poolside watching as the sole occupant swam with easy, effortless strokes towards the stainless steel ladder closest to them.

The man who mounted the ladder and emerged, dripping, from the swimming pool, had a well-muscled body, tanned and gleaming, and a completely bald head. Albert Klein was a good-looking man in his forties with bright blue eyes above a nose that had only the hint of a Jewish hook. "Don't fuss, Isaac, I can dry myself," he snapped as Gold draped a white towelling robe around his shoulders and patted his bald pate with an equally white hand-towel.

Gold stepped back deferentially and handed Klein the towel.

Glancing at Jack and Fuller, Klein made his way to a small marble-topped table in the corner of the poolroom, surrounded by four blue-painted wrought iron chairs with yellow seat pads. "Won't you join me, gentlemen?" Klein sat down at the table and pulled a cigar from a brown leather case. The attentive Gold was again on hand, cigar lighter primed. Klein ducked down and set the end of the cigar aglow, sucking in the smoke and rolling it around his mouth before puffing it out towards the glass ceiling. "Isaac tells me you're investigating a crime in your area. Hertfordshire?"

"Letchworth Garden City, yes," Fuller said, taking the lead.

Klein shook his head. "Don't know it. Is it nice in that neck of the woods?"

"Green. Very green."

Klein smiled indulgently and puffed again at the cigar. "So, what's the crime?"

"Murder. An actor was murdered. Tony Turner. You might know him."

Klein sucked on his cigar for a moment while he considered the idea, then he laid it down to rest on the lip of a chunky glass ashtray. "No." He shook his head. "Never heard of him." Turning to Isaac Gold who was hovering a few feet away, ready in case his services were required, he said, "Have you hear of him, Isaac, this actor, Tony Turner? Does the name mean anything to you."

Gold shook his head. "Means nothing to me."

Klein gave an exaggerated shrug. "Well, there you are, gentlemen. It seems you've had a wasted trip.

It was Jack's turn to speak. "One of our lines of inquiry has taken us in the direction of Thomas Usher, a name I'm sure you're familiar with."

A slight smile hovered on Klein's lips. "You seriously have old Tommy in the frame for this? You know he had a stroke a while back, don't you?"

"We were aware of that."

"Then forgive me for saying so, gentlemen, but you seem to be barking up the wrong tree." Klein got to his feet. "Now, if you'll excuse me I have to go and put some clothes on. I have a business meeting in a little while. We'll continue this shortly."

Before they could respond Klein disappeared into to a small dressing room leading off from the pool area, followed closely by Gold who turned and closed the door behind them.

Fuller gave a low whistle. "Well, he's a cool customer. Do you think he's right? About barking up the wrong tree?"

Jack sat, staring into the depths of the swimming pool, a

faraway look in his eyes.

"Sir?" Fuller prompted him.

Jack seemed to shake himself. "Yes. Probably. I don't know."

"Is something wrong?"

"Something's nagging away at the back of my mind. I know him from somewhere. I'm sure I've met Klein before but, as much as I wrack my brains, I just can't place where."

"Hardly a surprise. You've crossed swords with lots of villains in your time."

"But not one as wealthy as this." His arm encompassed the poolroom. "I'd remember."

They lapsed into silence, broken only by the steady hum of the swimming pool's pump and the occasional gushing sound as the inlet valves opened and allowed warm water in from the heater.

Eventually the changing room door opened and Gold stepped out, the robe and towel draped over his arm, wet trunks clasped in his fist. He walked past them without acknowledgment and disappeared back into the house.

Finally the door opened and Klein stepped out. He was dressed casually in a pink jumper over grey slacks with white canvas deck shoes on his feet. The bald head had been covered by a neatly cut blond wig that transformed his face, softening the hard features.

Jack stared at him as he approached them and let out a breath. "Albie Small," he said almost to himself as recognition finally dawned.

22 - MONDAY

"I wondered when the penny would finally drop," Klein said with a smile.

"You two know each other?" Fuller looked at Jack incredulously.

Before he could answer Klein said to him, "They say in the nick that you never forget the first copper to feel your collar. Your Chief Inspector here was the first rozzer to arrest me, that's right isn't it, Mr. Callum?"

Jack nodded. "You've done all right for yourself since those days, Albie."

"Albert now, Mr. Callum. Albie Small was a skinny little runt from Ponders End. A world away from this."

"You changed your surname too," Fuller said.

Klein shook his head. "Not legally. Klein was always my family name, but being recognizably Jewish in England in the twenties and thirties was not a good thing to be. Remember, Sergeant, this was the time of Oswald Mosley and his fascist Blackshirts. My father owned a tailor's shop in Palmers Green, and the Blackshirts would come around regularly and smash it up, and him into the bargain. When they firebombed it my mum decided enough was enough and persuaded the old man to sell up and move, hence we ended up in Ponders End, not the most salubrious area of North London, but a damned sight safer place for us than the snootier Palmers Green. We changed our name from Klein to Small and dad started a business working from home. The Blackshirts didn't bother us again."

"So why didn't you follow your father into the trade? Instead of becoming a hoodlum?" Jack said.

"Because I saw what tailoring did to him. A curved spine from hours hunched over whatever garment he was stitching, hands crippled by arthritis, and eyesight pretty much shot by the time he was forty. No." He shook his head. "Not for me. I wanted better out of life."

"And so you became a petty thief."

Klein smiled at Jack. "Fair play. That's what I was when you first collared me, but I seem to remember you used to wear blue serge with three stripes on your arm then, and look at you now. We evolve. We move on. Adolf Hitler changed my life."

Jack's eyes narrowed. "He changed a lot of people's lives. Mostly for the worst."

"And when a Nazi stick grenade landed in my Jeep and blew it to hell I thought it had mine, but I was invalided out of the army and sent home. For me the war was over. I was in hospital for the best part of six months while they patched me up, and they did a bloody good job of it. Most of the scars have disappeared now, but my insides were a mess and I'm still on daily medication. Funnily enough, the hair never grew back. Alopecia they said, brought on by the stress of the explosion and the resulting injuries. But God, as they say, works in mysterious ways his wonders to perform, and for me that was certainly the case. Wartime Britain was a land of endless opportunity for those with an eye for the easy profit." Klein gave a smile that was just the wrong side of smug.

"You became a black marketer."

"An entrepreneur," Klein corrected him. "I prefer to think of myself like that."

"I'm sure you do," Jack said sardonically.

"Sour grapes. Chief Inspector? Surely not. Not that I can blame your cynicism. Before I reconnected with my faith after the war and started using my God given name I'll admit I was pretty much a hopeless case, a profiteer with few scruples. But Judaism changed all that and helped me get my life back on track." He paused and looked at them both intently. "Ah, I can see the scepticism in your eyes. Shame. Let me try to convince you."

"In a moment perhaps." Jack reached into his pocket for the photograph of Isaac Gold and Simon Docherty taken outside *The Purple Flamingo* and laid it down on the table.

Klein picked it up and stared at it. "Why are you showing me this?"

Jack pointed to one of the figures in the photograph. "That's your man, Isaac Gold?"

"Yes, that's Isaac. I don't know who the other fellow is though."

"His name is Simon Docherty, legal advisor to Thomas Usher, and it was taken outside Usher's nightclub on the Tottenham Court Road. I was just wondering why your man was in, what seems to be, a deep conversation with the brief of one of your business rivals."

Klein dropped the photograph back on the table, shaking his head. "Isaac's his own man. I'm sure he had his reasons. Besides who he decides to converse with is entirely his own business. It has nothing to do with me, and certainly has nothing to do with the police."

"The man who gave me that photograph was the father of the young man who took it. He's a Jewish businessman like yourself, who is mourning the death of his photographer son, who died under the wheels of a bus in the very same spot the photograph was taken."

"Fate can be a swine sometimes. I hope you're not suggesting that this has anything to do with me."

Jack smiled at him easily. "Not at all. His death was deemed an unfortunate accident. It's just me, the way I work. I'm just trying to tie all the strands of this case together. You said that we appear to be barking up the wrong tree, but trees have branches, and I'm following those branches. Strangely enough, they all appear to lead to either Usher's or your businesses."

"A conundrum indeed," Klein said as Isaac Gold walked into the poolroom. "Ah, here's Isaac now. Show him your photograph. Perhaps he can shed some light on it. Isaac, if you could spare a minute."

Gold smiled and came over to the table.

"The chief inspector here has a photograph he'd like you to take a look at."

"With pleasure." Gold picked up the photograph and looked at it. "That's me. When was it taken? Some time ago I'd hazard. I haven't worn that suit in over a year. I ripped the pocket and never got it repaired."

"You should let me take a look at it, Isaac. I could

probably fix it for you. Invisible mending was one of my father's specialities. I did learn a few things at the old man's knee."

Jack steered the conversation back on track. "It was taken about eighteen months ago, outside *The Purple Flamingo* on the Tottenham Court Road.

"It's that nightclub Tommy Usher used to own," Klein said. "And apparently that's Usher's brief that you're talking with."

Gold shrugged. "Well, I'd hardly call it talking. He was just asking me the time. I thought he was just one of the club's customers so I obliged."

"And there was nothing more to it than that?" Klein said.

"No."

"Well, that clears that up then. Happenstance, Mr. Callum, nothing more and nothing less. A coincidence that has made you spend a morning trekking all the way over to Hampstead from the *very green* environs of Hertfordshire on nothing more than a wild goose chase." He shook his head sadly "I wouldn't want your job, Chief Inspector. It seems a very frustrating, unrewarding occupation to me."

"Someone has to do it. Thank you for your time, Albie." Jack walked to the door. "Just out of interest, where were you last Tuesday afternoon?"

"Oh, that's easy. I was at my uncle's house in Highgate, sitting Shiva for aunt Miriam, his wife, who died on Monday."

"My condolences."

"If you need that corroborated, Jacob Bloom, *Rabbi* Bloom was also there. He works out of the Golders Green synagogue. Or I can give you the names of the other mourners if you need more."

"That won't be necessary. Goodbye."

"But don't you want the grand tour of house and grounds. It's not often I get the chance to show off."

"Maybe the next time I come to see you."

Klein smiled and shook his head. "Oh, I doubt there will be a next time, Mr Callum. I doubt that very much. Good day."

"Would you mind telling me what that achieved?" Fuller said as they got back into the Wolseley.

"It was an itch that needed scratching."

"And that's all?"

"For the time being, Sergeant."

Fuller shook his head and started the car.

Myra Banks sat down at her desk, picked up the 'phone and called down to Elaine Simmons on the switchboard. "Elaine, could you get me Northrop Chemicals?"

"Give me a moment," Elaine's cheery voice replied. She was a 48-year-old spinster with an ample bosom that matched the rest of her curvaceous frame. Her naturally happy disposition was infectious and even the sound of her voice could melt all but the hardest of hearts. She was surrogate mother to all of the younger officers at the station, Myra included, a warm, wise matriarch, totally reliable, and a discreet shoulder to cry on. "I have the number, Myra love. Would you like me to me to put you through?"

"If you would, Elaine, and thanks."

"Do you want to go to the *Two Brewers* for a drink on Thursday? There're a few of us going. It's my birthday."

"I wouldn't miss it."

"Lovely. Connecting you now."

The switchboard operator at Northrop Chemicals was polite but had none of Elaine's warmth.

"I'd like to speak to the person in charge of advertising," Myra said. "The person responsible for the *Cadence* campaign a few years ago."

"I'll put you through to our marketing director. Who shall I say is calling?"

Myra introduced herself and a few seconds later a man came on the line. "Stephen Sullivan, Marketing."

"Hello, Mr. Sullivan, this is WPC Banks of the Welwyn and Hatfield police. I'm trying to get some information regarding Lois Franklin, your *Cadence Girl*."

"Yes, a very successful advertising campaign. I'm not

150

ashamed to say that I must take some credit for making Miss Franklin the success she went on to be. We went through a dozen hopefuls until we came to Lois. She had the perfect face, you see. It was a face that called out from the adverts. Beautiful, beguiling and yet unthreatening to the women our products were aimed at. I like to think that in Lois they could see themselves."

Well, I didn't, Myra thought, *and I used to use* Cadence.

"What can you tell me about Lois Franklin?" She cut through the advertising man's waffle.

There was a slight pause on the other end of the phone.

"Mr. Sullivan?"

"Sorry, I was just trying to remember. You see I didn't really get to know her that well. We had dinner a couple of times after the photo shoots, but they were very much group affairs, the photographer and his assistant, the make up girl and hairdresser. So Lois and I didn't really engage in any meaningful conversations. All I really knew about her was that she was an American and very beautiful. Of course, I found out more about her, as did everybody else, when that sordid little affair with that actor chappie was splashed all over the papers. We changed our marketing strategy as soon as the story hit the dailies." He laughed softly. "Not good for business, as you can imagine."

"I can indeed. So, apart from what I can find out by trawling through old newspapers. you can't tell me much about her?"

"Sorry. We engaged her through an agency. They would be the people to ask I suspect."

"And can you tell me which agency that would be?"

"Zoom."

"Pardon?" Myra thought she'd misheard him.

"Sorry. *The Zoom Modelling Agency*. It's based in London and pretty exclusive. I think all the girls we've used in our campaigns have come via them. Certainly those campaigns we've undertaken in the past five years."

"Could you give me their address and telephone number?"

"But of course." There was another slight pause accompanied by the sound of shuffling paper as Sullivan worked through his index cards. "Do you have a pen?"

Myra picked up the receiver and dialled the number Sullivan had given her. On the other end of the line a phone rang three times before being picked up. "Hullo?" A woman answered, a cut glass voice with no warmth.

"Hello," Myra said cheerily. "Is that the *Zoom Modelling Agency*?"

"It is. How may I help you?" The voice conjured up an image of a glacial blonde with a haughty demeanour and a condescending manner.

Myra pressed on. "I need some information about one of your models. Lois Turner, though you probably have her on your books as Lois Franklin, the *Cadence Girl*."

When it next spoke the cool voice had dropped several degrees. "I'm afraid Miss Franklin is no longer on our books."

"No, I didn't think she would be, but I still need any information you can give me about her."

"Who is this?" The voice was positively icy now.

"WPC Myra Banks. I'm with the Welwyn and Hatfield Police."

There was the sound of the mouthpiece being covered followed by the muted murmur of conversation. Suddenly a man's voice came down the line at her like a pistol shot.

"Who is this again?" Educated, perfect enunciation.

Myra repeated her name.

"How do I know you are who you say you are?"

"I assure you…"

"Assurances mean nothing." The man fired again. "Where is your proof that you are genuine? I know the way Fleet Street works. For all I know, you could be a reporter from one of those awful rags, trawling for a juicy bit of scandal to keep your moronic readers buying your newspaper."

"I could you give you the station's number and you can ring me back here so you can see that I am who I say I am."

"Again it proves nothing. You could give me any old number, with another hack on the end of the line, ready to corroborate your story. No, as you were told, Miss Franklin is no longer with us, but I still have a duty to respect her privacy."

Exasperated Myra said, "Who am *I* talking to?"

"Cedric Bannister. I *own* the *Zoom Agency*."

"Well, Mr. Bannister, I really need the information. It's regarding an investigation I'm working on. A murder investigation," she added heavily.

There was a slight pause and then Bannister came back on the line. "If you are who you say you are then you need to prove it, in person."

"You want me to come up there, to London?"

"Precisely, and bring identification with you. Do that and I'll see what I can do to help you."

You have to be joking, Myra thought. "I'll be with you first thing tomorrow."

"Very well. You know where we are? Holborn Viaduct?"

"I have your address."

"Then I'll expect to see you in the morning. Good day." The phone went dead.

Myra shook her head in disbelief and replaced the receiver.

23 - MONDAY

"Have you been in touch with Simon Docherty yet, Frank?"

Lesser spun round in his seat as Jack came into the squad room. "Not yet, Guv." Tracking down Simon Docherty was his task for the morning and so far he had drawn a blank.

Jack frowned. "How hard can it be to track down a solicitor. Criminals manage it, why can't you?"

"It's been nigh on impossible. Brick walls at every turn. He has an office in Belgravia, so I 'phoned there and they say they haven't seen him since the middle of last week, and they were reluctant to give me his home address. They got very snooty about it in fact, even when I told them I was police and I needed his help in a murder investigation I was working on."

"He must be in the telephone directory."

"You would think. But other than his office number I can't find him. It's the same story with the Law Society. They'll let me have the Belgravia address, but won't divulge any personal details, such as where he lives."

Jack sat down at his desk and opened the case file. "Have you tried Bob Lock? He might have Docherty's home address on file somewhere."

"I did and he hasn't." There was frustration in Lesser's voice.

"Give me the number for the Belgravia office. *I'll* call them and give them a rocket. Their reluctance to give us what we need is interfering with an ongoing police investigation. We can't have that."

With a sigh Lesser scribbled the telephone number on a piece of scrap paper and dropped it onto Jack's desk blotter.

Jack picked up the handset and dialled the number.

"Good day, this is Chief Inspector Callum of the Welwyn and Hatfield Police. I need to speak with Simon Docherty. It's a matter of great urgency."

"I'm afraid Mr. Docherty is not in the office at the moment," a female voice replied, speaking with a soft Belgravia drawl. "If you leave me your telephone number, I will make sure Mr

Docherty calls you as soon as he comes in."

"Can you tell me when that's likely to be?"

"I'm afraid I can't."

"To whom am I speaking?" Jack's voice took on a harder edge.

"This is Sara Gibson, Mr. Docherty's secretary."

"Well, Miss Gibson, I think when Detective Sergeant Lesser called you earlier today, he made it quite clear that this is a murder investigation we are conducting here and not being able to speak with Mr. Docherty is hampering our inquiries, quite seriously in fact, so please be good enough to give me his home address."

"I really am not a liberty to disclose that."

"Miss Gibson, what part of 'murder investigation' did you fail to comprehend? The killer's *modus operandi* in this case is particularly brutal, and we have reason to believe that he has targeted Mr. Docherty. The fact that he hasn't been in the office there since the middle of last week gives us great cause for concern, so, his home address if you please."

"Simon could be a target? His life could be in danger?" There was an edge of mild hysteria in her voice.

"It's a chance I'm not willing to take, nor, I am certain, are you."

Jack listened as the mouthpiece on the other end of the line was muffled. Finally Sara Gibson came back on the line. "Do you have a pen?"

"Indeed I do."

"Docherty lives in St Albans. 13, Devon Street." Jack put down the pen.

"I didn't realise Docherty's life was in danger." Lesser sat down heavily at his desk.

Jack smiled. "As far as I know, it's not, but his secretary doesn't know that, does she?"

"Very cunning, sir."

"It's called good police work, Frank, or bending the truth to achieve the result you want. They don't teach it at Hendon, but

I've found it works, more often than not. Now, Sergeant Fuller and I will go and pay Mr. Simon Docherty a visit."

Fuller came into the office, carrying an enamel mug of canteen tea.

"No time for tea, Eddie. We're going to St Albans to speak to Simon Docherty."

Fuller muttered an oath under his breath and put the mug down on Frank Lesser's desk. "A cuppa for you, Frank."

"You're too kind." Lesser picked it up and took a swig, before grimacing and spitting the tea back in the mug. "Hey, there's sugar in this!"

"Beggars can't be choosers, Frank." Fuller whistled cheerfully as he walked out of the office.

"Sir! Excuse me, sir!" Myra ran across the station foyer

Jack paused as he was about to push through the doors and follow Fuller out into the car park. "What is it, WPC Banks?"

"I'm sorry, sir. I nearly missed you. I've managed to locate the modelling agency that used to procure work for Lois Turner."

"Splendid. What information did you glean from them?"

"That's just it, sir." Myra shifted her weight from foot to foot, blushing slightly with embarrassment.

"Go on, girl, spit it out. What have you found out?"

"Nothing." She shook her head. "They won't speak to me unless I can prove I am who I say I am. They want me to go there in person, and they won't talk to me until they see I'm not a reporter trying to rake up some muck on their ex-client."

Jack took off his hat tiredly and ran a hand through his hair. "Where is this agency?"

"London, sir. It's the *Zoom Modelling Agency*. They're based in Holborn Viaduct."

"So you have to trek all the way to Holborn, just so they can see you're a policewoman asking genuine questions?"

"That's about the long and the short of it, sir. The man who runs the agency, a Mr. Cedric Bannister, is the very suspicious type. I wouldn't be surprised if he's been *had* before."

Jack shook his head. "There's a lack of trust in this world, Myra."

"Yes, sir. I said I'd go up there tomorrow."

His eyes narrowed. "Did you indeed?"

"I thought you'd want to know anything they can tell me."

He suppressed a smile. "Yes, I do. Fair enough. Go up there by train in the morning. Get a receipt for the fare and let me have it. I'll see that you're reimbursed. Come and see me when you get back and tell me everything they said."

"Very good, sir."

Jack pushed open the doors. "Oh, and, Myra."

"Yes, sir?"

"Good work."

"Yes, sir. Thank you, sir."

"You did yourself no harm there," Andy Brewer said from the desk as the doors closed behind Jack. He had witnessed the whole encounter.

"I wasn't sure he'd allow me to go." Myra smiled at him.

Brewer laughed. "Are you pulling my leg? It's common knowledge that you're Jack Callum's favourite. He was never going to say no."

"Now you're pulling *my* leg. I'm nothing special. Just an ordinary WPC doing my job, that's me."

"That's not what they're saying in the canteen," Brewer muttered under his breath, but she heard him.

"Just what are they saying in the canteen, Sergeant Brewer?"

"Come on, Myra love, don't play the innocent. You've got our
chief inspector wrapped around your little finger, or as my old dad used to say, you've got him on a piece of string. You tug it and he jumps. I should remind you, Constable, that he's a married man."

"What are you implying, Sergeant?"

"I'm only repeating what I've heard. You can play coy all you like, but you work in a police station, for heaven's sake. There are too many eyes around here, eyes used to uncovering dirty little secrets, for you to pull the wool over them all."

Myra felt the implication like a kick in the stomach. It took her breath away and hot tears sprang to her eyes. She clenched her fists, digging her fingernails into the heels of her hands to keep the tears from flowing down her cheeks.

"I don't know what gossip you have heard, Sergeant Brewer," she said steadily, fighting to keep her voice even. "But, I assure you, you are wrong. You are all wrong. DCI Callum treats me the same as any other police constable in the building."

"And if you believe that, girl, you'll believe anything."

Myra flushed and walked quickly from the foyer.

But I do believe that, she thought. *Really I do*. Andy Brewer's comments and the knowing wink he gave her had upset her more than she would have imagined possible. Worse, it brought thoughts to the front of her mind she had been trying to bury for months.

"Hello, Myra. What brings you to my humble abode?" Elaine Simmons said. There was one other person in the Dispatch room, an older woman called Esther, who had headphones covering her ears as she spoke softly into a microphone mounted in front of her.

"Are you all right, love?" Elaine said.

Myra glanced nervously at Esther.

"Pay her no mind. She's calling her husband. She thinks I don't know about her misappropriation of police resources, but I do. She'll be another half an hour yet."

"Can we go somewhere to talk? I need to ask you something. In private."

Elaine smiled at Myra indulgently. "Of course. It can't wait until we go for our drink tomorrow, but then, that won't be very private will it?"

Myra could not keep the desperation out of her voice when she spoke. "Please?"

"Okay, love. Let's go to the Ladies. We should be private enough in there."

The small lavatory smelt of disinfectant. There were just three stalls and Elaine pushed open all three doors to make sure they were empty and then she turned to Myra. "Okay, pet. What's the problem?"

Now she was here and about to bare her soul, Myra felt tongue-tied and foolish. She cleared her throat. "I...I don't know where to start," she began and then a wave of emotion swept over her. She shuddered and the recently suppressed tears began to flow. "I'm sorry."

"Hey now." Elaine wrapped a motherly arm around Myra's shoulders and hugged her. "Whatever's wrong?"

Myra sniffed. "I'm just being stupid."

"Let me be the judge of that."

Myra recovered herself slightly. "You take your lunch in the canteen, don't you?"

"Most days. Sometimes I bring sandwiches, but I usually go there to eat them. It gets me away from the 'phones and the radio for an hour."

"Have you heard the gossip, gossip about me?"

Myra felt Elaine pull away from her slightly.

"You have, haven't you?"

Elaine sighed. "You know what men are like when they all get together. The thing you have to do is to take no notice of them."

Myra sagged. "But none of it's true, Elaine, none of it. DCI Callum is just my boss. I can't help it if he gives me interesting stuff to do."

"Stuff that the other PC's would give their eye teeth for. I'm afraid that the preferential treatment Jack Callum shows you has put a few people's noses out of joint. I'm sure that wasn't his intention, but it has ruffled a few feathers."

"But that's not my fault. I never asked to be treated any differently to anyone else."

"But it doesn't alter the fact that he does treat you differently and people are beginning to resent it and, when resentment sets in, those same people start to ask why."

"There's nothing like that going on between us. Elaine you must believe that."

Elaine chuckled. "Oh, I do, love. I've known Jack Callum for years and I know that's he's a straight arrow. He's a loving husband and a committed family man. He wouldn't be interested in a slip of a girl like you, no matter how pretty you are. Lord knows, you're not that much older than Joan, his eldest daughter."

"So how do I convince the others and stop the gossip?"

Elaine pulled away from her and looked at her frankly. "Ah, there you have me. I really can't say. Once the rumours start circulating it's hard to know how to stop them without fanning the fires that give them life. Best just to let them smoulder for a while. Deprive them of oxygen and eventually they'll burn themselves out."

"And until they do?"

"Keep your head down and work diligently. Show the gossips in the canteen that you've earned the favours you're shown with hard work and nothing more. Show them that you are simply good at your job. Once they realise that fact the rumours will stop."

"I hope you're right."

"And if they come to me with such rubbish, I'll tell them straight out what I think of their tall tales."

"You'd do that, Elaine?"

"As long as I'm sure there's no truth to them, then of course I will. But I've seen the way you stare at him sometimes, when you think he isn't looking. Not that I blame you. Jack Callum's a very attractive, *older* man."

"Oh, hell!' Myra said. "Am I that obvious?"

Elaine smiled. "I'm afraid so."

"Hell!"

"Anyway, I have to get back to the 'phones. Esther's probably still on with her hubby and something important might come up."

"Thank you, Elaine."

"Any time, dear. And don't forget about drinks tomorrow."

Myra filled the hand basin with water and dunked her face in it, washing away the tears streaks on her face. Drying her skin with a handful of paper towels, she stared at herself in the mirror above the sink. "Get a grip. Myra. Get a bloody grip!"

24 - MONDAY

Devon Street was a well-kept row of Edwardian cottages half a mile away from the St Albans city centre.

"There's money here," Eddie Fuller said enviously. "I couldn't afford one of these places on my wages."

"You want to think about promotion, Eddie. I think you could make inspector easily." Jack climbed out of the car.

Fuller followed him out onto the street. "I'm taking the exams this October."

Jack turned to look at him sharply. "You kept that bloody quiet."

"I've been swotting up for weeks now. By October I should be ready."

"Why haven't you mentioned it before? I could give you a few pointers."

"I don't want to get anyone's expectations up."

"Meaning mine?"

"Yours, and the rest of the station. I already get enough stick from Frank Lesser without giving him more ammunition."

"It will be a different story if you make inspector though." Jack walked across the street and stood outside number thirteen. "If you get the promotion do you think you'll stay at Welwyn, or will you be looking to move further afield?"

Fuller shrugged. "I haven't decided yet. It depends on whether there's a place for me at the nick. I quite fancy the Met. Life in the big city has a certain appeal."

"And some very large drawbacks. I'd be sorry to see you go, Eddie."

Fuller stared up at the cottage. All the windows were closed, the curtains pulled tightly shut. "It doesn't look like there's anyone in." He pressed the brass bell push. A ringing sounded deep within the cottage.

They waited on the doorstep for a full minute before Fuller pressed the doorbell again.

Jack put his ear to the door. "We're wasting our time.

Docherty's not here."

"Either that, or he's seen who it is and he's not answering."

Further along the street an elderly road sweeper had parked his cart and was listlessly pushing his broom as he limped along the gutter, whistling tunelessly to himself. Jack went across to him. "Is this street part of your regular route?"

The road sweeper looked at him with rheumy eyes and rubbed at the day's worth of white stubble on his chin. "Depends who's asking." His voice rasped like two sheets of sandpaper being rubbed together. He hawked and spat a gob of phlegm onto the street at Jack's feet.

"Police," he said. "Now please could you answer the question."

Fear and cunning jostled for position in the old man's eyes. "It might be."

"Well is it or isn't it, man? The question is simple enough." There was impatience in Jack's voice. Whether it was irritation at the road sweeper's contrariness, or the fact that he'd been blindsided by his sergeant's bombshell he couldn't be sure.

"Come on, soldier." Fuller stepped in. "Just give the man a straight answer."

"I was at El Alamein, you know? Eighth Army. Served under Monty himself. Took a bullet that shattered my leg bone. Shovelling up other people's rubbish is all I'm good for now."

For the first time Jack noticed the two medals hanging from the old man's coat, the metal tarnished, the ribbons threadbare. He softened his attitude. "That's the Africa Star, isn't it?"

The old man straightened slightly. "It is."

"I got my star in Burma."

"What rank were you?"

"Captain."

The road sweeper took a step back and saluted. "Lance corporal, sir."

"So is this your regular route, Lance Corporal?"

"Yes, sir."

"And number thirteen over there." He pointed to Docherty's cottage. "Have you seen the man who lives there?"

The old man stared across the road. "Yes, sir. I've seen him.

Saw him last Wednesday morning, getting into a taxi with a suitcase. Haven't seen him since. I think he was disappearing off somewhere. He looked shifty. Kept looking up and down the street to see if anyone was watching him. He paid no mind to me though. I doubt he even saw me. Invisible I am, these days."

"You're sure it was last Wednesday?"

"I always do Devon Street Mondays and Wednesdays, and it wasn't Monday so I'm sure."

"Well, thank you, Lance Corporal…"

"Rogers, sir. Lance Corporal Ernie Rogers."

"I don't suppose you heard the address he gave the driver?"

Rogers looked slightly embarrassed. "He was a bit too far away for me to hear. My ears aren't what they were when I was in service, sir."

"Never mind. It was very observant of you anyway. You've been a great help." Jack proffered his hand and when the old man took it he pressed a folded ten-shilling note into Roger's palm.

The old man glanced furtively down at the note and stuffed it into the pocket of his battered overcoat, and then he raised himself to his full height and saluted smartly. "Happy to oblige, sir!"

Jack returned the salute and went to the car. "There's nothing for us here, Eddie. Best we get back."

Fuller got in behind the wheel and started the engine.

"Tony Turner is killed on Tuesday afternoon, and Simon Docherty takes a taxi to an unknown destination on the Wednesday morning and hasn't been seen since. A coincidence? I think not." Jack drummed his fingers on the dashboard of the car. "What are we missing, Eddie?"

"Do you think you might have been right when you told Docherty's secretary that he might be the killer's next target?"

"Or was Docherty himself the killer?"

Fuller changed down the gears as they approached a set of traffic lights. "Shall I take you home? It's after five."

"Drop me at the station and then get off yourself. We'll start again tomorrow. I just can't shake the feeling that this one is getting away from us."

Henry Lane was waiting for him in his office when Jack got back to the station. "It's been a week now, Jack. Tell me you're making some serious progress on the Turner case. Are you expecting to make an arrest soon?"

"We're making progress, sir. I've just come back from trying to interview Simon Docherty, Thomas Usher's brief."

"You say 'trying' to interview Docherty. I take it things didn't go so well."

"He's done a flit, sir. Moved out of his place in St Albans last Wednesday morning, heading for destinations unknown."

"That's not so clever, Jack. It can't be a coincidence that Docherty disappears the day after Turner's murdered."

"My thoughts exactly."

Lane glanced at his watch. "Ah well, I just needed to be brought up to date. I'm having dinner with the assistant chief constable tonight. He's bound to ask how the investigation is progressing."

"Tell him that we're following significant leads then, sir. That would be a good bone to throw him."

"ACC Hazelhurst is not a dog, Chief Inspector."

"No, sir."

"But it's a good enough line to keep him off my back for a day or so. Oh, and next time you decide to give an interview to the press, don't. Leave that to me. Some of us have a knack for that kind of thing, some of us don't, and I'd put you very much in the latter category."

"Yes, sir. Not my forte I'm afraid."

"Quite." Without another word Lane left the office closing the door behind him.

Jack had barely sat down at his desk when someone rapped on the door. "What now?" he grumbled quietly. "Yes?"

The door opened and Bob Lock came into the office smiling. "Yes, Bob?"

"Just call me David Nixon." The collator smiled and laid a photograph on the blotter in front of him.

The photograph showed two men walking out onto the street

from the doors of *The Purple Flamingo*. Both men wore their black hair in crew cuts and were dressed in almost identical expensive-looking black suits, smart white shirts with dark ties.

"Who am I looking at here, Bob?"

"Those two Herbert's are the O'Brien brothers, Fergus and Conner."

Jack stared at the photograph. "Sorry, the names mean nothing to me. What are they? Irish?"

"Irish American, from the Bronx in New York. They're the sons of Padraig, head of the O'Brien family, one of most notorious crime families on the East Coast of America."

"How did you recognise them?"

"When I looked at the photo for a second time, their faces set bells ringing somewhere in the back of my mind. I knew I'd seen them before, but just couldn't place where. It's taken me until today to finally solve it." He pointed to the chair on his side of the desk. "May I?"

"Please do."

Lock sat down on the chair and shuffled it up to the desk. "Every month or so Scotland Yard send out notifications to regional stations if there's a person or persons of interest they want us to be on the look out for. Normally I give the notes a quick once over and then file them away for future reference." He laid out a sheet of paper on the desk. "I had this filed under the wrong heading. I had it under 'undesirable aliens', instead of 'foreign villains we'd very much like to get our hands on'."

Jack picked up the sheet of paper and stared at it. There were two separate mug shots on the paper. Official photos taken of the two men at the time of their arrest by the New York Police Department. Both men were photographed holding cards with their names printed on them, neither of them looked happy.

Lock produced another piece of paper and glanced at it. "Those snaps were taken at the time of the brothers' arrest for a *knock down, drag out* punch up at an Irish bar in Brooklyn. They were arrested but never charged. Insufficient evidence apparently. New York's finest provided Scotland Yard with a comprehensive record of the O'Briens' suspected crimes. It makes for interesting reading. The family has a finger in every type of illegal activity; murder, racketeering, bootlegging, prostitution, narcotics. In fact you'd be hard pressed to find something dodgy they're not involved in."

"So why did the New York police tell the Met about them. Surely the O'Briens are very much their problem."

"They were tipping Scotland Yard the wink. Apparently, rumours had been circulating for some time that the family were looking to expand their criminal empire. Specifically, they were looking to expand it onto our shores. This photograph shows that the intelligence they provided was pretty spot on. Have another look at it. Use your glass."

Jack picked up his magnifying glass that was lying on the base of his desk lamp and scrutinized the photograph.

"Do you see?" Lock's could barely contain his enthusiasm. "Who's that coming out of the club behind the brothers?"

"That's Isaac Gold."

"And if you look closer, who's just behind him? Mind, you have to look closely as his face is mostly in shadow."

Jack peered through the magnifying glass. "Albert Klein."

Lock clapped his hands. "Give that man a coconut. So tell me, why are Klein and Gold coming out of Tommy Usher's nightclub, hot on the heels of two of New York's most wanted."

"You tell me, Bob. This whole thing is your narrative."

Lock sat back in the seat. "The way I see it, the O'Briens were meeting with North London's most notorious gang leader with a view of striking up some kind of deal or arrangement. Personally, I reckon it's drugs. The brothers are trying to open up an untapped market for their wares. By doing a deal with Klein they get North London and beyond, possibly as far up the country as Manchester. That's a huge market for them. If they get Usher on board as well they get the South of England, all the way down to the ports, thus guaranteeing their supply line. Klein and Usher would stand to make millions out of the deal."

Jack laid the magnifying glass down on the desk. "I like your thinking, Bob. It certainly seems plausible, apart from the fly in the ointment."

The smile dropped from Lock's face. "What fly?"

"Thomas Usher."

"But they're coming out of Usher's club, so obviously he's got to be involved." Lock was trying desperately to salvage his theory. He had been working on it all day, thinking it through since he had first made the O'Brien connection. Being a collator was a satisfying job, and one he had done without complaint for years, but he still missed chasing and catching criminals. That was what had attracted him to police work in the first place.

"Usher is the fly in the ointment. He won't have anything to do with drugs. He's hated them with a passion since he lost his brother Cyril to heroin. It's the main reason why he could never form any kind of business relationship with Albert Klein, because he could never square Klein's involvement with drugs with his own deeply held beliefs. So I can't see him having any truck with the O'Brien family if that's their business. There must be another scenario playing out here."

Lock looked crestfallen.

"Never mind, Bob. It was a good theory."

"But one that won't float." He got to his feet. "Well, I've taken up enough of your time. I'll let you get off home. Goodnight, sir."

"Night, Bob." Jack watched Lock walk dejectedly from the office and then went and took his coat from the rack. "Enough for one day, Jack," he said to himself. "Let's see what tomorrow brings."

25 - MONDAY

The atmosphere in the house when he arrived home that evening was strangely muted. He had expected to find his family gathered together on the settee, their attention fixed on a box in the corner with a glowing screen, instead the family room was in darkness and the only sign of life in the house was the sound of Annie's light soprano as she sang a fairly tuneful rendition of *Happy Talk* from Rogers and Hammerstein's musical, *South Pacific*.

He took off his hat and coat and made his way through to the kitchen, the only lighted room in the house. He walked into the kitchen with an enthusiastic, "Good evening, one and all," only to be greeted by the sullen faces of his children who sat around the kitchen table. Joan was reading a magazine, Rosie, a paperback Agatha Christie novel, whilst Eric had his nose buried in Bert Weedon's Play in a Day book, his guitar resting across his knee.

Annie disengaged herself from her task at the cooker and flitted across to him, still singing the Rogers and Hammerstein, which had taken on a new, ironic meaning.

"What on earth has happened here? Who's died?" he said as Annie pecked his cheek.

She broke mid-verse and half-said, half-sang, "They'll tell you."

He turned to his children. "Well? Would someone mind explaining to me why my kitchen resembles a dentist's waiting room, save for your mother here who for some reason has turned into Bloody Mary for the evening."

"Language, Dad!" Rosie looked up from her book.

"I'm not swearing. That was the woman's name in *South Pacific*. *Bloody Mary*. Though I will start swearing if someone doesn't tell me what's going on. Did the television arrive?"

"Oh, it arrived," Joan said languidly, barely lifting her gaze from the pages of her magazine.

"It's just a shame the aerial didn't," Eric said.

"So we can't actually watch it." Annie prodded the sausages in the frying pan forcefully with a fork, pricking their skins so they didn't burst. Jack felt for them.

"I didn't think," he offered.

"Evidently." Annie put the fork down on the counter. "Didn't Mr. Howard say anything to you about it when you went in there on Saturday? Something along the lines of, 'I trust you have an aerial on your roof, Mr. Callum?' or, 'Do you need an indoor aerial for that, Jack?'"

"I didn't see Mr. Howard. It was that Saturday boy of his and he seemed more intent on making sure I sign the rental agreement in the right place. Sorry. I've had a lot on my mind lately."

"No matter." Annie relented and smiled at him. "I called them. They're coming to fit an aerial to the chimney on Wednesday, and they'll lend me an indoor one for tomorrow evening so we can test the set out. I'll pick it up on my way home from work."

It took a moment for what she had just said to register in his weary mind. "Work! Yes, of course. How did your first day go?"

Annie looked around from the pan of sausages. "Not too bad."

"Not too bad?" Rosie said scornfully, laying her book down on the kitchen table. "The customers loved her, Dad, especially the lunchtime crowd. Our iced buns flew off the shelves and our muffins sold…"

"…like hot cakes," Eric said tiredly. "That joke was old when you told it the first time, Rosie."

"Suffice it to say, Dad, that mum was a hit." Joan finally looked up from her magazine. "A hundred per cent success. You should be very proud of her."

"I am." He looked across at Annie whose cheeks were colouring slightly.

"Don't make such a fuss." She dabbed perspiration from her forehead with the hem of her apron. "It's not as if I've never worked before."

"But not for years," Eric said. "Years and years."

"Careful, son." Jack shot Eric a warning look. "It's not been that long."

"But it is, Jack," Annie said. "Not since the war, and I was as nervous as a kitten when I went into Painters this morning. Luckily the customers seemed to like me, and I didn't make any mistakes on the till."

"So, Mrs Painter wants you back then? That's lucky."

She screwed up her face in an expression he'd always found adorable. "Go and wash your hands, Jack Callum. Dinner will be ready in five minutes."

"I'm home!" Myra called out as she let herself into the terraced house in Hitchin she shared with her parents.

"We're in here." Her mother's voice floated out from the front room. Myra pushed the door and peeked around it. Her parents were sitting in front of the small television, her mother knitting, the clacking of the needles drowning out the sound of the program that was attracting her father's attention as he leaned forward in his wheelchair trying to hear it.

"Why don't you turn it up, Mum? Dad can't hear it."

"He doesn't deserve to hear it. Not after the way he's behaved today."

Myra rested her head tiredly on the doorframe. Another day, another argument. She sometimes wondered how her parents had stayed married for so long, especially since her father's accident at the non-ferrous metal factory where he'd worked since he was fourteen-year old apprentice. The accident had left him paralysed from the waist down and confined to a wheelchair.

"What's he done today?"

"That nice Nurse Meadows came to apply the embrocation to his legs and he spent the entire time speaking at her in Welsh. The poor girl didn't have a clue what he was waffling on about. I wouldn't mind but he's lived in Hitchin since he was ten years old and hasn't been back to the Valleys since the day he left."

"Do you think he's all right?" There was genuine concern in Myra's voice. "You don't think he's going…you know?"

"Senile? What him? No. He was just being a cantankerous old

171

goat. As usual." Her mother tore her attention away from her knitting and the clacking stopped.

"Thank God for that," Mr. Banks muttered without looking round at his wife.

On the television a couple in scuba gear were examining the marine life inhabiting an under-sea wreck.

"Are you really interested in that, Dad? Is there nothing on the other side that mum might like?" Playing the role of peacekeeper in the house had become second nature to her since the accident had thrown her parents together twenty-four hours a day.

"She's all right. She's got her program on later. That'll do her."

"It's the Ann Shelton Show tonight," Mrs Banks said excitedly. "I love her voice. Oh, and your dinner's on the stove keeping warm. I didn't know when you'd be in, so we've had ours. It's herrings. I hope that's all right for you."

"Thanks, Mum." Myra grimaced and pulled the door shut, leaving them to their rancorous evening, and went out to the kitchen where a large aluminium saucepan simmered on the gas stove. Two plates sat on top of the steaming saucepan, the herring trapped in between them.

Judging from the condensation streaming down the windows and the disgusting reek of boiled fish that filled the room she guessed that her parents had eaten some time ago. Using a tea towel she lifted the top plate and gagged at the sight of an anaemic herring swimming in a cloudy sea of liquefied mashed potato. Grey peas added a few dots of contrast to the mush.

I can't eat this, she thought. She turned off the gas, took the plates from the saucepan and tipped the sorry mess into the sink. Turning on the tap she washed the liquid potato and peas down the drain, lifted out the drowned herring and threw it out into the back garden for next door's cat. Then, washing her hands to get rid of the fishy smell she went up to her room.

Her parents had lived downstairs since the accident so she had the entire top floor of the house to herself. It was only two rooms. Her bedroom, and the old master bedroom she had converted into a sitting room, with a second-hand sofa, a small

172

drop-leaf table and dining chair, and a Utility style sideboard. On top of the sideboard rested her one item of luxury, a *Dansette* record player with an autochanger. A small pile of records was positioned on the autochanger's post. She switched it on and waited for the first disc to drop onto the turntable. As the mellow voice of Pat Boone filled the room with *April Love,* she flopped down onto the sofa, opened her handbag and took out a packet of crisps. She opened the blue waxed-paper twist and sprinkled salt over the crisps. These and a chocolate bar would be her dinner tonight. *What did I do to deserve such luxury?* Well, at least hunger would take her mind off Jack Callum and the unfortunate rumours circulating at work.

She decided she would have an early night in readiness for tomorrow's jaunt up to London on the train.

Jack sat at the dining table, half a dozen photographs lain out before him. He had turned on the overhead light and in the bright 100 watt glow he stared at each of the prints in turn, looking for connections between them, and anything that struck him as odd.

In the centre of the group was the boxing photograph Charlie Somers had sent him, and he picked up each of the others in turn, looking to see if any of the patrons of *The Purple Flamingo* also attended the fight apart from the three he had already identified. He was reminded of the card game *Pelmanism* he used to play as a child where he would spread the cards face down on the floor and pick two at random trying to match a pair. As a game it took all his concentration to remember where he had replaced the cards on the floor. The game was markedly different to what he was attempting here, but the level of concentration was pretty much the same.

His neck ached from being hunched over the table, and his head was developing a nagging ache.

"Do we have any aspirin in the house?" he said to Joan as she came in to fetch another magazine from the rack at the side of the settee.

"I think so. There's probably a bottle in the bathroom cabinet.

Do you want me to look?"

"Would you?"

"I'll be back in a tick."

She returned a few moments later clutching a small brown bottle and a tumbler of water. She set them down beside him on the table.

"Thanks." He unscrewed the cap on the bottle, pulled out the cotton wool wadding and shook three white tablets into his palm. He tossed the pills into his mouth and took a gulp of water.

"Are you doing anything interesting?" Joan peered over his shoulder.

"Just work. Quite boring really."

"Hey, that's Tony Turner." Joan recognised the actor sitting in the front row at the boxing match. "Have you got any more like these? I'd bet the *News of the World* would pay for this, and any more you have of him."

"It's not for sale."

She reached across him and picked up the photo from the table. "Who's in the rest of the row?" She lowered the print for Jack to see, and he pointed to each face in turn.

"That's Charlie Somers, Eddie's old boss, and that," he jabbed at Thomas Usher, "is one of the most vicious criminals South of the river."

Joan seemed enthralled. "Imagine, policemen and criminals enjoying a night at the fights together Oh, I know it goes on. Fraternization, isn't that what they call it? I used to see policemen mixing with all types of dodgy characters when I worked at the pub. I used to call them Heroes and Villains nights. Have you got any more shots of the criminal? Oh, wait, there he is."

She swooped on the photograph of Lois Turner draped on Usher's arm. She stared at it for a few seconds. "False alarm. I thought it was the bloke in the boxing photo, but it's not."

Jack turned and stared at her questioningly. "But it is. That's Tommy Usher, leaving his club with Tony Turner's wife, Lois, and that's him at the boxing, chomping on a cigar."

"Sorry, Dad. You're wrong. I mean they look very similar,

and they could be mistaken for twins, in a darkened room, but two different men, definitely."

He snatched the photograph out of her hand and peered at it through the magnifying glass. "It beats me how you can say that. It's obviously the same man. Thomas Usher."

Joan shrugged. "Have it your way, Dad." She moved as if to go back to her room.

"Wait!" He grabbed her sleeve. "Pull up a chair and tell me how you reached your decision."

Joan smiled brightly and sat down next to him.

"When I was a kid," she began, "my favourite thing in my comic was the *spot the difference* game. You know the one, where they print two pictures side by side that look identical, but actually have ten or twelve subtle differences. Do you want to play?"

"I'm game."

"Right, put the photographs down side by side on the table."

He laid them down next to each other and offered her the magnifying glass.

"That's okay. I don't need it. Just look at the pictures closely."

Jack stared at them, not sure what he was supposed to be seeing.

Joan leaned in and with her index finger tapped on the nightclub photograph three times. "There, there and there. Look at the ears. He's got longer earlobes than him and there, if you look closely you can see that the one in the boxing photo has the tip of his little finger missing. You have to look hard because it's almost hidden by the fold in his jacket, and the chap leaving the nightclub has all his fingers intact, but the main difference is the nose. The man leaving the club has a slightly different shape of bridge to his nose than the man at the boxing match. Again it's subtle, but once you realise there are differences you start *really* looking." Joan sat back in her seat, a satisfied smile on her face.

Jack continued to stare at the photographs until the differences between the two men became so apparent he was stunned that he hadn't seen them before. "We could use you on the force."

"Why? Could your chief superintendent do with a shampoo

and set?"

"Ha!" He spun in his seat and hugged her. "Thank you, Joanie, You might just have cracked this case."

"How's the headache?"

"What headache." He kissed her cheek. "Would you like a cup of tea to celebrate?"

"I'd prefer champagne."

"I'm sure you would. I'll put the kettle on. I'll go and see if your mother wants one."

"She'll be easy to find. She's in the kitchen, doing the ironing."

26 - TUESDAY MARCH 24TH 1959

"I want another meeting with Charlie Somers," Jack said as Eddie Fuller came into the office. He had spent a largely sleepless night turning over the implications and possible ramifications of the discovery made by Joan yesterday evening. "What station does he work out of these days?"

"Kings Cross."

"Make the arrangements for us to go and pay him a visit."

"I don't think he'll be very happy with that, us turning up at Kings Cross nick for a chat."

"I couldn't give a tinker's cuss whether he's happy with it or not. He involved himself in our investigation. It's on his head if our lines of inquiry don't sit conveniently with him."

Fuller shrugged. He had seen his boss in this kind of mood before. Like a terrier with a ferret, he'd shake the idea to death before releasing it. "I'll call him."

"Good."

Ten minutes later, and one fractious telephone call later, Fuller came over and sat at Jack's desk. "He's agreed to see us but he wants us to meet him at a local pub, The Carpenters in the Kings Cross Road at midday."

"That suits me. We'll take a car. I want to go on somewhere else afterwards, while we're up in London."

With her uniform freshly pressed and her wavy hair swept neatly into a smooth French pleat by means of vigorous brushing and a liberal application of hair lacquer, Myra stepped out of the Holborn underground station and made her way smartly to the *Zoom* offices.

Despite its grand name the *Zoom Advertising Agency* offices were on the first floor of an undistinguished redbrick building above a cobbler's shop. The doorway was at the side of the shop and an enamelled arrow affixed to the wall pointed the way up a narrow, carpeted flight of stairs. At the top of the stairs was a half-glazed door with the legend ZOOM picked out in gold capital letters on the glass.

Myra tapped on the door, pushed it open, and her earlier confidence about her appearance evaporated like dew in the morning sunshine. She was in a small wood-panelled room, its walls adorned with framed colour photographs of some of the most beautiful and glamorous women she had ever seen. She felt her head sink down into her shoulders as a door in the room opened and an equally glamorous young woman walked in. About thirty, with short dark hair and an hourglass figure encased in a crisp beige silk suit, she was smiling and stretching out her hand. Her lips were red and the perfect teeth seemed to be lit from within. "Hello." She pumped Myra's hand. "I'm Marion, Cedric's secretary."

"WPC Banks."

"Yes, of course you are. I mean, who else could you be? It's not as if we have the police coming to our door every day." The secretary gave a girlish giggle. For all her apparent sophistication and movie star appearance, Marion didn't seem very bright. Myra chided herself silently for making such a premature assessment of the woman based only on an initial impression.

"Mr. Bannister is expecting me?"

"Indeed he is. If you could just take a seat." Marion pointed to a small hard chair in the corner of the room. "Cedric's in a meeting with a client, so Larry has agreed to see you."

"Larry?"

"Larry Barker. He and Wendy Worthing are Cedric's business partners. He'll be with you presently."

Myra thanked her and took the seat, crossing her ankles demurely, and Marion glided back out of the room on her four-inch stilettos.

Myra sat drumming her fingers on her knee, as the beauties adorning the wall continued to mock and intimidate her. A few minutes later the door opened again and a short man with brilliantined hair and a pencil-thin moustache hurried through the room and out of the offices. As he passed he gave her a furtive glance but, other than that, ignored her.

The door to the main office stayed open and seconds later another man entered the room. Young, tall and good-looking in an Errol Flynn type of way with thick wavy hair and a wolfish grin, Larry Barker stood just inside the doorway saying nothing, but watched Myra as she got to her feet.

"WPC Myra Banks," Myra offered in the hope of provoking some response.

Barker narrowed his eyes and looked her up and down. "Good figure. Nice pins. Pretty face though the eyebrows could use some work. Lovely eyes though. It's just a shame about the constipated hair. Is it straight or wavy? I can't tell with that style."

"Mr. Barker. I really don't see that my appearance has anything to do with the reason I'm here."

He put his fingers to his lips in a gesture for silence. "Never refuse a compliment. It's one of the first things I tell the girls. Compliments build confidence. Never forget that."

"I really feel we should get to the matter in hand," Myra said stiffly. She'd met types like Larry Barker before in dancehalls from Hertford to Hackney. They did not impress her, let alone turn her head.

Barker stared at the resolve etched on her face, in her steely gaze and in the taught line of her mouth. He inclined his head courteously. "As you wish. Come through to the office."

He led the way out of the room past a desk where Marion was sitting, her fingers flying dextrously over the keys of an Olympia typewriter. Myra noticed the secretary smile at Bannister adoringly as they passed by. Just another notch on his bedpost, she guessed.

The office was large and sumptuously furnished and Myra was surprised to see three desks, two of them occupied, one by a woman, possibly in her forties, although the impeccably applied makeup was a mask concealing her real age, and a man dressed in a well-tailored pin-striped suit whose blond hair gleamed under the harsh lights in the room. He was talking on the telephone as they entered the room and Myra recognised the voice of Cedric Bannister. He didn't look up as they entered. The woman, however, did.

"Must you bring that in here, Larry? Can't you see that we're working?"

Myra felt a chill from the icy voice she had encountered yesterday.

"Now, now, Wendy," Barker said. "Be polite. WPC Banks here has some questions for us." He turned to Myra. "Please excuse Wendy. She doesn't care for disruptions to the office routine."

"I promise I'll be as brief as possible," Myra said, hoping to mollify the woman and instead earned herself a cool stare from Wendy Worthing.

"My desk is here," Barker said. "Please take a seat and make yourself comfortable."

Myra did as he requested, sitting down at the desk, taking her notebook from the breast pocket of her tunic.

"Shall we begin then?" Barker made himself comfortable in a plush office chair across the desk from her.

Myra crossed her legs and rested the notebook on her knee. "Lois Franklin. What can you tell me about her?"

"We made her into a star," Barker said.

Myra wondered how many other people were going to take the credit for Lois's success. First Stephen Sullivan at Northrop Chemicals and now Larry Barker. She wondered how many others would crawl out of the woodwork before the end of this investigation.

"You see at the *Zoom Agency* we pride ourselves on being able to see the potential in what appears to be unpromising material." Larry Barker lit a cigarette and leaned back in his chair. "Rather like I did to you outside. When I first saw you, WPC Banks, I saw a young woman, confined by her uniform, destined to play an unglamorous role in life. One of the grey people who slip through the decades unnoticed, anonymous. Instead you should think of yourself as a lump of clay, raw material waiting to be sculpted and moulded into someone special, someone unique. Someone the camera loves; a sow's ear transformed into a silk purse. It's why we called the agency *Zoom*. Because we can take someone like you, someone who has good, but basic, raw materials that, with some slight alterations, a few tweaks, can then go, zoom! Up through the roof. A face and body that can sell anything from, plum puddings to platinum jewellery, from dumplings to diamonds. Zoom!" He raised his hand, his index finger pointing at the ceiling.

Give me strength, Myra thought, tiring of the agency sales pitch. "Lois Franklin?" She pressed him, trying to bring him back to the reason she was here.

"A case in point." Barker suddenly got to his feet and went across to a filing cabinet in the corner of the room. He pulled open a drawer and started to flick through a collection of files. Seconds later he was back, opening a file out on the desk and leafing through the papers and photographs inside.

He took out a colour photograph and laid it down for her to see.

It was a head and shoulders shot of a rather plain girl, with uneven, slightly discoloured teeth, bad skin and lank, mousy hair.

Barker watched Myra keenly as she studied the picture. "From that." He reached into the file again and produced another glossy colour shot, this one much more familiar to her; Lois Turner née Franklin as the *Cadence Girl*, with her shimmering golden hair, perfect features and flawless complexion. "To this." Barker beamed at her. "You see what I mean. The magic of the *Zoom Agency*."

Myra picked up the photographs and studied them. "They're the same girl?" She couldn't hide the incredulity in her voice.

"It's hard to credit isn't it? I must admit that even I was sceptical when she first walked in here, but all credit has to go to Wendy there. She saw something in that girl, something that many people before her had failed to spot.

Wendy Worthing heard her name mentioned and looked across at them curiously. Barker sensed her cold gaze on them and turned in his seat. "That's right, Wendy, isn't it? You spotted the potential in Lois Franklin from the off."

Wendy scowled at him. "That's right. I spotted her, the ungrateful little hussy."

Barker smiled at Myra. "I'm afraid Wendy's still bitter

181

because Lois left us."

Wendy came around from behind her desk and stood over them, glaring down at the photographs. "When I think of the time I wasted on that girl, it makes my blood boil. I gave her new hair, new teeth, contact lenses for her eyes. I reshaped her eyebrows, showed how to apply her makeup. I showed her how to stand, to sit and to pose for photographs. I even gave her a new name. Whoever heard of an international model called Bláthnaid?"

"Bláthnaid? How do you spell that?"

Wendy spelt it out for her and Myra jotted it down in her notebook.

"Horrendous, isn't it?" Wendy seemed to be fully engaged in the conversation now. The woman seemed to have an axe to grind. "It conjures up images of peat bogs and potatoes, and that awful fiddle music. The name had to go. Lois is much more sophisticated. It just oozes glamour."

"But Bláthnaid is an Irish name? I thought Lois Franklin was American."

Barker was rifling through the file again, found another piece of paper and started reading from it. "Born into a Irish family and grew up in Brooklyn, New York City. She came to us a month after she arrived in this country, looking for modelling work. Though why in God's name she thought she had any chance in this career is anyone's guess. But you saw the potential in her, didn't you, Wendy?"

"I saw the unformed lump of clay," Wendy said. "I've spent more than twenty years transforming clay into fine porcelain. I saw it as a challenge, nothing more."

"Agoraphobia?" Larry Barker said when Myra brought it up. "She's not still using that old chestnut is she?

"Do you mean she doesn't have agoraphobia?" Myra said.

Wendy smirked. "No, she does have it, like I've have two heads and the bubonic plague. That woman collects spurious ailments like other people collect stamps or cigarette cards."

"It's a ploy she's used before. Most notably when she was trying to get out of her contract with us."

Myra glanced round as Cedric Bannister, his phone call now ended, came from behind his desk and came to stand with his partners.

"But her doctor..." She flipped back the pages of her notebook. "Mark Francombe, confirmed it."

Wendy let out an exasperated sigh. "I do hope that the rest of our policemen and women aren't as naïve as you."

"Naïve? What do you mean?"

"The sudden onset of agoraphobia was a godsend for her. Actually I was rather surprised that she had the intellect to think it up. Obviously, by the very nature of the condition, she couldn't go to the surgery, so her Dr. Francombe would come to visit, usually when that drip of a husband of hers was away touring or shooting a film."

"I'm sorry, I'm still not sure I follow your drift." Myra used the end of her ballpoint pen to scratch an itch behind her ear. *I used too much hair lacquer.* The thought drifted into her mind and out again as she tried to keep track of the conversation.

Wendy Worthing shook her head incredulously "I don't know what kind of sheltered upbringing you've had, Constable Banks, so this may come as a shock to you, but she was sleeping with him."

"I'm afraid that Lois uses her sex appeal as a bargaining chip," Barker added. "I've seen her turn the most ruthless marketing director into a drooling mess with a bat of an eyelash. It's a powerful tool and she has no qualms about using it."

"But surely it didn't do her any good when she had the affair with Tony Turner. They were crucified by the newspapers."

"Which all but destroyed his career," Bannister said.

"And sent hers skyrocketing," Wendy added.

"Zoom indeed." Larry Barker grinned and pointed to the ceiling again.

"There was a mad rush to book her." Bannister had warmed to the subject. He sat back down at his desk, and was now totally immersed in the conversation. "There's nothing like a sex scandal to add value to a model's worth."

"But Lois wasn't willing to play the game," Wendy said bitterly. "After all the money we had invested in her, and all the hours I had put into grooming her, she decided she could go her own way and make more money freelancing, working for the highest bidder, so to speak."

"That was when the agoraphobia reared its ugly, and entirely fictitious, head again," Bannister said. "Only this time she used it to hamper the contract negotiations, missing meetings, that sort of thing. Not that her solicitor needed any help. He was running rings around my man, finding obscure loopholes in the contract that had totally eluded us. Sometimes it helps when your lawyer is your brother."

"Her brother?"

"Yes, and very good he was too. In fact, if he hadn't had a vested interest in his sister's career, I would have sacked my man and hired him myself."

Myra was scribbling down notes in her ersatz shorthand. *I really need to take a Pitman's course*, she thought. "And you think her marriage to Tony Turner was a sham?"

"I think it was about as genuine as everything else to do with Lois Turner," Wendy said. "I was there when they first met at a dinner party given by Noël Coward at the Savoy Hotel, and she had Turner eating out of her hand by end of the *aperitifs*. It was pitiful to watch."

"Like a lamb to the slaughter," Barker said.

"Can you give me the name of her solicitor?" Myra said, her pen poised over the page of her notebook.

"Docherty," Bannister said. "Simon Docherty."

"But you said he was her brother."

"And so he is." Wendy perched on the edge of Barker's desk. "I changed her name to Lois Franklin from the unappealing and very unmarketable *Bláthnaid Docherty*. As I said, peat bogs and fiddle music."

27 - TUESDAY

The public bar of the Carpenters was heaving for a Tuesday lunchtime. All the tables were occupied and there was queue at the bar. Three barmen were rushing backwards and forwards behind the long oak counter, dispensing trays of drinks, taking pound notes from customers and stowing them away in a cash register that seemed to be constantly ringing up sales. The air was heavy with cigarette smoke and the malty aroma of beer, and the general hubbub of conversation was punctuated with the occasional eruption of cheering.

Jack looked about him critically. The idea of having anything approaching a private conversation here was slim. "Are you sure he said to meet in here?"

Eddie Fuller shrugged, his eyebrows raised. "That's what he said."

Seconds later Charlie Somers was tugging at Fuller's elbow. "Sorry. Darts match. I forgot. Come through to the saloon bar."

Fuller attracted Jack's attention and they moved through the frosted-glass door to the oasis of peace that was the saloon bar.

"Find a table and I'll get them in." Somers walked up to the bar. "Half of bitter, Eddie? And you, Jack?"

"Orange squash. I'm driving."

They sat in a booth to one side of the bar and Somers put the tray of drinks down on the table between them. He sat down himself and took his pint of Guinness from the tray, pulled out his pipe and lit it with a match. Puffing the aromatic smoke, he finally got the pipe alight, shook his hand and dropped the spent match into the china ashtray that occupied a space in the centre of the table.

"So why the urgent visit to my home turf? Has something come up?"

"A couple of things." Jack leaned forward and pushed the ashtray to one side, leaving himself space to lay down the photographs he'd taken from his pocket. "I'd like you to take a look at these."

Somers glanced down at them. "Why are you showing me these?" He pointed to the boxing photograph. "That's the one I gave you."

"Bear with me." Jack took out the photograph of the O'Brien brothers and laid it down next to the others. "Recognise them?"

A slow smile spread over Somers face. "Fergus and Conner O'Brien. You don't think those two are caught up in all this, do you?"

"Very much so, Charlie. In fact I believe they're a large part of the reason for *all this*. Tell me what you know about them."

"Probably about as much as you do, if you saw the memo Scotland Yard sent round. Irish Americans, and not the type whose only connection to the mother country is to get pissed up every St Patrick's day and to sing a verse or two of *Danny Boy*. The O'Brien family hail from County Cork. When they were scrabbling around Ireland's illicit underbelly, they sent the crime rates soaring. The old man, Padraig, packed up the entire family and emigrated to the United States before the *Garda* could pull them in. If this photo was taken in London it would appear that the Yard were right. They did come over here." Somers leaned back in his chair and sucked on his pipe. "You're awfully quiet, Eddie. Cat got your tongue?"

Fuller shook his head. "I'm just wondering where all this is leading." He turned to Jack. "Guv?"

"All in good time, Eddie," Jack said and took a mouthful of orange squash. He said to Somers, "Tell me, when did Thomas Usher have his stroke?"

"About six months after that boxing match at the York Hall. The fifth of December 1956. An early, or some would say, very belated Christmas present."

"Interesting," Jack said. "According to Benny Talbot's filing system, this photograph..." He pointed to the shot of Lois Turner leaving *The Purple Flamingo* draped on Usher's arm. "This photograph was taken in 1957."

"Then Usher looks remarkably healthy for a man recovering from a stroke," Fuller said.

"I'd agree with you, Eddie. But that's not Thomas Usher."

Fuller picked up the print and stared at it for a long moment.

"Then if it's not him, it must be…"

"Tony Turner," Somers said. "Well I'll be… Here, let me look at that."

Fuller slid the photograph across the table. He, like Fuller, stared at it long and hard. "Stone me," he said. "Do you think you could be right? It certainly looks like Usher."

"I am right." Jack pointed out the differences in the two men that his daughter had spotted yesterday.

"It still doesn't make a lot of sense, Jack. It's common knowledge that Usher had a stroke and is pretty much gaga these days. What would be the point of impersonating him when everyone knows the truth?"

"Usher's stroke must have been very inconvenient for the higher ups running the firm, a power vacuum, and yet nobody stepped up to take his place. Did you ever ask yourself why?"

"I wondered but, as I told Eddie, my bosses were just relieved that Usher was out of their hair."

"Only he wasn't. See, there he is leaving the night club." Jack pointed to the photo.

"But it's not him," Fuller said.

"Yes, but the photo had us fooled. Turner's impersonation may have hoodwinked others into believing that Usher was still active; still a face. Usher's stroke was always regarded as a convenience. You thought so yourself, Charlie. A way to stop the investigation into his criminal activities and, let's be honest, it worked. The Met effectively wrote him off as a threat."

"Only after the stroke was confirmed."

"But what if the word was spread among the criminal fraternity that it had been a ruse all along and Usher was well and still running things in the South, and to confirm it Tommy Usher would be seen at his night club, fit and healthy. On the strength of his reputation alone, no one with any regard for their safety is going to question it. Quite the reverse in fact. He would be seen as a criminal mastermind, putting one over on Scotland Yard. He'd be hailed as a hero."

"Word would have reached the Yard if that were the case," Somers said.

"You mean Scotland Yard has a string of informers ready to

risk life and limb by telling you that Thomas Usher was still in charge and that the stroke was just one huge deception?"

"Fair point, I suppose." Somers sipped at his Guinness. "So who do you think is running the show now?"

"I have my suspicions," Jack said.

"Do you want to share them?"

Jack laid the photograph of Simon Docherty in conversation with Isaac Gold down on the table.

Somers stared at it.

"Gold told Eddie and me that Docherty was just asking him for the time, but I didn't believe it then and I don't believe now. I think they're working together."

"Which means Albert Klein would be running London, North and South."

"Yes, but covertly, along with Simon Docherty who has been Usher's right-hand man for a few years now. There are factions in south London who would never take orders from an American lawyer and a North London Jew. It would go too much against the grain. But if those instructions were thought to be coming from Usher himself, no one is going to complain or make waves."

"So Tony Turner dressed and made up to look like Tommy Usher appears every so often, just too make it seem that the boss still around?" Somers scratched his head. "It's a bit of a stretch, Jack."

"Not when you consider how high the stakes are, especially when you bring the O'Brien family into the equation."

Fuller drained his glass. "Now you've lost me."

"Usher's main objection to joining forces with Albert Klein was Klein's drug business. It was the one criminal activity he would have no truck with after the death of his brother. Suddenly the O'Brien family arrive on the scene, offering untold riches if they can bring London into their drug market, and Klein can't capitalise on the opportunity because he'd never get Usher to guarantee the supply line from the coast into London and the rest of the UK. The O'Briens would never risk exposing themselves in a venture that was only fifty per cent certain. So for Klein, Usher's stroke was both a godsend and a curse. On one hand Usher, the fly in the ointment, has been removed. On the other, the O'Briens would never be persuaded to commit to anything without dealing directly with both Klein *and* Usher. So they meet at Usher's nightclub, with Turner playing the role of *mein host*, the deal is done and all parties get what they want." Jack sat back in his seat, waiting for a reaction. "Well? What do you think?"

Somers and Fuller exchanged looks, and Somers shook his head. "Sorry, Jack. I'm not buying it. Obviously you've put a lot of thought into your theory, but too far-fetched. This is the London underworld we're dealing with here, and you're presenting us with a scenario of Machiavellian proportions. I doubt that any of the participants in your story have the intelligence to come up with such a scheme."

"And it still doesn't explain why Tony Turner ended up tortured and nailed to a tree in the middle of Letchworth," Fuller said.

"Agreed, Eddie, it doesn't explain that, but I must disagree with you, Charlie. If, as we suspect, it *is* Simon Docherty running the show in the South just remember, he's a trained lawyer, and his devious legal mind would be more than capable of thinking this thing up, and Albert Klein is no slouch in the intelligence department either. You don't go from being a snotty kid from Ponders End to being the head of North London's top criminal firm without having something special about you."

Somers drained his glass. "If you can find some evidence to support your crazy idea I'd be willing to suspend my disbelief, take it to my superiors and get them to restart the investigations, but all this Shakespearian drama stuff will get me laughed out of the chief constable's office and wreck what little reputation and credibility I have left. Sorry, Jack, but I can't help you on this."

"Ah, well," Jack said, draining the last of his orange squash. "It was worth a try."

"Shall I get them in again?"

Jack shook his head. "Not now, Charlie. We have to be going. Places to go, people to see."

"Fair enough." Somers got to his feet. "I'll leave you with one thought though. You mentioned the O'Brien brothers. The most infamous incident involving them that the New York police could never get a result on, was that of Joey the Fish, one of the bookies on the O'Briens' payroll. Joey swindled the brothers out of thousands of dollars and met an untimely end under the wheels of a Greyhound bus. The NYPD could never prove that it was anything other than an accident, but everyone knew that the O'Briens were just exacting their revenge. I might get in touch with Roy Armitage who led the investigation into Benny Talbot's death. He might be interested to know that not only were the brothers in the Tottenham Court Road area around that time, but Benny Talbot snapped them coming out of Tommy Usher's club, and I doubt they were much pleased by that. Who knows, it might lead somewhere."

28 - TUESDAY

"Is Mr. Callum in his office, Sergeant?"

Andy Brewer looked up at Myra bleakly. "He's out."

"Sergeant Fuller?"

"He's out too."

"Well, when they return, I'll be in the canteen."

"Don't expect them to come looking for you, girl. They have enough on their plates."

"I didn't mean they should…" Myra shook her head. "I'll find them when they get back."

"Yeah, you do that."

"Sergeant Brewer, have you got a problem with me?" She knew she couldn't let this situation continue. After a mostly sleepless night, tossing around the ideas about Jack Callum and their supposed flirtation, she had reached the conclusion that she could not let the rumours fester for much longer. She had to act.

"A problem? Whatever gave you that idea?"

"You're not exactly being very helpful."Brewer just looked blankly at her.

"Oh, never mind." She turned and started to walk towards the canteen.

"You're being paranoid, girl," Brewer said as she walked away from him. "My wife gets like it, once a month without fail."

She hesitated for a second, biting her tongue, before continuing her journey and not looking back at him.

She reached the canteen and the aromas of the meals being prepared whet her appetite. Her stomach growled. A reminder of the paltry dinner she'd had the night before. *You can't live on crisps and chocolate*, Myra, she chided herself.

"Shepherds pie, love?" Yvonne Morrison, the cook said to her as Myra came up to the serving hatch.

"Yes. Great."

A few seconds later she was carrying a plate piled high with mashed potato, minced lamb and onions. Garden peas and

191

sliced carrots made up the rest of the meal, all drenched in Yvonne's famous, and delicious, gravy.

Myra was salivating as she reached her seat at a table in the corner. As she laid her plate down on the blue Formica-topped table it struck her that she usually ate alone these days. How different to when she had first come to the station, when the camaraderie was strong and she was often invited to eat with her fellow officers. She was sure she wasn't imagining that the casual ostracization had started during her secondment to CID last year. Suddenly she was excluded from the mealtime banter of the others, and the feeling began to grow that she was being deliberately shunned. At first it was easy to shrug off, but she had encountered the odd barbed comment that she chose to ignore, but now the specific cause of the others resentment was becoming clear.

She ate her meal without really tasting it, aware of the occasional furtive glance and whispered aside. Finally she put down her knife and fork, picked up her plate and took it back to the hatch.

"Steamed syrup sponge with custard for afters," Yvonne said brightly. "Can I tempt you?"

Myra looked back at the canteen. There were only a few of her colleagues eating now. One of them was DC Trevor Walsh, Frank Lesser's number two.

"Just a small portion, Yvonne. That dinner filled me up."

Yvonne handed her a bowl of steaming dessert. "Enjoy it. It will put meat on your bones."

Myra smiled at her. "As if I need that."

She carried the bowl across to Walsh who was sitting alone at another table.

"Do you mind if I join you?"

Walsh shrugged and nodded to an empty seat across from him.

He was twenty-eight, a year older than her and had come through Hendon at more or less the same time. She had always enjoyed a kind of brother/sister relationship with him, though on one memorable occasion, at a drunken leaving do for a retiring officer, it had slipped from the comfortable platonic plateau into a alcoholic fumble and a few kisses, but they had quickly recovered themselves, apologised and the incident was never mentioned by either of them again. Now, Trevor Walsh was looking more than a little uncomfortable by her close proximity. He had a newspaper propped up against a tomato ketchup bottle and seemed totally engrossed in the racing results as he ate his meal.

"There's nothing going on you know? Between Jack Callum and me. Nothing at all."

Walsh looked over the top of the newspaper at her.

"Okay." There was an edge of scepticism in his voice that he tried but failed to mask.

"Honestly, Trev. I wouldn't lie to you. We've known each other too long."

"Okay." The scepticism was still there.

Myra slapped her forehead and stood up, knocking her chair over. "Christ! What do I have to do to convince you all?"

Her outburst and the clatter of the upended chair drew the attention of the other diners in the room. Even Yvonne was staring at her from the serving hatch.

"It might help if the chief inspector stopped giving you all the plum jobs and shared them out among the rest of us," Chris Tate said. He was a uniformed PC like herself, and was taking his plate back to the hatch. "It's bloody obvious you're his favourite. We can't help it if we draw the obvious conclusion."

Myra looked across at Walsh, beseeching him to say something, to lay this nonsense to rest once and for all.

"He's got a point, Myra."

Her mouth dropped open. "You too, Trev?"

Walsh shrugged and Myra glared at him and the others. "I state categorically, here and now, that there is nothing like that going on between DCI Callum and myself. Has it ever occurred to any of you that I get given the *plum* jobs because I just happen to be a good police officer, or can't you accept that a woman can do this job just as well as the rest of you?" She stared around at room and got nothing but cynicism in return. "Well, Jack Callum believes in me, and I don't need to open my legs to convince him." With tears of anger and frustration stinging her eyes she dropped the spoon she'd been holding like a weapon and stormed from the canteen.

She reached the Ladies toilet and locked herself into a stall, taking deep, disinfectant-tinged gulps of air as she fought to get herself under control. After a minute or so of fighting, she gave up. The tears burst from her eyes and shoulder-heaving sobs wracked her body. "It's not fair," she said to herself. "It's not bloody fair."

The doors to *The Purple Flamingo* were being held open by mop and bucket. Jack negotiated his way around them and entered the dimly lit foyer.

"Is there anyone around?" Fuller said as he stepped over the bucket.

"Sorry, we're not open yet." His question was answered by an elderly man dressed in shirtsleeves and stained dungarees who emerged from a toilet to the left of a smart reception desk. The man was almost completely bald apart from a semi-circle of fuzzy white hair that sat on his head like a fallen halo.

"It's all right, George. I'll handle this," another voice sounded, and from the gloom behind the counter a younger man emerged. Younger, fitter, with a thick neck and pugilistic features, he regarded Jack and his sergeant with hostile eyes. "We're closed. Anyway, it's members only. Are you two members? Do you have your cards?"

Jack took out his warrant card and waved it under the thuggish man's nose. "This is the only card I need."

The man glanced at the card and gave a derisive snort. "Plods. I might have known. I didn't think you looked like our regular punters."

"What gave us away?" Fuller smiled at the man.

"Your feet are too fucking big for one thing," he said. "Fucking flatfoots."

"And what charm school did you attend?" Jack peered at the brass name badge on the man's lapel. "Irving?"

"Didn't go to no fucking charm school."

Jack smiled. "No, I thought not."

Irving leaned back on his heels and gave them an appraising look. "What do you want?"

"We'd like to have a look around your club."

"Got a warrant?"

"We don't need a warrant. We don't want to search the place, just a general look around."

"Well I say you can't, so you can just sling your hook."

"Irving! Irving, that's no way to treat our guests." Another man appeared out of the gloom. He was prissy, slightly built, wore a purple silk suit and too much cologne.

"Are you the Purple Flamingo?" Fuller said.

"Miles Clarke. I'm the manager here." He stuck out a hand.

"They're old bill." Irving said morosely, miffed at being denied the chance to crack heads together.

Clarke smiled benignly but dropped his hand. "Ah, gentlemen from London's finest. What can I do for you?"

"We'd like to take a look around your club," Jack said.

The smile widened but the eyes were watchful. "And why would that be?"

"We're looking for a venue for the next policeman's ball."

"Really?" Clarke gave the impression that he might expire from excitement. "I must say it would be an honour for us to host such an event. Whatever made you think of us?"

"Word has it that you can organize a good 'do'. I'd just like to check the place out first."

"Of course, of course. Why don't you come through to the club itself?" Clarke walked across to a pair of half-glazed door and pushed them open. "Please come through."

They found themselves in a very large room with a small stage at one end and tables and chairs surrounding a rectangular, highly polished dance floor. There was a balcony on one wall and opposite the stage was a raised area with three booths each containing luxurious looking sofas and more tables. Purple was the dominant colour scheme, from the silk drapes that hung at regular intervals on the walls to the flamingo motif picked out in fluorescent tubes above the stage. Even the grand piano that occupied one side of the stage had been painted purple and doused with a quantity of glitter. *Subtley is a complete stranger*

195

here, Jack thought as his gaze drank in the amethyst excess.

"And where does Mr. Usher sit when he comes in?" Jack said.

"That's his private booth in the centre," Clarke said pointing up at the raised area.

"I suppose since his illness he doesn't get in much these days."

"On the contrary, he was in only last wee…" His voice drained away as he suddenly remembered to whom he was talking. He gave a brisk shake of his head as if to dismiss the words that had just poured like diarrhea from his lips. "Oh, Mr. Usher, who used to own the club. Him. No. He hasn't been in here since his stroke."

Jack smiled at him. "Yes, that's what I thought." He walked out to the centre of the dance floor, stared up at Usher's booth and called Fuller over. "Pretty gloomy," he said quietly, pointing at the subdued lighting. "Anyone could be sitting up there but, unless you were told who it was, you wouldn't have a clue." He beckoned for Clarke to come and join them. The man dutifully obliged. "There might be a small presentation on the night of our do, and we'd like to make it somewhere where everyone can see. Can anything be done with the lighting up there?"

Clarke considered the question for a moment before shaking his head. "No' All the bulbs are low wattage I'm afraid. We like to keep the lighting in that area discreet to ensure privacy for our patrons, should they need it."

"Well, I think we've seen enough. We still have a couple of venues we need to check out while we're in the area. Thank you for your time."

"My pleasure," Clarke said unctuously. "And you promise you'll keep us in mind?"

Jack shook Clarke's rather clammy hand. "I assure you, I'm moving you up to the top of the list."

Clarke beamed. "As I said, it would be such an honour to host your event."

Jack inclined his head and moved to the door. Seconds later they were out on the Tottenham Court Road and walking back to where they'd left the car.

"Do you still think my theory was off kilter, Eddie?"

Fuller shook his head. "I don't know, Jack."

"But you heard him yourself. Usher was in the night club last week…last week, Eddie."

They reached the car. "I suppose you could be right," Fuller said as he climbed into the passenger seat. "Let's get back to the station. I hate London. It gives me the itch."

"I thought you were considering the Met as your next possible port of call."

"Just an idea, and not a particularly good one."

"As I said, London has its drawbacks."

29 - TUESDAY

"Please give this to DCI Callum when he gets in," Myra said, handing Brewer a sealed brown envelope.

Brewer took it from her and turned it over and over in his hands, as if he could tell what was in the envelope by touch alone. "What's this? Your resignation?"

Myra regarded him coolly. She had washed her face to get rid of the signs of her tears. "Please just see that he gets it as soon as he gets in." She turned on her heel and walked to the doors, pushing through them and letting them swing shut behind her.

"Hey, where are you off to?" Brewer called, but Myra was already crossing the car park towards her Morris Minor. She climbed inside, slammed the door behind her and drove quickly out onto the street.

Andy Brewer slipped the envelope into one of the pigeonholes on the wall behind the desk and went back to tidying the forms in the wall racks.

Leaving her car parked in the road, Myra slipped in through the gates of *Elsinore* and approached the front of the house. She noticed immediately that the door was ajar but pressed the doorbell anyway and waited for someone to answer it. As seconds turned into minutes she nudged the door open with the toe of her shoe and looked inside.

When she saw the body of Hester Gough sprawled on her back in the centre of the hall carpet, she took a step to one side and pressed her spine against the wall as her heart thudded in her chest. It took her a few moments to gather her thoughts and, when she felt she had regained her self-control, she turned back to the door and pushed it wide open.

Had she been driving a pool car with a radio she would have called in to the station to ask for back up and advice on how to proceed, but she wasn't. She was driving her stupid, battered Morris Minor, with no way of contacting the station and help. She was on her own. Angry at her stupidity and lack of foresight she entered the house cautiously.

Jack and Fuller walked into the station and went straight to the canteen for a cup of tea. They took their drinks to a table in the corner.

"All right," Fuller resumed the conversation they'd been having in the car on the drive back from London. "Supposing your theory is right. It's like I said before, it still doesn't explain why Turner was killed. Even if the rest of it makes some kind of sense, that part doesn't. If you're using Tony Turner as some kind of puppet in order to put one over on the O'Briens or whomever, why then kill him? It's like cutting your nose off to spite your face. I can't see that Docherty or Klein would have anything to gain from it."

"Excuse me, sir, I thought I saw you come in." Andy Brewer came into the canteen and stood at their table.

"What can I do for you, Sergeant?"

"WPC Banks asked me to give you this, sir."

Jack took the letter from Brewer, picked up a knife from the table and slid it under the flap and slit it open, taking out the single sheet of notepaper from inside. He started to read.

Sir,

This is the information attained from the Zoom Modelling Agency.

1)   Lois Turner does not have agoraphobia. She uses it as a ruse so she can carry on an affair with her doctor, Mark Francombe. Whether or not her husband was complicit in this charade is not clear, though I suspect not. Why should he be as it was him she was cheating on?

2)   Lois is not her birth name, which was Bláthnaid. Her surname is Docherty. Thomas Usher's solicitor, Simon Docherty, is her brother

In the light of this information I think another interview is in order. You are out at the moment and Sergeant Brewer can't give me any idea when you might return. As time is of the essence I am going along to Elsinore to confront her with these newly acquired facts. I will report to you on my return.

WPC Banks.

Jack folded the letter in half and slipped it into his pocket.

"Has she come up with anything useful?" Fuller said.

"You could say that. She's gone out to *Elsinore* to have another chat with Lois Turner." He turned back to Brewer. "How long ago did she leave this for me?"

Brewer shrugged. "An hour ago? Ninety minutes?"

Jack glared at him. "Well, what is it?"

Brewer looked up at the clock on the wall. "Ninety minutes, sir. Ninety minutes."

"I should be there," Jack said to Fuller. "Coming?"

They walked towards the door.

"Sergeant Fuller." Henry Lane appeared at the top of the stairs.

"Yes, sir."

"If I could see you in my office?"

Fuller exchanged looks with Jack.

"When you're ready, Sergeant," Lane said, sensing Fuller's hesitation.

"You'd better not keep the chief super waiting. Eddie," Jack said quietly.

"Looks like I'll have to catch you up."

"Okay. You know where it is." Jack went out to the car park and signed out a pool car. Moments later he was heading towards Letchworth.

Hester Gough was very dead. Her eyes were open wide. The look of mild shock in her eyes made her expression look almost comical. In the centre of her forehead was a neat, almost blood-free bullet hole. What blood there was had pooled at the back of her head and was slowly soaking into the carpet. Instinctively

Myra reached out and closed the staring eyes with her fingertips and then she looked about her, listening hard for any noise in the house. All she could hear was the sound of her own breathing and the rhythmic thud of her heartbeat. She pushed herself to her feet, still looking about her.

All the doors leading off from the hall were closed except the door to the conservatory. Moving around Hester's body, she crept on tiptoe across the carpet towards the open door. She approached the doorway, glancing into the room and ducking back out of sight as she saw the tableau inside.

Lois Turner was slumped face down on the bamboo couch, blood and brains from a head wound dribbling down the chintz upholstery and forming a pool on the Italian-tiled floor. Pressed up against the piano was a wheelchair. There was a figure in the wheelchair, Thomas Usher, his legs covered by a plaid blanket, his greying head slumped to one side, eyes open but staring into nothingness, spittle dribbling down one side of his chin from a mouth that gaped open lopsidedly.

He didn't move, not even to acknowledge her presence as she stepped into the room and crossed to Lois Turner to check her pulse. Feeling nothing Myra let the wrist drop, got to her feet and froze as a voice sounded behind her.

"I must admit, you're prettier than most of the plods I've had on my tail over the years."

Myra spun round and stared into Thomas Usher's very alert and smiling face.

30 - TUESDAY

Usher was sitting upright in the wheelchair, his eyes bright and clear. He'd wiped the drool from his chin.

"I…I thought…"

The smile widened. "Yes, so did everyone. I think I've played the role of the pathetic invalid quite well, don't you? Better than Tony Turner could have done anyway. Driving is still a problem for me, but one of my lads brought me over here. He's waiting in the van, just up the road by the phone box so I can call for him to pick me up when I finish here."

Myra just stared at him.

"What's your name by the way?"

"Banks. WPC Banks."

"Well, WPC Banks, do you have your handcuffs on you?"

Myra nodded.

"Good. Go over to the wall behind you, sit down on the floor and cuff yourself to the radiator."

As she shook her head and opened her mouth to protest, Usher took his hand out from under the blanket to show her that his fingers were curled around the stock of a black revolver. He twitched it. "I won't tell you twice," he said, still smiling benignly.

When she didn't move he squeezed the trigger and fired, the bullet kicking up dust and chips of ceramic as it buried itself deep in the tiles at her feet.

Myra threw herself back against the wall and, winded, slid down until she was sitting on the floor. She took out her handcuffs and threaded one cuff through the pipes of the cast iron radiator, and then closed it around her wrist.

"And the other wrist." He twitched the revolver again and watched her closely as she attached the other cuff. The radiator was on and pumping out steady heat. The cast iron was burning her skin and she strained to keep her wrists away from the scorching metal.

"That's better." Usher lowered the gun. "I hate using these

things." He nodded at the weapon. "I always feel it makes me less of a man, but, as you see, I'm hardly in a position to use my strength to persuade you."

"I thought you said you were acting."

"Ah, you misunderstand me, WPC Banks. My stroke was real, very real, and left me with certain disabilities, but it could have been so much worse, and I've let people think that it was." He gave a short sharp belch of laughter. "At least it got you lot off my tail for a while. 'Poor old Tommy Usher. He's a cabbage now I hear'. You wouldn't believe some of the tales that have built up around me."

"You were very convincing. I've heard some of those tales myself."

"As was my intention. Plods like yourself were never the sharpest chisels in the toolbox. Your governors just use you like blunt instruments, letting you do all the donkey work while they stand around and wait to collect the glory."

Myra shifted on the floor. The burning pain in her wrists was becoming unbearable and she bit the insides of her cheek to stop herself crying out. She would not give Usher the satisfaction.

"What about *your* governor, Miss Banks, is he a uniformed glory-seeker?"

"Jack Callum's a damned fine policeman," she snapped at him and instantly regretted it as she saw a light flare in his eyes.

"Chief Inspector Callum." He rolled the name around in his mouth, as if he were savouring a fine wine. "*He's* your boss? I know the name but not the man. So it's him you have to thank for your current predicament."

Myra tilted her chin pugnaciously and glared at him. "He's got your number."

"Really?" Usher smiled, and cupped a hand to his ear. "And yet I can't hear the bells of approaching salvation, so perhaps your faith in him is misplaced."

"Why did you kill Tony Turner?" Myra said suddenly, trying to steer the conversation away from her boss and his investigations.

Usher spun around in his chair.

"Because he was becoming a bloody nuisance," Usher said

savagely.

For the first time Myra glimpsed behind the urbane mask, and it scared her.

"His impersonations of me were fun at first and could be very useful indeed, but he took it too far. It's remarkable that what started out as a skit, a spoof at my fortieth birthday party at the *Flamingo,* could prove to be such a boon in the years to come.

"He and a couple of his actor cronies wrote and performed this short comedy sketch with Tony portraying me as some kind of Al Capone figure. I don't remember the exact details apart from a few gags about tax evasion, but I saw how accurate Turner's impersonation of me was, and I saw the potential. I realised that here was the instant alibi. Christ, the fun I had, out pulling job after job all over the South and on every one of them I had about twenty or thirty witnesses telling your lot that I was at my club all evening and never left my private booth, not for a second. Tony didn't complain. His career had hit the skids and was sliding all the way down the toilet, plus he owed me for pulling out of the escort business, leaving me high and dry.

"But, like all good things, it came to an end once that bastard stroke got me. At least I thought it had. Simon bloody Docherty had other ideas. When they brought me back from Switzerland and Brussels – Christ what a boring country that is – he staged a welcome home party for me at the *Flamingo*, with a guest list of some of the nastiest bastards in the South London underworld, some of the major faces. There was I in my private booth, the picture of health after my miraculous recovery in foreign parts. In actual fact I was in a nursing home by the coast – bloody Dymchurch of all places. Somewhere I used to go when I was a nipper – Tony Turner took my place that night and for many more nights afterwards. All the guests were sworn to secrecy on the understanding that if news leaked out that I was back in the game, the police investigation would start again, and no one wanted that.

"You have to hand it to Simon. It was something of a masterstroke. He could carry on with business, supposedly sanctioned by me, but without having to involve me at all. I was out of the way at the seaside so he had a free reign to do as he liked.

"And it all worked out fine for a while. I was playing the role of the pathetic invalid. Docherty and his bitch of a sister would come to visit me and speak freely in front of me, thinking I couldn't understand what they were saying, and even if I could I couldn't do anything about it. But they were wrong. I understood totally what they were planning. Even down to the deals they were making with that piece of slime Albert Klein, that maggot Jew with his drug dealing; getting kids hooked on the filthy stuff without a care that he was probably killing them. Kids like my brother Cyril."

Usher lapsed into silence, his eyes brimming with tears.

If she didn't know that Usher was a murdering psychopath, Myra could almost feel sorry for him.

Now he had stopped talking her mind started to refocus on her scorched wrist. "So what did you do?" she said to snap him out of his reverie. "There was Simon Docherty and his sister effectively taking over your business, and there's you in a Dymchurch nursing home not being able to do a damned thing about it."

Usher suddenly snapped back to the present. "Ah, but that's where they were wrong. I still had people who were loyal to me. Jimmy Dymond for one. Jimmy and I went to school together in Peckham. He wasn't given much in the way of brains, but he was a big kid for his age, and tough. So when we were growing up he was my protector. In return I saw that his schoolwork was always done on time, and done to a reasonable standard. The school never caught on, so he never got into trouble with them. When we left and I started my own business – money lending it was – I took Jimmy on as my debt collector, and he's been at my side ever since, loyal to a fault.

"It was Jimmy who came to tell me that Docherty, Klein and Turner had restarted negotiations with those American Micks, the O'Briens, and I didn't like the sound of that. I needed to know what they were planning, but the meeting last Tuesday was a strictly private affair, so Jimmy and a couple of his lads followed Turner back here to Letchworth and took him over the Common to find out what they'd been discussing. As I said,

Jimmy's not intellectually blessed but he does have a knack for extracting information from reluctant subjects."

"So he nailed Turner to a tree and tortured him," Myra said.

"Did I mention that Jimmy has got an awful temper? I don't think he intended to kill Tony at the outset, but Jimmy had watched them playing out this bloody game for so long, he figured they were just taking the piss out of me, and his natural protective instinct just got the better of him."

"So Jimmy Dymond killed Tony Turner, not you."

Usher nodded his head. "But that's not the way it will play. I have my reputation to think of. Mind you, had I done it myself I would have cut off his balls and sent them to that bitch of a wife of his."

"I heard she spoke very highly of you too." Myra shifted her arms again.

Usher gave another bark of laughter. "My word, I like you, WPC Banks. You've got spunk. I'll give you that. Not a lot of sense, but spunk. I admire that in a woman."

31 - TUESDAY

Usher wheeled himself across the floor until he was a yard away from her. He reached down and lifted one of her wrists, pulling it as far away from the radiator as her other cuffed hand would allow. She winced as he ran his finger over the scorched skin.

"Nasty. I think that's going to blister," he said matter-of-factly and let her arm drop.

"Are you going to kill me?"

He looked at her steadily, raised an eyebrow but said nothing. Instead he turned the wheelchair to roll back to the centre of the room.

He turned to face her once more. "There's no rush is there? I rarely get a chance to talk to people these days, keeping up this bloody charade. You don't mind me bending your ear, do you?"

"I'm only too happy to listen." She was buying time. If she could just keep him talking, she might be able to find a way out of this mess, and in doing so save her own life.

"Good." Usher clapped a hand down on his knee.

"I'd be happier though if I could move away from the radiator. The burning is distracting me."

A thoughtful frown creased his brow. After a moment he said. "All right." He rolled back to her and held out his hand. "Key?"

"It's in my tunic." She nodded at her left-hand breast pocket.

He reached into the pocket and took out the key and slipped it into the cuff securing her right wrist, at the same time he produced the gun again.

"When I unlock it, very carefully take the cuff from behind the radiator and secure yourself again. If you try anything stupid, or reckless I'll put a bullet between your eyes. I may not like these bloody things but I know how to use one, as I'm sure you noticed when you came in." He twisted the key in the lock and the cuff fell free.

All thoughts of making a dash for it froze in her mind as he tapped her gently on the forehead with the barrel of the revolver.

With a resigned sigh she hooked the cuff over her wrist and closed it again.

When she was secured once more he said, "Now, what shall we talk about? As you can see, I've killed Lois and the old biddy that lives with her. Perhaps I'll tell you what I'm planning to do to her brother. If he thinks he can bring the O'Briens' filthy drugs onto my manor, he has another think coming."

"Yes, Tommy, tell us how you plan to kill Simon Docherty," Jack said from the doorway. "I've already heard enough to see that you finish your life at the end of a rope."

Anger flared in Usher's eyes and he raised the gun, his other hand thrusting down on the wheel to turn himself, ready to fire. As he turned Myra kicked out with both feet and connected with the wheelchair, sending it spinning. The impact jarred him and his finger jerked on the trigger, firing the revolver. Myra grunted as the bullet slammed into her and she fell backwards onto the floor.

Jack launched himself across the room, diving on top of Usher, knocking the gun from his hand, the momentum carrying both men to the floor, where they landed in a tangle of arms legs and wheelchair. Jack tried to move but his body was trapped beneath Usher's and, as he tried to heave him off, Usher's hands came up and grabbed him around the throat. All urbanity had gone from Usher face which was now a mask of white hot rage as he pressed his thumbs into Jack's windpipe, cutting off his air supply, and no matter how much he bucked and kicked out he could not shift Usher's dead weight.

"Fucking rozzer!" Usher hissed at him and gritted his teeth to make one last effort to kill him. Then, as if someone had thrown a switch, a shadow moved behind his eyes, the left side of his face sagged and he gave a strangled cry, pitching forward, his finger's releasing Jack's throat, his ruined face smacking into the tiled floor.

For a second or so they lay there, frozen in the moment, and then Jack finally managed to roll Usher off of him and get to his feet. Without a backwards glance at Usher's dead body he crouched down beside Myra, cradling her head in his arm while he searched his pocket for a handkerchief. He found it quickly and folded it into a pad that he pressed against the hole in the shoulder of her tunic from which blood was leaking in a steady flow.

"Bloody hell!" Fuller exclaimed as he walked into the room. "What happened here?"

Jack spun round. "Call for an ambulance, Eddie!" he shouted.

Fuller stared down at the dead body on the floor. "I think Usher is beyond their help."

"It's not for him. It's for Myra!"

Fuller stared and the full importance of what he was seeing finally struck home. He turned and dashed out to the car to use the radio.

"Myra," Jack said softly, and her eyes fluttered open.

"Hello, sir," she managed to croak.

"That was quick thinking, kicking the chair like that. You saved my life,"

"It's the same chair my dad has." She said weakly. "They turn on a sixpence if you give them a shove. Wasn't counting on getting shot though." She glanced down at the bloody handkerchief, gave a soft sigh and passed out.

Somewhere in the house a telephone started to ring. After a few seconds a disembodied voice sounded.

"This is a recording. Lois Turner is not here at the moment to take your call. If you would like to leave a message, you can do so after the tone."

There followed a short beeping sound.

"Lois, it's Simon again. Lois? Lois? Damn it, Bláthnaid! Pick up the bloody 'phone! I hate these machines. Okay, perhaps you're not there. Well, I'm still at the hotel, but I have to leave now to get to the airport. Our flight leaves in just over an hour. If you don't make it in time I'll leave your ticket at the check-in counter. Hopefully you will."

The line went dead.

"Looks like you'll be travelling alone, old son," Jack said quietly as the bell of an approaching ambulance cut through the afternoon silence.

Jack and Fuller sat in the car and watched the ambulance, its bell ringing urgently, pull out of the gates and take a right onto the road.

"Is she going to be all right?" Fuller said.

"It was a clean shot to the shoulder. The bullet went straight through, missing her collarbone so, according to the ambulance-man she should make a full recovery. It means she'll be out of commission for a few weeks, and in considerable pain for a few weeks longer than that, but it could have been a lot worse. She was lucky."

"You sound relieved."

Jack frowned. "I am. It doesn't say a lot for my leadership skills when one of my officers makes a rash decision and puts her life at risk."

"I don't think you could have foreseen her actions. I think Myra had something to prove."

"Such as?"

Fuller leaned forward and started the car. "It doesn't matter."

"On the contrary, Sergeant, I think it matters a lot."

Fuller made great play of putting the car into gear and following the ambulance out through the gates. "Just let it lie, Jack."

"Sorry, not good enough, Eddie. You're keeping something from me. What did I say to you the other day about me being able to trust my sergeants? Spit it out, man."

Fuller pulled onto the main road and took a breath. "I suppose you're aware of the gossip going around the station about you and Myra?"

Jack laughed. "Yes, Eddie. I'm aware of it."

"And it doesn't bother you?"

"If I was bothered about all the old toffee that's said about me, I wouldn't be able to do my job."

"Nevertheless, you can't just let the rumours carry on."

"Trust me, Eddie, I won't, but I squash them in my own way and in my own time. They're just stories, made up by people who feel that, perhaps, their careers aren't going the way they'd hoped. Myra's an easy target because she's female and is doing well, and a lot of men can't stand that, and some of the other women as well. The stories don't bother me and they certainly don't bother Mrs Callum."

Fuller looked at him sharply. "You've told her about them?"

"She's my wife. Of course I told her about them."

"What was her reaction?"

"She laughed too. The thought that I could be involved with a girl young enough to be my daughter tickled her."

Fuller gave a low whistle. "She's quite a woman."

"That's why I married her. I'm fortunate enough to have a handful of remarkable women in my life, and I include Myra Banks in that handful. I told you the other day that she reminds me of my Joanie, and I can imagine Joanie being just as reckless as Myra."

Fuller pulled onto the A1. "I don't know how you do it."

"How I do what?"

"Command that kind of loyalty from your wife. Judy doesn't trust me at all."

Jack smiled. "It's easy. I just remember the answer my old man gave on the day of his golden wedding anniversary. Someone asked him how he had managed to stay married to the same woman for fifty years. Do you know what he said?"

Fuller shook his head.

"'Whatever you do, never take them for granted.' And you'd do well to remember that, Eddie, if your relationship with Judy Taylor ever makes it off the starting blocks. Never take her for granted. I use that in my personal life as much as I do at work. At the end of the day, it's all about respect, and if we don't respect the people we surround ourselves with, then there's no hope for us."

"You're a lucky man, Jack."

"And don't I know it. By the way, what did the chief super want?"

It was Fuller's turn to laugh. "He'd just seen that I'm going for promotion. He seemed rather pleased and he wanted to reassure me that I have his backing and has put all the resources of his office at my disposal."

"Generous of him."

"He also wanted to make it clear that if I do make inspector, there will be a job for me at Welwyn."

"Despite all the budget cuts?"

"Apparently."

"Well. Good for you. I'm pleased."

"Really?"

"Yes, really. Good number twos are hard to come by."

"You mean that?"

"You know me. Eddie. I wouldn't have said it if I didn't believe it."

Simon Docherty slammed down the telephone, irritated. It was time to get out of this Godforsaken country. Going back to the United States was no longer an option for him and his sister. The O'Briens had pulled out of the deal that he and Albert Klein had worked so hard to put together, and were now after his blood. If he stayed here the people who killed Tony Turner no doubt had him marked as their next target. He just could not see how things could have gone so wrong. But the flight to Canada was booked and in a few hours time he'd be jetting off across the Atlantic.

There was a knock at the hotel door.

He glanced around. "Who's there?"

"Room service."

"I haven't ordered anything."

The knock came again.

Furiously Docherty walked to the door and yanked it open. "I told you, I haven't…"

The sentence was cut short by the fist that smashed into his mouth, splitting his lips and knocking two of his front teeth down his throat. He didn't recognise the two men who barrelled in through the door but he guessed their intent. The man who followed them into the house was instantly familiar and Docherty's bladder emptied.

The two thugs hauled him to the floor and pinned him there by his shoulders.

Jimmy Dymond stood over his fallen victim. "Oh, look, lads. He's wet himself. Pissed his pants like a little baby."

Docherty's head twisted from side to side, looking desperately for some means of escape. Pathetic mewling sounds were coming from his ruined mouth.

"I think baby needs changing," Dymond said matter-of-factly. "Would you do the honours, boys? Relieve him of his trousers."

One of the thugs unfastened Docherty's belt while the other one pulled the sodden slacks down over his thighs.

Docherty was struggling, kicking his legs, but an open-palmed slap to his face sent his thoughts reeling and the fight drained out of him.

Dymond leaned over him. "I suppose you're wondering how we found you."

Docherty couldn't speak but the confused look in his eyes was answer enough.

"You seem to forget, Simon. This is my home turf I have hundreds of eyes out there waiting to tell me what I need to know."

Docherty whimpered.

"The good news, mate, is that it happens to be your lucky day, " he said, his voice heavy with menace. "I have a present from a mutual friend of ours. Want to see what it is?"

Docherty shook his head frantically.

"No?" Dymond said. "I think I'll show you anyway." He took a step backwards and threw open the heavy coat he was wearing. "Surprise!" Dymond exulted. "Tommy sends his regards."

When Docherty saw what the coat was concealing his eyes widened and he managed to say one word. "No!" and then started babbling incoherently.

Dymond took the freshly honed garden shears from his belt and opened them, smiling in wonder as the blades reflected the sunlight as they scissored. "Playtime," he said and advanced on Docherty who gave a low howl of anguish. The howl rose in volume to a shrill scream that echoed off the walls before being brutally cut off.

32 - SATURDAY MARCH 28TH 1959

"Almost there," Jack said.

From the back seat of the Morris Oxford Eric peered out through the window. "Shillington? What's at Shillington?"

"Just some people I have to see."

"Do they know we're coming, Jack?" Annie said, checking her lipstick in the mirror of her powder compact.

"I telephoned first thing this morning. They know."

Laurence Turner opened the door to the bungalow while the echo of the doorbell was still hanging in the air. "Jack," he said. "So good of you to come, and you've brought your lovely family. Splendid."

Jack was taken aback. This was a different Laurence Turner to the man he had met just over a week ago, a man whose curtness bordered on rudeness, a man so consumed by bitterness there didn't seem space in his heart for any light. Not only had his whole character changed but he actually looked a good ten years younger.

"You're looking well, Mr. Turner."

"Now, Jack, please, call me Laurence. And thank you. I certainly feel well. Especially now this ghastly business with my son and his wife is over."

"He's a changed man, Chief Inspector, since Gerry came to live with us." Jean Turner appeared at her husband's side.

"Were done with formalities, Jean," Turner gently chided her. "It's Jack, and his lovely wife is? I'm sorry I didn't catch your name, my dear."

"Annie," she said. "And this is our son, Eric."

"Well, what are we doing standing out here? Come in, come in."

They followed the elderly couple through the hall and into the sitting room. Gerry Turner was on the sofa, her legs curled underneath her, a folded sheet of manuscript paper resting on her thigh on which she was adding crochets and quavers with a fine-tipped ballpoint pen.

"Look, Gerry, Chief Inspector Callum has come to see us, and he's brought his family," Jean Turner said.

Gerry Turner beamed up at Jack, laid the manuscript paper down on the sofa and stood up. She was wearing jeans and a tee shirt and had tied her hair up in a ponytail. She too looked different, Jack thought. The tension that had creased her forehead into an almost permanent frown had gone, and her cheeks had a ruddy glow of a child used to playing outside in the sunshine.

Jack said hello and introduced her to Annie and Eric. "Eric's a musician too," he added, which earned an embarrassed, "Dad!" from his son.

"That's all right, son. Gerry's a fine pianist, and I'm sure her grandparents never tire of singing her praises."

Laurence and Jean Turner nodded in agreement.

"What instrument do you play?" Gerry asked Eric directly.

"Guitar," Eric said diffidently. "I've not been playing that long. I'm not very good."

"From what I've heard you don't seem too bad."

"Dad!"

"Would you like to hear me play?" Gerry asked him. "I don't get much of a chance to *talk* to other musicians, let alone show off to them." Her enthusiasm was infectious and Eric found himself nodding. "Come on. We'll go in the back room where the piano is and leave the grownups to their chattering." She grabbed a rather bemused Eric by the hand and led his from the room.

"Well they seemed to hit it off," Turner said.

Annie laughed. "Judging from the expression on his face I don't think he knew what hit him. She's very confident, your Gerry."

"She is now," Jean agreed. "You wouldn't recognise her as the girl who arrived here in a taxi last week after running away from that hell-hole she called home. Shall I put the kettle on?"

"That would be lovely." Annie said. "I'll give you a hand."

Turner took Jack's arm and led him to the French doors that looked out onto a beautifully tended garden. "Talking of hell holes, I'd like your advice."

"I'm listening."

Turner opened one of the doors and they stepped out into the garden. "Are you a gardener, Jack?"

"I potter." He paused. "Actually, no I don't. Gardening is something of a passion for me. It's the perfect antidote for the type of work I do."

"Yes, I can see that. I had thirty-odd years in the Civil Service before I retired and had I not had the garden I swear I would have cracked up. Planting and growing my flowers kept me sane."

"And the problem you want me to help with," Jack prompted him.

"It's Gerry. It looks like Jean and I will be made her legal guardians."

"That seems the most likely outcome."

"We're thinking of taking her back to *Elsinore* – bloody stupid name for a house, pardon my French – her music room is there and I know she's missing her piano."

"But surely you have a piano here?"

"Yes, we do, but it's a rather ancient overstrung jobbie; more suitable for playing *Roll Out The Barrel* than a Rachmaninoff concerto. I know from growing plants all these years that seedlings need nurturing. Give them the best in the early days and they'll reward you with succulent blooms year after year. I want Gerry to have every opportunity to succeed in her ambition to become a top class pianist so taking her back to her piano and her music room seems about the best we can do for her. But Jean is worried that all the horror that's happened in that house might have some adverse effect on her. What do you think?"

The delicate sounds of *Clair de Lune* floated through the warm spring air. The music was pure Debussy but the tone was closer to Winifred Atwell. "See what I mean?" Turner said.

"I take your point." Jack said. "If you want my advice, I'd get the whole house professionally cleaned from top to bottom, move back in there and start a new life as a proper family, something I don't think Gerry's had since her mother died, and then sit back and watch her bloom."

Laurence Turner smiled and slapped Jack on the back. "Thank

you," he said. "That was what I hoped you'd say."

"Tea's up," Annie called from the sitting room.

"What did you think of Gerry?" Jack asked his son as they pulled out of the Turner's cul de sac.

Eric was thoughtful. "Hmm," he said. "She's very talented. She puts me to shame."

"Oh, Eric," Annie said don't be so hard on yourself. "You've only been playing a few months, she's been doing it for years."

"I suppose so."

"Of course so," Jack said. "Listen to your mother. She's quite right…as always."

Annie smiled and tapped him playfully on the arm. "Just you watch it, Jack Callum. You're not too big for a smack."

"Anyway," Eric said, ignoring the flirtatious behaviour taking place in the front seat of the car. "She said that when she's moved back to Letchworth I can go around to her house and practice my guitar there. She's got a big music room."

"That's right, she has. I've seen it," he said, trying to blot out the memory of Lois Turner lying dead on the bamboo couch, blood and brains dribbling from a bullet hole in her skull, and Thomas Usher lying dead on the floor, a look of complete surprise on his lopsided face. He wondered now if he had given Laurence Turner the correct advice.

Annie noticed the faraway look in his eyes as he relived the events of just a few days ago. "A penny for them."

"Eh?"

"A penny? For your thoughts?"

"Trust me. Annie, you wouldn't want them. Really you wouldn't."

33 - SATURDAY JUNE 14TH 1959

"You don't need a tie, dad." Rosie said. "It's St Mary's Youth Club not the Royal Albert Hall. Wear that pullover mum got you for Christmas. That's plenty smart enough."

"Talking of your mother, where is she?" Jack stared at himself in the mirror for a few seconds more before removing the tie and hanging it back on the wardrobe rail.

"Downstairs in the back room. Joanie's doing her hair for her."

"*Joanie* is doing her hair?" Jack said, surprised. "I thought I heard Avril arrive earlier."

"You did. It's a team effort."

Jack gave a slight frown and shook his head. He should be used to the vagaries of female beauty regimens by now but the women in his life always came up with something new to surprise him. "Shouldn't you be getting down to the club to rehearse? Eric will be wondering where you are."

"There's no rush. I've only got two songs this evening and I know them backwards. Besides they're debuting a new member of the group this evening so they want to run through a few things before I get down there cluttering up the stage, so I've got plenty of time. I might even cadge a lift from you."

"What's wrong with your bike?"

"Nothing. I just thought it might be nice to arrive in style for a change." Rosie grinned at him.

"I'm not your chauffer."

"Ah well. It was worth a try."

Jack sat in his armchair listening to the radio The new television glowered at him from the corner of the room as if challenging him to switch it on and get sucked into its time-consuming void. He had wondered how television would change their lives, for change it would. He'd been less than enthusiastic about the idea, but he was equally determined not to be perceived by his family as a curmudgeon, so went along with Annie's idea. He quickly became aware that moments like this, sitting in his favourite armchair listening to a classical concert on the BBC's Third Programme, were precious and would soon to be consigned to history. The thought made him slightly melancholy.

The door opened. Joan came into the room, stood by the doorway and cleared her throat. "Tonight, John '*Jack*' Callum, father, policeman, catcher of criminals, scourge of the Hertfordshire underworld, and husband, tonight *This Is Your Wife*. She stood to one side, glanced back over her shoulder, gave a low bow, and made a beckoning gesture with her arm. "Now, Mum," she hissed.

Jack got to his feet and stood as Annie, his wife of twenty years walked hesitantly and shyly into the room. He felt his jaw slacken and his mouth start to drop open. He snapped it shut.

Self-consciously Annie patted her newly shorn and permed hair. "Do you like it, Jack?" she asked, her eyes beseeching him to say yes.

Jack swallowed and crossed to the doorway. He stretched out his hand, his fingers gently pulling at a curl of hair at the nape of Annie's neck, marvelling slightly as the hair straightened and then sprung back into a curl on its release.

"Hey, you," Joan protested. "Don't you go spoiling the style with your great banana fingers."

"Jack, do you like it?" Annie said urgently. "Avril cut it for me and Joanie permed it. What do you think?"

Jack took a breath. "I think you look beautiful."

"Yes, but do you like the hairstyle, Dad?" Joan said to her father impatiently.

"Yes." Jack nodded his head slowly. "I love it."

"You see, Mum," Joan crowed. "I told you he would."

Annie looked hard into her husband's eyes, "I wasn't sure you would."

"It makes you look younger." Jack recognised his wife's uncertainty and tried to assuage it. "Like a new woman."

Annie shook her freshly coiffed head. "I'll settle for younger, but I don't want to be a *new woman*, Jack. I want to be the same old Annie Callum, wife and mother."

"And sexpot," Jack said with a twinkle in his eye.

The two women chorused. "Jack!" "Dad!"

"A man's entitled to his opinion." Jack glanced at his watch. "Anyway, we have to get going. Eric will kill us if we miss the beginning of the show. It's his big night." He went across to the radiogram and turned it off.

"I'll get my coat." Joan skipped happily from the room and called back over her shoulder. "Can I get yours, Mum?"

"If you would, love. I'm wearing my navy duster coat tonight." Annie encircled Jack's waist with her arms. "Do you *really* like it, Jack? I was so scared when Joanie suggested it. I know you always preferred my hair long."

He wrapped his arms around her. "Times are changing, pet." He kissed her on the forehead. "It wouldn't do if we don't change with them, and yes, I meant it. I think your hair looks lovely. Come on, let's go."

She disengaged herself from his embrace.

"And I meant what I said when I called you a sexpot too."

She glanced back at him with, what his mother would have called, *an old fashioned look*, and shook her head. "Jack Callum, you're incorrigible."

He smiled. "I know."

By the time they got to St Mary's church hall there was already quite a throng of people inside. Thirty or forty bodies, milling about the dusty, cavernous room, most of them jockeying for position to get near the stage, a small platform set at one end of the hall. Many of the faces were young, Eric's school friends mostly, but there were a handful of adults, mostly standing at the back of the hall.

"You see," Annie said. "We're not the oldest ones here. Phillip Langton's parents are here, and they're older than us."

They looked towards the stage as Reverend Williams, a short, rotund man with ruddy skin and thinning hair, climbed onto it and positioned himself at its centre, clapping his hands once for attention. "Ladies and gentlemen, boys and girls." The chatter in the hall quietened and the vicar continued. "Thank you all for coming to this… this…concert, which will help us raise funds for St Mary's Youth Club."

A small smattering of applause rippled through the audience.

Reverend Williams bowed his head slightly in acknowledgement and then continued. "When Eric Callum came to me with the proposal that his skiffle group put on a show for you all I must admit that at first I was sceptical."

A few of the adults in the hall smiled and nodded.

"But since then I have heard them play, and I'm sure you're in for a treat this evening. So, if you'll put your hands together and welcome to the stage, Eric and the Vikings."

"*Eric and the Vikings?*" Joan's eyes widened incredulously. "When did he dream that one up?"

Annie shushed her.

Jack just smiled.

The crowd parted and, from the back of the hall, Eric Callum, the strap of his guitar slung over one shoulder, led his group to the stage to the applause from the audience.

"This will go straight to his head." Joan raised her eyes to the ceiling. "He's going to be impossible. I suppose at least Rosie's there to keep his feet on the ground."

As the group started their first number, an up-tempo song Jack hadn't heard before but had his foot tapping, Rosie came to the front of the stage and started to sing, slapping her thigh in time to the music, but Jack was not watching his daughter. Instead his gaze was fixed on the pianist who sat hunched over the keys of the piano at the side of the stage. The piano filled out the sound of the group and, in Jack's opinion, was a one hundred per cent improvement from when he had last heard them.

Annie followed his gaze. "Isn't that…?"

"Yes, it is." Jack was smiling indulgently as the pianist turned from the keyboard and stared into the audience, finding his smile and returning it. "Well done," he mouthed.

Gerry Turner winked at him broadly and turned her attention back to the keys.

"I thought, when I introduced her to Eric, her classical influences would rub off on him. Seems I was wrong," Jack said

221

quietly to his wife.

Annie gripped her husband's hand and squeezed gently. "He's his father's son. Ploughing his own furrow. Would you have it any other way?"

Jack smiled broadly. "Not at all, Annie. Not at all."

CPSIA information can be obtained
at www.ICGtesting.com
Printed in the USA
LVHW011615240921
698679LV00021B/1691